# GOIN' SOUTH

*A Dusty Rose Series Book 5*

To Maggie,
Hope you enjoy!
Susie Drougas

SUSIE DROUGAS

**Goin' South**



Layout and design by Katherine Ballasiotes Rowley
Edited by Heidi Thomas
Cover Photo by Susie Drougas
Back Cover Photo Mike Drougas
www.SusieDrougas.com

Published by Diamond Hitch Press in the United States of America

Cochise Stronghold
Goin' North
Equestrian Camping Area
Forest Road 795
To Highway 191
Iron wood Road
CAVES
Equestrian Trailhead
Stronghold Divide
Halfmoon
TR 279
Equestrian Connecting Trail
FR 688
Trail 279
W
Public Campground
[no horses]
Cochise String
Forest Road 687
Trail 277
TR 387A
FR 345A
TR 697
Forest Road 345
Forest Road 689
Forest Road 345
Goin' South
Arizona
1/2 mile

# Acknowledgments

Thank you to my readers. I really appreciate your kind words and encouragement. Writing can be a long, lonely process. You guys light the way and make it all worth it!

And thank you to Yakwriters. Without you I would not be a writer today.

Gloria Kruszka, a special thanks to you for proofreading and punctuation. You've helped me so much, and I really appreciate it.

Duane Knittle, thank you for reading of the transcript and suggestions, enormously helpful.

Katherine Ballasiotes Rowley, my dear friend since second grade, I always wished I could draw like you – well, I can't, but I am so blessed to have you as my graphic designer! Thank you for your hours of hard work and perfection on my covers and maps. You make this series come alive!

Special thanks to my cousin, retired Detective John Clark, for reading my book and your suggestions.

Thank you, Mary Trimble for reading my book. You've helped me so much over the years! Meeting you at my first writer's conference when I wanted to write a book, until now, after my fifth novel, your insights and encouragement have been so enlightening. Writing and understanding the business of writing are two separate but dependent endeavors and a neverending learning process.

# Dedication

I would like to dedicate this book to my brother, Mark Anderson. Thanks for being my older brother, I can't imagine growing up without you.

Eagle Scout, National Merit Scholar, University of Washington graduate and finally a law degree from the University of Chicago, School of Law. I'm always in awe of your intelligence and hard work. I guess the only criticism I would have is that you don't pack and ride horses in the mountains.

Thanks for all your help and feedback on my books, I really appreciate it.

Love, Susie

# Goin' South

# Chapter One

Dusty drove his Ford 350 flatbed, towing his living quarters horse trailer down U.S. 84, keeping it just above the speed limit. He looked ahead and let out a contented sigh. Another road trip with the horses. *It doesn't get much better than this.* He glanced over at the seat next to him. The sun struck Cassie's light brown hair as she slept. His riding buddy. A lump rose in his throat. He never thought it would happen. Staring at the road in front of him he felt warmth in the pit of his stomach. Dusty first met Cassie in the Seattle courtroom and hadn't even noticed her as other than opposing counsel. But after winning the case for his clients, in maybe not the best way, he winced inwardly as he remembered the exhibits entered at the last minute. But the professional way she'd carried herself through the loss, and then later seeing her riding her horse at Basin Lake, had sealed the deal for him. Still, the last year had been confusing, pulling Cassie to him and pushing her away, but it all seemed to take him where he needed to be. And thank God shc was patient.

He shifted in his seat. It was a long drive to Arizona. He could have followed the coast down I-5, starting in Eagleclaw, but it made more sense to cut right over the pass at Crystal Mountain and then drop down to Pendleton.

Dusty focused on the clear blue October sky above the horizon. Although a balmy 70 degrees today, it could change quickly. The summer riding season seemed to slip through their fingers and he and Cassie weren't ready to let it end just yet. They decided to go to Arizona for a month. Mike had agreed to watch his place, and Terri was keeping an eye on Cassie's. Two furry forms sat in the truck; he threw a quick glance at the two dogs in the backseat.

Scout and Sammy had never seen cactus before, but Dusty was sure they would figure it out. Cassie wasn't convinced. With the only option of leaving her dog for a month, Cassie quickly came around to the fact that Sammy was an Australian Shepherd, and Aussies were smart dogs. Dusty had a crew cab, so they had plenty of room.

As the rig pulled up Cabbage Hill—also known as Dead Man's Pass because of the sharp curves and steep grade for truckers—Dusty sat back in his seat, his hands loosely holding the wheel. The roads were bare. He may not be so lucky on the way back, but no need to worry about that now. As he drove past the sign for the Blue Mountains, last summer played vividly into his mind. Dutch, the outfitter, and his daughter Stevie, her boyfriend Nick, and/or Buck, he corrected himself, since she was dating both men. What a crazy adventure that had been. Dusty ran his hand through his hair. *I wonder how that worked out for Nick.* Buck had died in the shootout. Nick was probably left with a really bad taste in his mouth about the whole thing. The case had started with a wrongful death at the Eagle Cap and ended up with an ill-fated lightning strike. Dusty stole another glance over at his companion. He'd almost lost her.

Cassie seemed to sense him. She opened her eyes and smiled sleepily. "Hi." She straightened. "Did I sleep long?"

He smiled back at her. "About an hour."

"Where are we now?" Cassie looked out the window.

"The Blues."

"Oh." She raised an eyebrow.

"Just passing through," he assured her.

"Good."

Funny how that worked: as bad as the trip into the Eagle Cap ended, it was a catalyst for this. Now they were going to relax and ride together and just see how it worked as a couple for them. Warmth pooled in the pit of his stomach. Contentment was a foreign emotion to him, but he was willing to give it a try.

"How much further to Ontario?"

"Probably a couple hours." Dusty glanced at the console clock. "We'll get there after dark."

Cassie's eyebrows drew together. "I'll be happy to spell you driving."

"I got it, just relax."

She sat back. "I always drive. This is going to take some getting used to."

"In a good way, I hope?"

She smiled. "Yes, in a good way."

As they approached La Grande, Oregon, Dusty pointed at a truck stop. "We need fuel. You want to stop in there? Looks like they have a restaurant. We could probably get something to eat and not worry about it when we hit Ontario."

"Sounds good."

They pulled into the pump and Dusty fueled up the truck. Afterwards they moved to an area in back, lined by big trucks.

Cassie lowered her window a couple inches and talked to the dogs in the back seat. She snapped the leashes on their collars, let them out of the truck, and turned them to some patches of grass in the parking lot. Both dogs strained to pull ahead, Dusty walked over and took Scout. "He hasn't had a whole lot of training on a leash."

"Sammy hasn't either." Cassie laughed, "I don't use one for trail riding."

They spent a few minutes with the dogs and after each had found a bush, they returned to the truck. "We'll be right back, you guys." Cassie said. Both Aussies stood at attention, wanting to bolt, barely restraining themselves. "Be good and we'll bring you a treat." She slammed and locked the door. Dusty waited for her in front of the truck. As she joined him, he put his arm around her and they walked together into the building.

The restaurant's interior was finished off in brown rough wood siding. The waitress popped up and seated them, handing them a couple of menus. "Coffee?" she chirped.

"Always." Dusty turned the cup upright.

Cassie nodded. "Yes, please."

"I'll be right back with the pot."

Dusty and Cassie looked over the menu and made their selection. The waitress came back and filled their coffee cups. "You headed far?"

"We're going to Arizona with our horses." Cassie's cheeks turned pink.

She was always beautiful, Dusty smiled, but the excitement in her voice made her even more so.

"Really?" The middle-aged waitress had her curly-brown hair pulled back into a ponytail. "Well, you're the lucky ones. I'd give anything to go on a trip like that with my horses." She pulled out her note pad. "As it is, the biggest place I ride is out here in the Wallowas, or the Eagle Cap."

"I never thought I'd be doing it either. You just never know." Cassie smiled at Dusty.

"If my husband rode, I'd probably be a lot closer to doing that. You are really lucky." The waitress nodded at Cassie.

Dusty's stomach tightened. *Husband? I hadn't even thought about that one.*

Cassie had gone from pink cheeks to a bright red complexion. Dusty had to stifle a laugh. Didn't appear it had occurred to her either.

After the waitress left to fill their orders, Cassie cleared her throat and took a drink of coffee. An awkward silence fell.

Dusty was enjoying himself, regardless. He was too old at this point to be swayed by any comments people may make. He knew his own mind. If and when he wanted to marry Cassie, he would ask her. Finally, he broke the silence. "Hey, wife."

Cassie stared at the table, then looked at him, her expression enigmatic. The corners of her mouth turned up. "That was different."

"Not in a bad way," he said, fighting to look serious.

Cassie changed the topic. "So we're staying in Ontario tonight and then going to Alamo?"

"Hopefully," said Dusty. "It's going to be a push for the horses, but it would be nice to cover some ground while they're fresh."

A table full of truckers sat down not far from them. It soon got too loud to talk over the guffaws and wild stories. Dusty and Cassie finished eating and left the restaurant. Cassie had brought part of her sandwich and split it between Scout and Sammy. By putting it on either side of the back seat, the dogs managed to eat it with a minimum of competition.

Cassie chuckled. "Scout's such a gentleman."

"He can be."

"Oh, like his master," Cassie teased.

"How did you know?"

The highway wove down the mountains surrounded by thick green trees on either side. As they lost elevation, the trees gave way to prairie.

The sun was gone and the city lights were on by the time they pulled into the Ontario fairgrounds. Dusty opened the gate, and idled the engine in front of the caretaker's house. A young, blonde woman came out, wearing a large brown Carhartt jacket that made her look small.

"Dusty Rose," he said. "We called ahead."

"Oh, yes, I thought that would be you. You can put them in the barn in the back." She pointed. "There's plenty of shavings. No lights in the stalls, but there are a couple power poles with lights outside."

"That's good. Who do we pay?"

"You can pay me right now if you like. It's $15 per stall."

Dusty handed her the money and drove around to the back of the property.

The fairgrounds were deserted and dark. Cassie pointed at the bright lights in the distance. "What's that? A factory?

"I think that's a state prison," said Dusty.

"Seriously? No wonder it looks so depressing around here."

"Yeah, it is depressing. To top that off I read somewhere that Ontario is the most dangerous city in Oregon with the highest crime rate. They estimated in the article your chances of becoming a victim in this city is one in twelve."

Cassie grimaced. "Lovely."

Pulling into the end row of stables, Dusty felt the hairs on his neck stand up and instinctively rubbed it. He parked next to a power pole and turned off the engine. Turning on the trailer lights, they walked back to unload. Prince first. Dusty went in and slowly backed the big gray Tennessee Walker out. Cassie picked up his lead rope.

"Just take any stall?" Cassie asked hesitantly.

"That's what she said."

"Okay." Cassie walked over to the closest one, opened the half door and walked into the pitch-black darkness, Prince following behind her.

Dusty put Muley in the next one. The heavy-muscled blue roan laid his ears back in the direction of the other horse as a warning. Dusty chuckled. It was all a bluff. The horses wouldn't be able to see each other, but they could hear, and that would be a comfort, despite Muley's actions to the contrary.

Dusty's hair still stood up on his neck, as he filled up the water bucket and fed Muley. Ignoring it, he went into his trailer and extended the slideout. The trailer was big enough to store their belongings, so it was just a matter of walking in.

He pulled out the coffee pot. Unlike most people, coffee relaxed him, and he always had one cup before going to bed. He poured water into the pot and put in the grounds. As he turned to the stove, a high-pitched scream rent the air from the direction of the stalls. The dogs barked and snarled. The coffee pot slipped from his hand and crashed to the floor. Dusty pushed out of the door and leaped to the ground at a run.

# Chapter Two

The single light on the pole shone dimly over the horse trailer. The row of stables sat in a line, the half doors closed, except the two they were using. Muley's big head hung over the top of the Dutch door, gathered and ready to explode through the flimsy wood. Dusty drew in a sharp breath. Scout and Sammy barked loudly and feet scrambled in Prince's stall. Dusty stepped through the open door, into pitch black darkness.

*Dang it, why didn't I grab my light?* His mind raced as he tried make out forms in the dark.

Prince slammed into him with such force, Dusty staggered backwards, almost falling over. Pain sparked through him from the impact. Gathering himself, he turned his shoulder into Prince's chest and grabbed onto the halter. He leaned into the horse, light-headed. Slowly he stroked Prince's neck and talked in low tones to the shivering animal.

"Cassie," he called out. Silence. Speaking calmly, not wanting to make a bad situation worse, he tried again. "Cassie, are you okay?"

He felt rather than heard her in the corner. Finally, a faint, "Yeah. Do you have Prince?"

Relief flooded through him. "Yes. I'm going to take him to the stall on the other side of Muley. I'll be right back for you." Without waiting for an answer, Dusty led the shaking animal to the other stall. Muley, for once, didn't try to bite the passing horse. Instead, his little black, silver-tipped ears pricked forward as he watched the gray walk by.

Closing Prince in the stall, Dusty ran into the darkness to Cassie. She lay in a corner on the left side of the stall. Dusty scooped her up in his arms. "What happened?"

"There's something in here," she said weakly.

"Where?"

"Over there," she pointed to the opposite side. As I lead Prince around, it smacked right into me. It's really huge."

Dusty forced his eyes to focus on the area she'd indicated. A large dark shape loomed in the corner, but he couldn't make out what it was. He picked up Cassie and carried her out of the stall. "I'll get you to the trailer."

"I can walk. Prince just knocked me down. I'll be okay," she said softly.

Dusty kept going. The door of the living quarters still hung open as he'd left it. Walking up the steps, he set her on the dinette seat. Flipping open the cabinet, he grabbed his .45 Colt Vaquero revolver and put on his headlamp. "I'll be right back."

Cautiously this time, he walked back to the stall. Uncertain of what was there, he stood carefully to one side of the door. His gun at low ready, he flashed the light into the right corner. A deer carcass hung from the ceiling, dried blood on the hide. And something else. He saw movement. Swarms of little bugs! Relief coupled with revulsion flooded through him. Cassie had walked right into it. Not what you would expect in a stall. The odor of fresh sawdust flooded his nostrils along with something else—the smell of death. It was obvious, now that he knew. Scout took a tentative step toward the deer, and Dusty said, "No, Scout." The dog backed up.

"Hey!" The sound came from behind him and Dusty almost jumped out of his skin. His gun still down, he whirled around. Scout came to life and ran in front of Dusty, barking.

The large brown Carhartt coat was almost next to him, a

flashlight burning his eyes. "What's all the commotion out here?" The woman from the caretaker's house. She'd added a stocking cap that came down almost over her eyes. Scout's barking just about drowned out her voice.

"Scout, no." His dog gave him a double take as if to say: Are you sure? But he stopped barking.

"I was just putting the kids to bed and I heard a loud scream."

Before Dusty could say anything, she added, "We got rules around here about quiet times."

"Do you have any rules about sending people to horse stalls that are already occupied?" Dusty asked in a voice that was much calmer than he felt. That was one benefit from being a lawyer as long as he had. Excess emotion in communication only got in the way.

"What?" The caretaker seemed confused. She walked past him and flashed the light in the stall. "Well, gol darn him." She turned to Dusty, her arms out. "I'm real sorry about that. My husband went hunting. I mucked out these stalls last week and no one has been in since. It seems he picked out the stall with the fresh shavings to hang his deer."

"Yeah, apparently so."

"I hope no one got hurt. I heard the screaming."

"My girlfriend's horse knocked her down." Dusty still hadn't gotten used to referring to Cassie as his girlfriend, but it was getting easier. "In fact, I need to get back to the trailer and check on her."

The woman dropped her head. "I'm sure sorry." She turned to walk away. "I just told him that thing's so full of ticks, I wasn't letting it near my shop."

*Ticks, great. That's what we need in the trailer.* Dusty quickened his pace back to Cassie.

She sat at the dinette, her cheeks red and her hair disheveled with bits of sawdust in it. "What in the heck was it? And who were you talking to?"

"A dead deer hanging in the corner." He turned to the control panel and flipped on the hot water switch. "That was the caretaker lady. Apparently, her husband put it in the stall when she wouldn't let him hang it in the shop." He paused. "Because it was covered with ticks."

Cassie's face instantly filled with horror. "Ticks?" Her hands went to her hair. "I thought I felt itchy."

"I just turned on the hot water tank. You can take a shower in about twenty minutes."

She stood up and then her hand went to her back.

"You okay?" Dusty asked.

"Yeah, yeah. Just a little stiff. I'll be all right." She walked for the door. "My clothes are in the back of the truck."

Dusty picked up the remains of the coffee pot and cleaned up the floor with some paper towels. He refilled it, put it back on the stove, and lit the burner.

A knock sounded at the door.

"You don't have to knock," he said as he opened the door.

She stood with her duffel bag in hand. Her eyes flickered with uncertainty. "I'm not sure what to do. I don't want to go back in there if I have ticks on me."

Dusty grinned and wiggled his eyebrows. "I'd be happy to check you for ticks."

"So considerate of you." She looked toward the back of the trailer. "I might take you up on that later, but right now I want to get rid of my clothes and shower."

Cassie set her bag down and rummaged in it, pulling out a towel. "Could you unlock the back door to the bathroom? I'll just come in that way. I'll put my clothes in the horse area."

"Sure thing."

She handed him the bag. "Just leave this in the trailer."

Dusty's living quarters had a bathroom and shower with a walkthrough door to access the horses. He made sure the door was unlocked. The coffee had started to boil and he turned it down. It was quiet in the back and he finally called out, "Is everything okay?"

"Yes, just waiting for the water." Cassie's voice came through the door.

Dusty opened it. Cassie stood with only a towel wrapped around her. He pulled her arm. "You can come into the bathroom at least. You're going to freeze out there."

"I was afraid."

"I think the water's done anyway." Dusty turned on the bathroom sink and hot water shot through. "You're good."

"Okay."

Dusty heard the shower water rushing through the pipes. The living quarters was filled with the smell of fresh perked coffee. He poured himself a cup and waited.

A short time later Cassie emerged from the bathroom, towel around her middle, her long brown hair dripping down her back. "I need to get my clothes now."

"Oh, yeah?" Dusty teased. "Did I tell you my horse trailer is clothes optional?"

"Really?" She spoke with mock sincerity. "I thought that was just for hot tubs."

"It's for hot tubs and horse trailers."

"Good to know." She turned. "I'm going for the clothes option. It's way cold in Oregon right now."

"Yeah, maybe that will sell better in Arizona."

"Maybe." Cassie shut the bathroom door.

"Coffee?"

"Sounds good."

He set the other cup on the table. Then asked hopefully, "What about the tick check?"

Laughter came through the bathroom door.

# Chapter Three

Dusty's phone alarm buzzed loudly in his ear. Sleepily, he reached in the dark and shut it off. Cassie lay asleep next to him, her light brown hair fanned out on the pillow. *I could get used to this.* He didn't want to get up just yet, but the horses needed to eat before they could leave. That would take at least an hour. He eased himself out of the bed and onto the camper floor, dressed quickly, put on a pot of coffee, and went outside. Gray sky. It was early yet, but looked like it could snow. Dusty hoped not. It would be great to get all the way to Arizona without it. They'd been lucky so far. But the middle of October, the weather could do anything at this point.

The horses eagerly tore into the hay as he tossed it into their stalls. The smell of alfalfa permeated the frosty air. Dusty went to the back of his LQ horse trailer and opened the door. The dogs bounded out, happy to be free. He fed them and went back to the trailer. The coffee was perking and he turned the burner down.

Cassie sat up in the bed. "Good morning."

"Good morning, beautiful."

She smiled brightly. "This might not be so bad after all."

"That's encouraging." He grinned.

"I don't know, after prisons and dead deer, I was starting to wonder."

Dusty gestured toward the stove. "Got some coffee just about ready."

"Yup, that would do it." She threw back the covers and hopped down from the bed.

"Are you still stiff?"

"No, I'm pretty good now." She walked by him to the bathroom.

He could smell her shampoo as she passed him in the tight quarters, and he couldn't help himself. He caught her and turned her into his arms. "Hmmm, I love that scent." He buried his face in her hair.

She hugged him back. "Thanks, you're not so bad yourself."

He reluctantly let go of her. "I'll pour you some coffee."

The small towns flew by as they drove down the highway, soon giving way to arid foothills. The sky looked like a blue glass dome on the horizon, joining the earth at a distant point. Snowcapped peaks lined the distance. Occasional fences and log ranch entrances were the only signs of humanity.

"Wow," said Cassie. "I never realized there was so much land out here."

"Yeah, it is something, isn't it?" agreed Dusty. "We're coming up to Ely, Nevada, pretty soon. Life magazine called this highway 'The loneliest road in America.'"

Cassie looked around. "Well, I can see why."

"The Pony Express came through here too."

"That would have been some crazy riding." Cassie tossed her hair back. "I think I would have liked it."

Dusty glanced at her appraisingly. "I think you would have."

She looked at him sideways. "And what about you?"

"Stagecoach. I just like that feel of a running team in front of me."

"And bullets flying?"

He grinned. "That too."

She leaned back in the seat. "High risk, bad boy, why am I always attracted to that?"

Dusty smiled into the afternoon sun. "You want to stop, get fuel and something to eat in Ely?"

"Heck, yeah. There's a town and we don't have to be lonely anymore?"

"Yup." Dusty stretched and sat back.

After fueling, they drove down the main street. "The guy at the pumps said if we follow this road around it will take us into town. I guess this is the outskirts."

The McDonalds and modern hotels turned into western front brick buildings. "Wow," said Cassie. "This looks like the Old West." Jagged mountains and blue sky framed the structures resembling the set of a western movie.

Dusty turned left and came up to a large gravel parking lot, where a couple of RVs were parked. "Here we go." He pointed down the block. "There's supposed to be a good restaurant over there."

"Great," said Cassie. "No fast food."

They parked and walked down the street toward a red brick building with faded signage saying "Hotel" in western block print. Dusty opened the door for Cassie and they walked inside. Immediately the smell of beer and cigarettes greeted them in the dimly lit room. Pops and beeps sounded from a room full of gambling machines in front of them.

Cassie gazed around the room. "I forgot gambling's legal in Nevada."

They followed the arrow to the left for the restaurant. "Yeah, I stay away from it," Dusty grimaced. "I don't need any other vices. Besides, I find myself mostly funding other people's payoffs."

As they stood and waited for the waitress to seat them, Dusty felt eyes on him. It was a small town, he reasoned, so watching strangers was always a pastime for the locals. He stood closer to Cassie and put his arm around her protectively.

She smiled at him. "Pretty exciting, huh? A real western?"

"Yeah, let's hope there's no shootout scene."

The waitress came bouncing up, a young girl in her early twenties. She was thin with dark hair pulled back in a ponytail, and a nose ring. "Two?"

"Yes." Dusty nodded. "Nonsmoking, if you have it." It seemed unlikely since the cloud over the machines wafted down the narrow hall into the restaurant.

"Sure thing." The ponytail turned, and they followed her toward the back. The light was dim with small lamps on the tables. Dusty found it impossible to tell the time of day.

They sat in a dark booth and ate lunch. "How much farther?" asked Cassie.

"It's only about three hours now to Alamo."

"The horses will be happy to hear that." she smiled.

"Yeah. They did a remodel on the fairgrounds. If nobody's using the arena, we can turn them out for a run before we go to bed. Lots of room to kick up their heels."

"The dogs will love that, too." Cassie pushed back her plate. "I'm going to hit the restroom before we leave." She opened her purse.

Dusty watched her. "I've got it."

She hesitated. "Dusty, I don't mind paying for things, too."

"I'm an old-fashioned kind of guy, I guess. When I invited you to come to Arizona for a month, I mean just that, invited."

Cassie's mouth turned up at the corners in the now familiar smile. "Okay, boss. But just so you know, I'm willing."

"Got it." Anxious to be done with the conversation, he picked up the bill.

Cassie rose out of the booth. "See you out front."

He glanced at her as she walked away—tall, lean legs, and her silky light brown hair cascaded down her back. It wasn't even so much her appearance, as the way she carried herself. It hit him hard in the gut. She was stunning. *And she's with me.* Dusty paid the bill. He stopped in the restroom and then waited in the foyer between the restaurant and the casino. Time dragged on. He thought Cassie would be waiting for him, but she wasn't. He busied himself reading some local announcements tacked to the wall. Uneasiness crept into the pit of his stomach. Finally, he'd had enough. Something wasn't right. He walked down the dimly lit hall to the restrooms. The men's bathroom in the front and the women's sat back around a dark corner. As soon as he turned the corner, his adrenaline kicked into full force.

A skinny, drunk cowboy had Cassie pushed against the wall. He was tall and wiry with droopy mustache, which he pushed into her face. Cassie twisted violently, trying to shove him away.

"Come on, honey. Don't be so uppity," the cowboy wheedled.

Anger burned up his spine and exploded in his chest. With an animal roar, Dusty threw himself forward, grabbed the cowboy by his shoulders and whirled him around. Ignoring the dumbfounded look on the man, Dusty punched him in the face and landed a second fist in his gut. Stale beer breath whished out as he doubled over. Dusty picked the cowboy up, held him by his neck against the wall and pulled his fish back to land another blow. Suddenly from behind, two hands bit into his shoulders and he found himself propelled forward, his head ramming into the wall. Adrenaline pumping, Dusty pulled himself to his feet. Somewhere far away he heard Cassie screaming. A cue stick slammed him in the side of the head. He moved back and tried to focus. It looked like two men, but maybe it was four—liquid running into his eyes made it difficult to see. He rubbed his face with his shirtsleeve and charged the cue stick man. More screaming and everything faded to black.

# Chapter Four

Feeling a sharp pain in his jaw, Dusty opened his eyes. In the dim light, he could make out a ceiling. He realized he was lying on his bed in the trailer. He tried to rise on his elbows, but his temples throbbed. He dropped back down.

"Dusty," came a tentative voice from below him. "Are you awake?"

"Yes." His voice came out soft and crackly. As more strength flowed through him, he added, "At least I think so."

"Good. I was afraid you were going to sleep all night."

"Cassie?" he asked as if to confirm.

"Yes," she answered in an amused voice. "Who else?"

"Just making sure."

Her voice moved closer. "Can I get you something? Coffee? Water?"

Dusty considered. Coffee would be a commitment to getting up; he wasn't sure he was ready for that yet. He wasn't sure of a lot of things at this moment. "Just give me a minute and I'll be down."

"Are you sure you should?" Her voice was heavy with concern, "The doctor said—"

"Doctor, huh?" Dusty frowned. *What have I done?*

"Yes," Cassie answered in a subdued voice. "He checked you out before they helped me get you back to the trailer."

Icy fingers of dread crept up his spine. Dusty searched his mind frantically, trying to piece together what she was talking about. The last thing he remembered was seeing that skinny cowboy all over Cassie. He knew he'd lost it. Now he remembered nothing. He thought that kind of anger was something he'd left far in his past. He could only recall a couple of times in his entire life that he'd lost control, and even then, never like today. He grimaced; emotions could be crazy powerful things.

He finally sat up and rubbed his eyes. He was wearing the same clothes he'd had on that afternoon, but his boots were off. Dusty slowly slid down from the bed onto his feet. Dizziness buzzed in the back of his head, and he grabbed onto the bed.

Cassie rushed over to help him. "Put your hand on my back to steady yourself. I'll help you to the table."

Dusty obeyed, and despite his battered condition, her sweet smell wafted by him. He held her closer than he needed to, as he slowly made his way to sit down.

Cassie efficiently washed out the coffee pot and refilled it. Dumping the basket, she put in four heaping tablespoons and set it on the burner. Turning on the gas, she lit the flame. Dusty intently watched her, she saw him as she turned around. "Soon."

"You're catching on."

She smiled. "It's not that difficult."

Dusty glanced out the window at the darkening sky. "Guess we'll be staying in the parking lot tonight."

"I checked with the casino owner when we brought you over. They said it would be no problem."

"I'm glad he's understanding," said Dusty tentatively, not knowing yet what he'd done.

"She," corrected Cassie.

"We're going to be off a day, spending the night here, but it won't be that big a deal."

Cassie's eyes were shiny, "It's more important that you're okay, Dusty."

"Yeah, I'm fine," Dusty murmured looking away.

The coffee perked and the aroma filled the living quarters. Dusty already felt much better, mentally anyway.

Cassie got down two cups from the shelf and filled them with hot coffee. She set one down in front of Dusty and hers on the other side of the table.

Gathering strength from the coffee, Dusty waited a few minutes. "Okay, so what did I do?"

Cassie swallowed a sip of coffee and crinkled her eyes.

"Careful, it's hot."

"Yes, it is." She straightened in her seat. "Well, as you probably remember, I had gone to the restroom."

"I remember."

"It's set up in the back of that hall and not very well lit. I remember thinking it wasn't all that safe." Cassie shivered. "I'm just glad nobody followed me in there."

"The last thing I remember is that skinny cowboy grabbing you."

Revulsion crossed Cassie's face. "Yes, he was." She put her hands around her cup. "I hadn't made it more than a couple of steps into the hall when he popped out. I kept thinking he was mistaking me for someone he knew—really well. He immediately started touching me and trying to kiss me."

Dusty felt a flame rise again up the back of his neck. Just the thought of another guy treating Cassie like that made his anger start all over again.

Cassie, watching him, joked, "The whole time all I could think is where is my gun when I need it?"

Dusty smiled. "He would have been toast."

Cassie's face became serious. "Um, I think he is toast."

"Oh-oh, I was afraid of that. What did I do?" Dusty held his breath and closed his eyes, not wanting to know.

"I remember trying to push him off, but he was stronger than he looked." Cassie pushed her hair from her face. "He reeked of beer and cigarettes, too." Her face paled. "He kept trying to kiss me. It was disgusting."

She cleared her throat. “Just when I didn’t think it could get much worse, there was a large roar. You, I think. And Skinny went airborne.”

“Then what?” He grimaced. It was going to get worse.

“You kept punching him. He wasn’t landing any back. I think you caught him completely by surprise.” She hesitated. “Finally you held him up against the wall by his throat. I thought you were going to kill him. I kept trying to get you to put him down, but you weren’t listening. Then four of his friends showed up with cue sticks.”

Cassie took a drink of coffee to steady herself. “I thought they were going to kill you. They hit you with a cue stick. When you got up from that, one of them cold cocked you and you went out flat on the floor. Before they could do anything else, the owner showed up. Apparently, she heard the commotion and shooed them out. They helped Skinny get up and leave, so he was okay.”

Dusty hadn’t realized he’d been holding his breath; he let it out with a large whoosh. “Thank God for that.”

“Yeah.” Cassie nodded. “The owner had the bouncer and another guy help me get you back here.” She nodded at the parking lot. “She owns the parking lot too and said you were welcome to spend the night.”

“I’m going to have to do that, I don’t feel like making the drive to Alamo right now.”

“He got you pretty good, Dusty.” She frowned at his jaw. “Do you want an ice pack for that?”

Dusty touched his tender jaw and winced. “Yeah, I might take you up on that, and a couple of Advil.”

“Sure thing.” Cassie walked over to the small refrigerator.

He put the ice pack on his cheek and thought about it. Fighting. The last fight he’d been in—he felt a rush of shame—the bar fight in Oregon when he and Mike stopped to eat on the way to the Eagle Cap. It wasn’t much of a fight. He got knocked out cold. He winced. *But I deserved it.*

Later that night, Dusty tossed fitfully in his bed and dreamed about the summer he spent in the Pasayten Wilderness when he was twelve.

*Uncle Bob threw another log on the fire. "Sit down, boy. I want to talk to you."*

*Dusty obeyed. It was the first time he'd been able to spend the entire summer with his Uncle's outfitter service. Tired of arguing, his dad said he could go. His family went to Europe without him, and he was finally free to do what he wanted.*

*Dusty knew when Uncle Bob wanted to talk, it was going to be big. He sat and waited quietly.*

*The flames from the fire flickered against Bob's face. "You're going to come across a lot of situations where you're not certain what to do. You're going to want to do the right thing."*

*"How am I going to know?"*

*"Well, a lot of times I have to sleep on it. I know in the morning." Bob raised his cowboy hat with one hand and ran his hand through his hair with the other.*

*Dusty considered it. "What does sleep have to do with it?"*

*Uncle Bob looked at him. "It removes you from the situation and lets you weigh all the possibilities, I suppose. The most important thing is that a man always holds himself accountable. Remember, you wake up with yourself in the morning."*

Dusty groaned and turned on his side. His cheek throbbed.

# Chapter Five

The sun crested the rocky mountaintops as Dusty left the trailer. He fed the horses, went back inside, and quietly put on the coffee pot. The rhythm of Cassie's breathing sounded faintly from the bed. He checked his watch, only 8:00. They were hoping to get an early start, but the incident at the restaurant had slowed everything down.

Pouring a cup of coffee, he looked out the window. A few more trailers had pulled into the lot. Overnight parking didn't appear to be abnormal here after all. They were the only occupants with horses and hay bags tied to their trailer though. Taking a last drink, Dusty set his cup down, put on his Stetson and walked out, shutting the trailer door softly behind him. Checking on the horses, he saw them standing by the trailer tearing and munching their hay. *Cassie must have double fed them last night.* He straightened, took a deep breath, and walked to the restaurant.

He pulled open the front door; the now familiar smell of cigarette smoke and stale booze rushed to meet him. Gambling machines pinged and ponged in the background. The restaurant was open for breakfast. Dusty walked over and stood by the "Please wait to be seated" sign. The smell of greasy bacon and eggs filled his nostrils. He suddenly felt hungry, but he pulled himself up short. *Maybe later, that's not what I'm here for now.*

A waitress bustled up to him with a menu under her arm. It was a different woman from yesterday. This lady had dyed black hair, heavy mascara, and lips painted bright red. As she looked at him recognition sparked into her eyes. "Hey, cowboy, how are you doing this morning?"

Heat fused into his cheeks. "Fine." He averted his eyes, hoping to put the conversation behind him.

The brunette wasn't ready to stop. "You are some fighter. Poor Luke didn't have much of a chance." She batted her eyes. "I like a man that will protect his woman." She pursed her lips. "You just don't meet many of them anymore."

Dusty cleared his throat. "Um, yeah."

"Where would you like to sit? The bar or a table?" She looked past him hopefully. "Are you alone this morning?"

"No–I mean, yes." Dusty looked up. "Actually, I'm not here for breakfast, I wanted to speak to the owner."

"Oh?" The waitress raised her eyebrows.

"Do you know where I could find her?"

"Sure." The brunette set the menus down and pointed down the hall. "Her office is right over there. And you're lucky, she's an early riser. Came in a couple hours ago."

"Thank you." He walked in the direction she'd pointed.

A dark hallway. In the dim light he barely made out a door labeled "Private." Dusty hesitated and then knocked.

A woman's deep voice said, "Come in."

He firmly turned the handle and pushed open the door.

A big-boned platinum blonde sat behind an old-fashioned wooden desk. She had bright red fingernails and lots of makeup. Dusty was no expert, but he could have sworn she looked like a madam. "Good morning, I'd like to speak with the owner."

A smile pulled at the creases of her eyes. "Well, good morning again, cowboy. I guess you don't remember me." She sat back in the chair. "We already met once."

Dusty felt his cheeks burning, but he laughed wryly. "You're the owner, I take it." He took off his hat.

"Big Kate." She stuck her hand out as she spoke.

"Nice to meet you." Dusty shook her hand.

Kate enfolded his hand in a firm grip, which surprised Dusty as her fingers appeared like fat sausages in his hand.

"Not to be confused with "Big Nosed Kate either." She pointed at him playfully. "There's a world of difference." She laughed. "We live in different times anyway." Dusty didn't know what to make of what she said and decided not to comment.

"How can I help you?" She held her arms out. "At your service!"

Dusty looked at her soberly. "Kate, I'm sorry about fighting at your place." He shifted his hat in his hands. "If I destroyed anything, I'd like to pay for it."

Kate looked at him, her face unreadable for a moment. She did have a large nose, and her left cheek sported a brown mole, painted or real. She wore a low-cut, black, V-neck dress with ample cleavage exposed. Her was hair pulled back into a chignon and wrapped in black lace. She topped it off with long dangling earrings.

The large woman's body quivered and the earrings shook. A loud guffaw erupted from her and filled the room. "I keep thinking I've seen it all, and then there's always another first." She put her pudgy hand on her chin. "Mr. Dusty, you are some kind of man. Not only are you very easy on the eyes, but you've got manners." She shook her large head. "I never."

Dusty stared at her in amazement. He'd expected to come in, fill out a check, and leave.

"Have a seat," Kate commanded. "Would you like some coffee?"

"Sure," Dusty replied automatically.

Kate picked up the phone and within a couple minutes a soft knock sounded at the door and a woman carrying two cups of steaming coffee walked in. She set one down in front of Dusty and one in front of Kate.

"Thank you, Jessie."

"My pleasure." The young woman wore a black skirt with a low-cut white blouse. Dusty assumed she came from the restaurant. She was attractive, large doe eyes and long brown hair pulled into a ponytail down her back. She smiled, her eyes resting on Dusty for a second longer than necessary, turned and left.

Dusty turned back to Kate and saw her nod approvingly at him, "You have good taste in women." She took a sip of coffee. "I saw your friend yesterday."

Not sure what to reply, Dusty elected to take a drink of coffee. It was rich and delicious. "Good coffee."

The older woman smiled at him. "I like the best in everything." She seemed to drift off momentarily and then refocused on him. "As for yesterday, I appreciate you coming back and apologizing. It means more to me than you will ever know. As a matter of fact, it's never happened before. Ever."

"I like to take care of my debts."

"In this case, I believe I owe you. That old drunk has been causing a lot of trouble with my girls—my waitresses—my employees." She finally seemed to settle on a term. "You did me one big favor. Now I have a concrete reason to eighty-six him from my place forever. And that's exactly what I told him."

As he listened to her, the true nature of Kate's business dawned on him. This wasn't just a restaurant in a western town, this was a modern-day whore house. And legal in Nevada. The thought had never crossed his mind.

"So thank you, Dusty. I'd like to pay you back. I know that any one of my girls would be happy to entertain you—and it would be on the house." Her voice lowered conspiratorially as she waved toward the hall.

Dusty did his best to hide his shock. "That's very generous of you, Kate." He took a drink of coffee. "And if the situation was different, I might take you up on it."

Kate nodded sagely. "The beauty you were with yesterday."

"Yes." He shifted in his chair. "But I would love to hear some of the history of this place, if you had the time."

"Oh, absolutely." Kate launched into the background story and it turned out sex for money had a long history in her family and establishment.

Dusty found himself captivated. Reading about the Old West was one thing, but this was living it.

The old madam had an easy way of talking. Dusty felt like he'd known her forever. The time flew by. His eyes finally drifted to the ornate clock on the wall. "Is that the right time?"

"Yes, it is. That clock has been here for years and never missed a minute." Her eyes sparkled.

Dusty jumped up. It was getting late and he'd left Cassie sleeping. "I really enjoyed talking with you, but I need to get back. My…my girlfriend was asleep when I left and she doesn't know where I am."

Kate stood up slowly. "Sorry to see you go, Dusty. You're welcome to stop by anytime you're out this way. I'll see you to the door."

She walked with him down the hall to the front doors and stopped. This time Dusty noticed smiles from several of the women. Some were seated at the gambling machines, others with a drink, seemingly girlfriends out for brunch. Another sat alone at the bar. All were striking in their different ways. All their smiles were directed at him. He hadn't even noticed before. He shook his head. *Cassie's the only one.*

Dusty shook hands with the old madam. "I'm really glad I came."

"Don't be a stranger." Kate pulled him closer. "There's going to be a lot of disappointed women here." She laughed uproariously. "But that's a good thing, they would have fought over you anyway." She turned to walk back to her office, and Dusty pushed out the glass door to the street.

Walking to the trailer, he thought about it. I'm not sure this is what Uncle Bob had in mind when he talked about settling your debts, but making new friends is always a bonus. His step felt light as he hurried back to the trailer, the morning sun warm on his back.

# Chapter Six

Cassie worked outside the trailer raking manure. The horses stood near her, eating from their respective hay bags. As Dusty approached she stopped and squinted at him in the morning sun, "I thought you left for Arizona."

"It's still kind of a long walk. Besides, I would have left the most important thing here." He took the rake from her hand, leaned it against the trailer, and pulled her into his arms." He loved the feel of holding her. The smell of horses and Cassie, he swore it was an aphrodisiac—or at least to him.

"What?" came a muffled voice from his chest. "Your horse?"

"That too," Dusty said in a husky voice.

"Movin' up. What about Scout?"

Dusty's stomach felt light and laughter overtook him. "You really know how to ruin a moment," he said playfully, releasing her. "Let's get going or we'll have to run through the entire town of Eagleclaw before we leave."

Cassie looked down. "Just checking." The corners of her mouth turned up in her enigmatic smile.

Loading the horses into the trailer, he thought back to Kate's place and all the beautiful women. Nope, not one of them was Cassie's equal. *And I'm the lucky one, because I know it.*

Back on the road again, Cassie looked out the window as the

country sped by. Bright blue sky lit up golden hills. "This is pretty amazing country, it goes on forever."

"Sure does." Dusty slowed the truck as they came to a small town. Tiny houses crowded both sides of the road, with small porches in front, and every so often a few old men were gathered on one. They waved as Dusty drove by. He raised his hand in greeting.

"Wow," said Cassie. "People really have time to sit on the front stoop and watch the world go by. What a relaxing life."

"Wouldn't it be nice. And look at the scenery you'd live in."

"All these little towns seemed to have a school, a few churches, a store and rodeo grounds. My kind of place." Cassie smiled.

"Yeah, they definitely have their priorities in order." Dusty ran his hand through his hair. "It's fun to come down here, but nothing replaces the high mountains for me."

Cassie seemed to think it over. "I agree."

They came to Alamo in early afternoon. "We could keep going to Vegas and be a lot closer," said Dusty, "but I really like the rodeo grounds here. They recently updated them and put in hookups. It's a nice place."

"Looks good to me. We're not in any hurry." Cassie sat back in her seat.

Dusty turned the rig past the combination gas station-restaurant-grocery store. The streets were old and potholed. The houses were small and needed paint. A banner hung in one yard cheering on the high school football team. Christmas lights hung on the poles, far too early. Probably a year-round fixture.

"How do you know where to go?" asked Cassie.

"Friends have given me directions over the years, and most of these towns are the same." The street opened up in front of them to a brand-new elementary school on top of the hill on the right, and to the left, the rodeo grounds.

Dusty drove in. "Ah, yes, county property, schools and fairgrounds. Way better than jails."

"Ugh, that reminds me of Ontario." Cassie shook her head in

disgust and threw her hair back. "I bet the horses are going to enjoy this."

"Yeah, let's turn them out for a while." Dusty pulled in next to some small pens on the right, with the large rodeo arena on the left. He scanned the area. "Looks like we lucked out. It's empty."

"At least until the kids get out of school." Cassie jumped out, closed the door behind her, and then opened the back door to let out the dogs. "Come on Sammy, Scout. You'll love this as much as the horses."

A few minutes later Dusty leaned against the corral fence watching Muley and Prince running up and down the arena. Scout and Sammy ran after them barking in excitement.

"Muley's going to be okay with Prince, right?" Cassie's brows drew together.

"Yeah, I think so."

She became rigid. "You think so?"

"He's married up." Dusty shrugged "He's traveling with Prince now, and that's his best friend. Doesn't take long."

"Oh, are you talking about Muley now?" she asked with mock seriousness.

Determination flashed across Dusty's face. "Yes." He scooped up Cassie in his arms and walked purposefully toward the large water trough.

"Wha...what are you doing?" Cassie squirmed.

"You seem like you might be hot." Dusty tossed her into the trough.

Cassie shrieked as she flew through the air and landed with a large splash. Greenish water sloshed out around her. She got up, soaked and spitting out the brackish water.

Dusty stood laughing at the side of the trough. She made quite the picture. Her hair streamed across her face in long strands, and she furiously brushed it out of her eyes. He realized his mistake too late. Cassie picked up a bucket by the side of the trough and filled it. Before he had a chance to get out of the way he got soaked. In rapid succession the buckets of water came at him. He just got his eyes cleared when another volley came. Finally, unable to shield himself any other way, he stepped over the side and into the trough. He wrested the bucket out of Cassie's hands. It was no easy feat; she was bent on his destruction.

Upon rendering her defenseless, they stood panting. Cassie had mud and green algae caked in her hair and clothes. Her light blue eyes flashed like ice. He pulled her into his arms and kissed her before she could grab anything else. At first, she resisted him, possibly suspecting a trick and more dunking, but the intensity of the kiss was so strong she put her arms around his neck and pulled him down to her.

"We better go in the trailer and, um, change," Dusty said as soon as he came up for air.

"Good idea," Cassie agreed.

Not wanting to lose contact with her, Dusty picked her up again, and carried her to the trailer. Rather than get the inside soaked, he kicked open the horse door and walked in from the back. Kissing, they pulled off their wet clothes and went inside.

The sound of girls' voices woke Dusty. He lay on the bed with Cassie in his arms. The horses! He'd left the horses and dogs out in the arena. Dusty felt so comfortable and relaxed, moving was the last thing on his mind. Cassie was asleep, her hair spread over him. The realization of how much he cared for her hit him by surprise. He shivered involuntarily. Letting out a deep sigh, he carefully moved her over, and set her on the bed.

"What's up?" Cassie said sleepily.

"I hear kids' voices. They're probably here to practice rodeoing, and we left the horses out in the pen." Dusty jumped down and pulled on a fresh pair of pants and a clean shirt.

Cassie sat bolt upright. "The horses. The dogs."

"I'll get them." Dusty pulled on his boots. He stopped, looked quickly in the bathroom mirror. His hair stuck out and his cheeks were flushed. He quickly wet a brush, ran it through his hair, and pulled on a ball cap. He dashed out the door, leaving Cassie looking for her clothes.

As he walked up to the pen, he saw three young girls who looked to be around twelve, all mounted. The barrels had been laid out in the middle of the arena and they were practicing runs. He scanned the area for Muley and Prince. It didn't take him long—they were in a side pen. The dogs were tied with baling twine to the fence.

Dusty walked over and leaned against the fence as one girl finished her ride. "Sorry to leave my horses out so long. I guess I fell asleep."

"No problem," said the girl closest to him, a strawberry blonde with freckles across her nose. "We just moved them over."

The brunette that had just finished the barrels rode up to him. "That's a pretty nice appy you got, mister. Ugly, but nice."

"Thank you." Dusty smiled.

"What would you take for him?"

"Not for sale." He spoke firmly.

"You sure? With his attitude, I think he'd probably make a good barrel horse." She squinted over at Muley. "He looks to have a lot of can do."

Dusty laughed. "That he does. But I need him for riding in the mountains."

"The mountains?" The girl snorted. "What's in the mountains?" She gestured at the rocky foothills surrounding her.

Dusty looked at the surroundings. "Those aren't mountains where we come from, but they look like they'd be okay riding."

"Thanks for putting our horses up." Cassie walked up behind him.

"Oh, surc." Thc brunette shrugged.

The little blonde in the back sitting quietly on her horse broke her silence. "You sure are pretty."

Cassie flushed. "Thank you."

Dusty smiled. "Yes, she is."

The little girl continued. "I was kind of hoping you might not come. I would really like to have your dogs." She gestured over at the fence. Scout and Sammy strained at the twine to come back to their owners.

"Honey, I'm sorry," said Cassie. "They are part of our family. We could not give them away."

"Kind of like my horse?" the girl asked.

"Exactly," said Dusty kindly.

"I was 'fraid of that."

"I told you, Sophie, horsemen don't get rid of their dogs." The brunette spoke up with finality.

"We'll let you girls get back to practice, and we'll just take the dogs." Dusty walked over to untie them from the fence. "We'll move our horses over by us too. Sorry again for leaving them."

"No problem," asserted the brunette spokesman. "Your turn, Sophie."

# Chapter Seven

Dusty and Cassie moved the horses to the pens next to their living quarters. They each fed and watered their horse and finished at the same time.

"What now?" Cassie gazed around the arena.

"We passed that combination store/gas station coming into town. Do you want to check that out for some dinner?"

"Sounds like a plan." She hesitated in front of the pens. "Do you think the dogs and horses will be okay here?"

Dusty glanced over at the girls still running barrels on their horses. "I'm thinking if those girls are okay, our animals are going to be okay, too."

"That's a good point," Cassie agreed. "Let me just run a brush through my hair and I'll be ready."

Dusty leaned against the pen and watched Muley eating. Scout stood by, looking up at him expectantly. "I guess I better put you in the trailer too, boy."

Scout cocked his head, concern seemed to knot his furry brows.

Dusty laughed. "It's okay. It's not going to be very long. We'll be back." He headed toward the trailer with his dog following. Stopping he looked at Scout. "Besides, Sammy's a pretty cute dog." He winked. Scout wagged his tail.

"Who are you talking to?" Cassie walked out of the trailer.

"Nobody, just Scout and I." Dusty smiled conspiratorially.

"I don't think I want to know. Come on, Sammy, load up." She gestured at the rear door of the horse trailer and her Aussie leapt in.

The sun hung low in the sky as Dusty and Cassie walked through town. The asphalt had large potholes and the sidewalks were cracked. Even with disrepair, the town had a homey feeling to it.

"Do you think you could ever live in a place like this?" asked Cassie.

Dusty took a deep breath and looked around. "It's a beautiful area. But I couldn't live here full time."

"Why not if it's beautiful?"

"Trees and mountains."

"It always comes down to that, huh?" Cassie pressed.

"Yes, I guess it does." Dusty winced.

"Well, this is pretty spectacular." She pushed against him playfully as they walked. "But I'm with you. I guess when you're born in the Pacific Northwest, some things just become the bottom line."

"Is that it?" Dusty wondered. "Well, that's okay. It's going to be fun riding down here too." He put his arm around her and they walked to the store.

It was a busy place. Trucks pulled in and out of the gas station pumps and mothers with children pushed carts of groceries in the store. A combination fast food/bakery sat just inside the door with booths in front of it.

Dusty stopped to read the menu. "Well, this is convenient. Cheeseburgers and fries."

"Salads, too." Cassie grinned.

As they sat with their food, Cassie announced, "I like this restaurant better than Ely."

Dusty felt his cheeks flush. "Why is that?"

She looked at him amused. "No cigarette smoke and stale booze."

Guilt shot through him. "Oh, yeah, it's a lot better."

"Why?" she asked innocently. "What else would it be?"

Dusty recovered quickly. "It's the Old West, could be just about anything, couldn't it?"

Engrossed in each other, they missed the trucker who came in behind them. Short and dark skinned with black hair, he wore an LA Dodgers ball cap and a faded jean jacket. He looked like he'd been on the road for a while. While waiting to order his food, the striking light brown-haired woman caught his eye. He studied the flyers on the wall next to the order window, glancing at her covertly from time to time. When his order was done, he picked up his burger and fries and slowly ambled over to a table that would afford him a good view, without being obvious. Dirt ringed his fingernails and filled the creases of his hands. He gave it no mind as he bit into the thick hamburger and watched the couple.

Dusty and Cassie finished their meal and threw the remains in the garbage can. Dusty hesitated. "Do we need something from the store?" He gestured at the other half of the building.

"I can't think of anything." Cassie laughed. "I'm so used to camping I think we better stock up, but shoot, there's a store around every corner now. So until we get where we're going, there's probably no point."

"Yeah, it's a different mindset all right." Dusty agreed. They walked toward the door. Cassie added, "As long as we've got coffee, creamer and dog food, I'd say we're good.

"Dusty kissed her on the head. "We're so compatible." He took her hand and they walked out the sliding glass doors.

The man finished his meal, chewing thoughtfully. That woman fit the description El Patron had given him. It was important that he bring the right one. The risks in the United States were considerable for kidnapping, a lot stiffer than simply transporting migrants across the border. But the money, how could he not? He had to find out more about her. If this was the woman El Patron wanted, he would be a rich man. He took a final sip of his drink and hurried out into the parking lot, leaving all the trash on the table behind him.

The large furniture truck sat out in the stall. It was a perfect foil for what he did. People, furniture, they all had to be moved at one time or another. Some willing and some not so willing. He stomped on the gas. The old truck sputtered and the gears engaged. He wasn't sure exactly which way the couple had gone. Judging by the size of Alamo, he'd bet it wasn't far. He turned out of the lot toward the center of town.

It was a good guess. A block ahead of him he saw the brown-haired man, holding the woman's hand. The way they walked it was apparent they were together. The trucker stroked his beard thoughtfully, perhaps a new couple at that. He sighed. Love wasn't always meant to be. What was really important was how much money a woman like that could bring to his life." He thought about his wife, Maria, and his child. He'd promised them he'd be back and he would. His beautiful daughter, Marisol. She needed a father. He straightened his back, a father who could provide for them. He would be all that when he returned. This money could even provide indoor plumbing. He puffed up his chest at the thought. They would be the first in the neighborhood with indoor plumbing. All would know what a good husband and father he'd be then. How proud his family would be. With all of his thoughts, he almost missed that the road ended in the rodeo grounds.

The man and woman from the store walked up a slight incline to the trailer parked by horse pens. He paused at the bottom. What to do? Before he could decide, the large man called to him.

"Are you lost?"

*Thank you, perfect.* He stuck his head out the window of his truck. "Yes, as a matter of fact I am." He hesitated. "Is this the rodeo grounds?"

"You found it. Are you planning on spending the night?"

"Yes," the trucker replied.

"There are hookups over on that side of the arena, if you need power."

"I'm self-contained, but thank you. I'll check it out." He put the truck in gear and drove around to the other side of the large arena. He needed to find out where they were going, but one thing at a time, he cautioned himself.

"That's kind of strange," said Cassie. "Do people usually camp in furniture hauling trucks?"

"Yeah, I was thinking that too." Dusty scratched Muley's head as the big blue roan plunged into his hay. "But these days who knows what people sleep in."

# Chapter Eight

Dusty woke, but lay for a while enjoying the warmth from Cassie's body next to him. It had been a long time since he had been in love with anybody. At this point he wondered whether he ever had before. He had met his first wife, Sarah, in college. At that age who knew? She was pretty. He was in his last year of law school and marriage was the next step in his perfect life plan. Sarah was a good partner. Although she'd never liked horses and despised living in the country, she'd put up with it for the most part. Putting up was a whole lot different than liking it. Dusty rubbed the sleep from his eyes. He couldn't fault Sarah for that. She had been an excellent mother. And years ago, when alcohol had overtaken him and he really needed someone to get him help, she'd been there. For that he'd always be grateful to her.

Dusty slowly eased his way out of the bed, taking care not to waken Cassie. Thoughts of the intervention with his wife and kids played back through his mind. He tried to forget that part of his life, but sometimes it managed to wiggle through his thoughts. It wasn't supposed to be something that people were ashamed of. He'd had that pounded into his head in treatment. It was a disease. Something you were born with, and you were to turn it around into a growing experience. It was an easy decision: you grew or you died. Dusty thanked God every day that he got the chance. Having his daughter Katie sobbing and begging him to stop made the choice obvious for him. It was easier than his son Nick's aloofness. The cold way he had appraised his father during the intervention reminded him of himself. He had been a good teacher. The astounding part was the amount of pain Nick's standoffishness inflicted. Dusty had never been on the receiving end before. It almost made him feel sorry for his own father—but not quite.

Putting on the pot to reheat last night's coffee, Dusty walked into the bathroom and slipped on his jeans and shirt. He brushed his teeth and ran a comb through his hair. He stopped to appraise the image. Tan skin, blue eyes with just a hint of crow's feet in the corners. His teeth were white and straight and he had what he'd heard referred to as laugh lines around his mouth. He never thought much about what he looked like. It seemed whatever it was, women made a big deal over it. He picked up his hat, sitting crown down on the dinette table—the only important thing now was what one woman thought of him.

Pulling on his jean jacket, he slipped out the trailer door. The sun lit up the dark, bare foothills around the rodeo pens. Muley and Prince neighed encouragement to him as he walked by. "Just a minute." He pulled open the back door of the horse trailer, and the two Aussies bounded out. They immediately chased around and took off to places beyond, barking in excitement. "Scout, no," commanded Dusty to the quickly retreating furry form. Scout shot him a contrite look, but didn't slow down.

Dusty tore off a couple flakes of hay from the bales on the back of his flatbed and carried them over to the horses. The second the hay went in the bags, the equines tore into them like it had been years since they had been fed. Dusty filled their water buckets from the spigot by the pens. He looked again at the sky. As the sun rose, dark purple clouds moved aside to let orange, then yellow colors rise. The hills changed from black to blue, and finally a reddish brown as the morning began to take shape.

"It's a beautiful morning, no?" said a deep voice from behind him.

Dusty jumped involuntarily. The short dark-skinned man had surprised him. He hadn't heard him approach.

"Ye—yes, it is beautiful." The water had overflowed the top of the bucket, so he reached over and turned it off.

The man leaned against the corral. "Where are you headed?"

The question seemed odd to Dusty. *Normally, didn't people usually ask you first where you were from?* He answered guardedly, "South." Passing the man, he filled Prince's water bucket. "What about you?"

"Oh." The dark face beamed, exposing yellow teeth. "I, too, am heading south."

Dusty didn't want to continue the conversation and wished the man would leave, but he didn't seem close to that.

The man fished in his pocket for a cigarette. Striking a match, he lit the end of it and inhaled deeply. Smoke poured out his nose and enveloped his head in the crisp early morning air.

"My name is Javier Mendoza."

"Dusty Rose."

Javier continued. "The woman you are with, she is very beautiful." He took a deep inhale of cigarette. "Is she your wife?"

Feeling the hair raise up on the back of his neck, Dusty tried to reason with himself. It was an innocent question. Why was it so offensive? "Pretty much," he said curtly.

Javier threw back his head and laughed deeply. "Oh, senor, I'm sorry. I always ask too many questions."

Before Dusty could respond, the LQ door flew open, and Cassie walked out. Her light brown hair shone in the early light. She wore a dark jean jacket, green plaid shirt, and a black silk scarf tied around her neck. Both men's eyes were riveted on her. Cassie looked at the second man and surprise crossed her face. She quickly looked at Dusty, a question in her eyes.

"This is Javier, our neighbor in the furniture van," said Dusty.

"Oh, good morning, Javier," she managed a faint smile.

"And this is Cassie Martin." Dusty hesitated and plunged ahead. "My fiancée."

"Pleased to meet you." The man dipped his head respectfully. "You are a very beautiful woman." He turned to Dusty. "And you are a very lucky man."

Cassie turned pink. Dusty was pretty sure it had less to do with being called a beautiful woman than being called his fiancée. He'd heard her called the former several times in his presence, but it was a first for the latter. Dusty didn't even know why he said it, but he had an overwhelming desire to protect her. And that was the best thing he could give her at the moment. Of course, if things changed, he wouldn't hesitate to employ force.

Javier took another deep drag on his cigarette and threw it to the ground. He gave a half-hearted stomp with his heel on the smoldering embers.

"Are you delivering furniture?" asked Cassie.

Confusion crossed the man's dark face, and then he looked over at his van. "Oh, that." He gestured at the truck. "Yes, it is for deliveries, but not always furniture." He winked at Dusty conspiratorially.

Not knowing what the man was talking about—human trafficking seemed like a good guess—Dusty walked over to Cassie and put his arm around her. "Well, it's been nice talking with you. We've got to get to breakfast now." He steered her back to the trailer door, without looking back, escorted her inside ahead of him and closed the door.

She sat down at the dinette. The corners of her mouth turned up in a smile.

"I'll get us some coffee." Dusty opened the cabinet and took out coffee cups. He filled them and reached into the refrigerator for vanilla creamer. He set the coffee down in front of her.

"So when's the big date?" asked Cassie.

Dusty asked slowly, "What date?"

"Our wedding," Cassie responded with a straight face.

Heat flooded Dusty's face, "Oh, that. Sorry," he said with a mixture of apology, embarrassment and something else, which he couldn't place. He sat down with his coffee. "That little guy is a creep. He asked a lot of questions." He poured vanilla into the cups.

"Questions about you. I just wanted to put a stop to it."

"Really." Cassie raised her eyebrows. "What kind of questions?"

"I didn't let him get that far, but he seemed too interested in you."

Cassie laughed nervously. "Well, good. Because I don't want to end up in the back of a furniture van."

Dusty put his hand on her arm. "And you never need to worry about that."

A far-off barking interrupted their conversation. Cassie stood. "Where is Sammy?"

They looked out the window of the trailer. Javier walked toward his truck with both dogs following right on his heels. "That's not like Scout." Dusty jumped up and rushed out of the trailer.

They got outside just as the man got to his truck. He opened the back door, pausing for a minute to reach into his pocket. He tossed something on the ground and the dogs ate it hungrily. He reached into his pocket again and threw something on the inside of the van. Dusty couldn't hear him, but he could see him coaxing the dogs to go inside.

"Scout," Dusty called, his voice ripping into the morning silence. Midway into the door Scout froze and pivoted on his back legs.

Cassie put her hands up to her mouth and called, tension rife in her voice. "Sammy, come." Her dog stopped and whirled, following Scout. They both ran across the arena to their owners.

Behind the rapidly approaching dogs, Dusty saw Javier quickly shut the back door of the truck and run around to the driver's side. He hopped in and gunned the engine. With a couple of black puffs of smoke from the exhaust pipe, the big truck lumbered away.

Cassie threw her head into Sammy's neck. "Oh, my God! That horrid little man tried to steal our dogs." The blue merle Aussie licked Cassie's face enthusiastically, unaware of the close call she'd just had.

Dusty put his arms around Scout and held him. Scout's heart beat against his chest. "Unbelievable. Right out the window in plain sight."

"What if we hadn't looked just then? They'd be gone."

Dusty buried his head in Scout's neck. "We're just going to have to keep an eye on them more closely."

"There's nothing we can do either," Cassie dropped her head. "Attempted dognapping would be difficult to prove."

Dusty stood up. "At least now we know who to look for."

"Where did you tell him we were going?" Cassie's forehead creased.

"I just said south. That's it."

"Good, that's a big place. And I think we'd notice him if he tries to follow us." Cassie stood up. "Did you want to have some breakfast?"

"Let's load up and head down the road," said Dusty. "I don't like it here as much as I did before."

Cassie nodded. "Me either."

They fed their dogs. The horses finished eating, and they tied them to the trailer while they cleaned out their pens. The day was warming up fast, and Dusty was in his shirtsleeves before he finished.

Cassie loaded the dogs in the back seat of the pickup truck. Dusty started the truck to let the engine warm up, and he loaded the horses. They drove around the arena past the overnight camping area on their way out. Dusty noticed empty bags and bottles lay in the spot where the furniture van was parked earlier. Javier had apparently decided to dump his garbage in the parking space rather than use the garbage cans a short distance away. He shook his head in disgust.

As they turned down the residential street back to the highway, they passed kids carrying backpacks and heading toward the school. The street guards held up their flags for the children to cross while Dusty waited. The warm, small town atmosphere began to overtake the feeling of violation that Javier had brought to their stay.

"I'm just going to top the fuel off at the station." He pulled the truck and trailer once again into gas station/store.

He got out to fill up. The pump beeped and directed him to go inside. "I'll be right back. Do you want anything inside?"

"No, I'm good," said Cassie, "Thanks."

A stocky young woman stood behind the counter. Dusty handed her his card and waited for her to approve it. "Have you heard of anyone trying to steal dogs around here?"

Her face turned white and she hesitated. "Did you have a problem?"

"Yes. We were down at the rodeo grounds and this guy with a furniture truck almost stole our dogs."

"Oh, no," she breathed, "Not again."

Dusty perked up, "Again?"

The woman gathered herself, finished with his card, and handed it to him. "It's been happening off and on around here. I've heard, depending on the breed of the dog, it can bring a good price to some people down in Phoenix."

"Is that so?" He tucked the card back in his wallet. "Well, they almost got a couple more." He turned to walk out and smiled at her. "Thanks for the info." A flush reddened her cheeks and she nodded back.

Dusty slid back into the truck. "Our dogs weren't the first victims of possible dognapping."

"Really?" Cassie raised her eyebrows.

"Yeah, I guess there's a market for them in Phoenix."

Cassie reached back and stroked Sammy's head. "We're just going to have to be more vigilant."

"Yes, we are." Dusty put on the turn indicator and got back on their route. As they passed the end of town, a large "A" sat high up on the hillside.

"Alamo." Cassie turned in her seat to face Dusty. "What's next?"

Dusty put on his sunglasses and gave her a devilish smile. "Vegas, baby."

# Chapter Nine

The highway wound through arid farmland and sliced through quasi-mountains. Cassie studied the landscape through the window. "I'm not sure what I'd call those hills."

"Pretty close to mountains," said Dusty.

"Yes, there's even snow on top of some of them." She stared out the window again.

"It's a beautiful landscape. Feels lonely, though."

Dusty pointed over the hills in front of them. "All of it falls by the wayside up here, we're almost to Las Vegas. Loneliness is over."

"Oh." Cassie frowned. "There can be a lot of loneliness there too, I've heard. Depends on what you're doing, I guess."

"True. None of that lifestyle has ever appealed to me." He settled back in his seat. "I've gone to a few Continuing Legal Education conferences in Vegas over the years, but it's always the same thing. I'm not a gambler."

"I've been there too." Cassie shook her head. "It's never done much for me either."

The highway dropped over a hill into a metropolis with tall buildings jutting into the skyline. The road became alive with vehicles, at times bumper to bumper. Dusty sat up, his full attention now on maneuvering the horse trailer in and out of traffic.

"Geez, I guess we hit rush hour." Cassie grimaced.

Dusty glanced at his watch. “Noon.”

“Guess they’re in a hurry to eat.”

They made it through the city traffic and drove across the bridge at Hoover Dam. Cassie gestured at the window again. “Why is there wire caging up the sides of the bridge?”

“Maybe they’re trying to head off the depressed gamblers from Vegas,” suggested Dusty.

“I never thought of that.” Cassie nodded. “Good idea.”

The sun was warm and relaxing, and Dusty felt himself drifting. “How about we take the next stop and get some lunch? And coffee.”

“Sounds good to me.”

An old weather-beaten house appeared on their right with a sign “Good Eats” on the front. Dusty pulled into the gravel parking lot and got out of the truck. Next to the restaurant a flea market featured blankets and several other items. They walked up the creaky wooden steps to the house.

It was dark inside and a few round tables took up the space that had probably once been the dining room and living room. An order bar sat in the back of the room with handwritten menus and specials hanging on pieces of paper. The air was rife with the smell of bacon and eggs. A couple patrons sat at one of the round tables, drinking coffee and reading newspapers.

“Hi,” Dusty greeted the middle-aged woman behind the counter.

“Good morning.” She hesitated. “Or whatever it is.” She pulled her pencil out and got ready to write. “You just missed the morning special, sorry to say.” She tucked a few dark strands of hair behind her ear and smiled. “But that’s okay, it’s all good.”

“I’m sure it is.” Dusty smiled and turned to Cassie. “What would you like?”

Cassie flushed. “Dusty, I can pay—”

Not waiting for her to protest, Dusty cut in, “Looks like they have some great salads.”

“Yes,” she said finally. “Okay, I’ll take your club salad.”

The waitress beamed with pleasure. "What kind of dressing would you like?"

"Ranch would be great. Thank you."

"And you?" The woman turned to Dusty.

"Well, since I missed the bacon and eggs, how about a bacon cheeseburger? That ought to make up for it."

"You bet." The waitress winked at him. "And since you missed the special, we'll throw a little extra bacon on it for you."

It was Dusty's turn to beam with pleasure. "That would be wonderful. You never can have enough bacon."

They got their drinks out of the coolers and sat down. "I like this place," announced Dusty. "Extra bacon."

Cassie rolled her eyes. "Of course you do."

Trucks rolled down the highway outside the little restaurant. The hiss of airbrakes sounded close by. Looking out the window, Dusty noticed a fuel stop not too far away. The door creaked open and a group of men walked in. By the looks of them, he'd bet they were truckers. Their clothes were rumpled, they wore ball caps pulled down on their heads, and their pants hung low. One of them was almost falling off.

Cassie took a bite of salad as low-pants turned around to show a perfect plumber's assembly. She quickly averted her eyes and looked at Dusty. It was all he could do not to explode laughing at the pained expression on her face.

The truckers picked up on Cassie's presence quickly. One nudged the other and pretty soon three smiling faces beamed at her. She smiled back briefly and sat her fork down. "I think I'm done."

Dusty was still working on his burger with extra bacon. As far as the truckers were concerned, he didn't exist. He couldn't figure out why he found that so funny this time, but he did. "Just about there," he mumbled, grabbing his Squirt and washing down the rest of his burger.

A girl who didn't look more than fifteen hurried up with a tub. "Are you done?" she politely asked Cassie.

"Yes," said Cassie.

The girl scooped up her dishes and whisked back behind the counter.

"Must be a family business," Cassie watched her leave.

Dusty tossed his napkin down on the counter. "Train 'em young." He stood up. "You want to see what they've got out back?"

"Why not?" Cassie stood up.

Dusty threw a couple bills down on the table. "We can stop at the truck stop next door and I'll get some coffee on our way out." He held the door open and they walked into the market.

Cassie was oblivious to the truckers' disappointed faces as she breezed out the door.

The flea market turned out to be larger than it appeared, featuring almost a full city block of wares in the aisles. Busier too, with parking on the backside, and people buzzing through the vendors. Jewelry, concrete statuaries, and colorful blankets hung on the booths.

Cassie paused at a jewelry stand and admired the turquoise. She touched a delicate bracelet, aqua stones with inlays of silver feathers. "This is beautiful. I've always loved turquoise."

"That's a nice piece." Dusty admired the bracelet.

They walked the short distance to the truck and got in. Dusty turned the key and then stopped. "Oh, man, I forgot my coffee. Why don't you wait here for a minute and I'll go get some."

"Okay."

"Do you want anything?"

"No, I'm fine, thanks." Cassie smiled.

Dusty ran back into the flea market. He returned a few minutes later with a large cup of steaming coffee.

"I didn't know they had coffee in there? I thought it was at the truck stop."

"They have coffee everywhere. It's what makes the world go around."

"I see." She nodded. "At least in Washington State anyway."

They continued down the highway. Cactus began to appear with more regularity the farther south they drove.

"We're going to be coming up to Wickenburg in a little bit," said Dusty. "That's where all the ropers winter."

"I've heard about that place. A lot of people love it."

Mobile homes and houses gathered together on the roadsides, and traffic increased. Soon they were in a town with a distinct Western motif.

"We can come back here later on, but right now I think we should keep going so we can hit Apache Junction before it gets too late." Dusty negotiated the trailer through the islands in the center of town as they passed through. Tourists, intermingled with people dressed in cowboy garb, populated the streets.

Leaning forward and looking out the window, Cassie said, "I'd like that."

Dusty looked at her amused. "What don't you like?"

She paused and answered honestly. "A lot of things, Dusty."

"Name them," he challenged.

"Well, since I have a little time, okay." She flipped her hair back. "Shopping malls, big cities, formal dinners, social events, really high heels that hurt my feet, doing things that are socially required." She hesitated. "Court motions with arrogant attorneys…"

Dusty was caught off guard—suddenly he got it and laughed. "I have a feeling who that could be." She was talking about when they first met in a motion hearing a couple years ago in King County. It seemed so long ago now. Still, he felt the burn of embarrassment that he came across so badly to Cassie. *Maybe I'll never live that down.*

Cassie smiled like the cat who ate the canary. "Hmm, if the shoe fits, I guess."

"I need to stop up here and use the bathroom." He motioned at the approaching rest area.

"Coffee again." Cassie teased.

Dusty pulled the living quarters into the truck parking, and they walked to the building.

He got back first and walked around the trailer to check on the horses. Muley and Prince stood quietly, fly masks on their faces.

He knew people traveled for longer periods with their horses, some would drive for twenty hours, but he liked to give the animals a break. Traveling could be stressful and Dusty didn't want them to get sick.

Colic was a common ailment that caused extreme cramping in the horses' intestines, like the flu. The problem was horses could not throw up. Instead, they would go down, kicking at the pain in their stomachs. That activity could cause a "twisting of a gut" which was fatal. More than once Dusty had heard a horse go down and start kicking. He hurried and got the horse back up again. In days past, walking the horse would take care of the pain. It was a long process. The drug Banamine now quickly took care of the problem with a lot less walking. He always carried a tube with him.

Dusty walked to the cab. Cassie was just coming with the dogs. She opened the back door and commanded, "Load up." Both Aussies jumped in. Scout smiled at Dusty.

"Wow, now you've even got my dog." He put his hands on his hips.

Cassie laughed. "I think Sammy might have something to do with it. He's pretty fond of her."

Dusty got ready to start the truck and then stopped.

Waiting, Cassie said, "If you're tired, I can drive too."

Digging around in his pocket, Dusty pulled out a small bag.

Cassie gasped. "What did you do?"

"You know that guy in the King County courtroom? I want to make sure you know it wasn't me." He picked up her wrist and fastened a bracelet on.

"It's beautiful." She smiled, admiring the silver and turquoise standing out again her tan skin.

Dusty undid her seatbelt, pulled her over and kissed her. His head exploded with the fragrance of her hair. Fir trees and fresh air. The need for her was overwhelming and he completely forgot where he was. If Cassie hadn't broken away from him, he wasn't sure where it would have ended.

"Whoa, Dusty." She sat up, breathless, her hair messed up and her shirt unbuttoned. "I think this is probably not the best place for this."

It took him a minute to reorient himself. Letting go of her wasn't easy for him. He sat up in his seat. "Sorry about that." He cleared his throat. "I've never met a woman like you in my life." He turned the ignition, smoothed his hair, set his Stetson back on, and straightened his dark glasses. Flashing her a grin, he said, "Let's go to Red Rock Stables."

# Chapter Ten

The setting sun outlined the hills in reddish gold and the skyline darkened as they entered the freeway traffic of Phoenix.

Dusty shifted in his seat. Stiffness had settled in his back after the long drive. He sighed. Now bumper to bumper traffic lay in front of him.

"So we're going to ride horses here? Cassie frowned.

Dusty stretched, careful to keep his foot on the brake. "We're not quite there yet. We've still got an hour and a half."

"Or longer." Cassie flopped back on the seat.

"Yeah. At least we don't have to worry about rain obliterating our sight."

Cassie frowned. "From what I've read, when it does rain here it does a little more than cloud your vision. It picks up your whole car and washes it away."

"I've heard that too." Dusty chuckled.

The red taillights in front appeared endless, and like a big snake, its eyes blinked off and on as they inched forward. Dusty stole a glance at Cassie who was staring out the window. What was she thinking? They'd talked a lot in the truck during the twenty-five-hour drive. It was stunning how much alike they were. She was easily the brightest and most capable woman he had ever met.

"You can go, Dusty," Cassie prompted.

He shook his head. "Highway hypnosis." He crept up the ten feet in front of him and stopped again.

By the time they entered Apache Junction it was dark, and the moon inching up in the sky. "We'll just stay on the Apache Trail. There's a western themed town right across the street from the RV park. Watch for those signs."

"Oh, you mean Goldfield Ghost Town?"

"How did you guess?"

"We just passed a sign back there."

"Did it say how far?"

"Two miles."

Lights appeared from the ghost town, burning brightly among old styled buildings and various pieces of mining equipment. On the right, they almost missed a small sign said "Red Rock Stable."

Dusty turned in and slowly drove down the road. It forked and a sign with an arrow pointed left to the stables. As they pulled into the clearing, a huge Saguaro cactus stood in front of them, illuminated by the barn lights. It appeared to be supported by an intricate system of belts and cables.

Cassie leaned forward. "That's interesting."

"Yeah, they're protected. You have to get permission to move them for any reason. And if you get it, you have to transplant them."

"I hope it works out."

"They're really slow growing," said Dusty. "The first arm takes seventy-five to a hundred years to grow and they can live a hundred-fifty years. They are a very old plant."

A small man walked briskly to the truck. He carried a flashlight. "Hello."

"Hi, I'm Dusty Rose and this is Cassie Martin."

A smile lit the fine-boned features of the man's face. Dusty thought he appeared Vietnamese. "I am Bob, and welcome to Red Rock Stable. We've been expecting you."

"Thank you, Bob. It took us a little longer than we'd anticipated."

Bob waved it off. "That traffic in Phoenix, it gets worse every year." He turned toward the stables. "Come, I'll show you where to put your horses and park your truck."

Dusty and Cassie followed. Dusty stretched, glad to finally be able to walk again. The air, cool despite the warm day felt good on his skin.

"You put horses here." Bob gestured his light on two empty stalls. They were open air with a roof. "You can water there."

Dusty saw the plastic half barrels under the water faucets, which obviously doubled as water troughs.

They unloaded the horses and Bob directed them over to a parking spot. Dusty backed in, and the utilities—power, water, and septic—were on the side ready to hook up. There were a few rigs there, but it looked like there was room for a lot more of them. "Are other people coming?"

"Oh, yeah," said Bob. "The place will be full by the end of the month. Reservations already full for next year."

"Wow, we were lucky to get in."

Bob nodded enthusiastically. "We had a cancellation." He flashed the light for Dusty to hook up to the water and sewer. "I'll let you get settled. See you tomorrow."

"Yeah, thanks a lot, Bob." Dusty slowly walked into the trailer. He sat down hard on the dinette cushion.

Cassie had already taken care of the slideout and coffee perked on the stovetop.

"It smells good in here."

"I would offer you dinner, but I'm not sure what we have." Cassie opened the cabinets. "Aha." She pulled a package of buns off the shelf. Turning around, she opened the refrigerator and took out a package of brats. "I think these might go together."

Dusty laughed. "You're going to put Mike out of business if you get any better at detective work."

Cassie smiled. "I may have a way to go yet, but you're right; finding brats and buns is a good start."

In spite of being so tired, a warm satisfaction pooled in Dusty's stomach. The coffee was good, the brats were decent, and the woman in front of him was entertaining. *I can't believe I even had to think twice about asking her out.* He finished his coffee. "If you don't mind, I think I'm going to turn in. That was a long drive."

"Yeah, I'll be right behind you. It was an awfully long sit." She winked. "I had to keep my eyes open for furniture trucks."

Dusty smiled. "Good girl. Always keep a lookout."

He just began to drift off to sleep when he felt the bed move and a faint whiff of shampoo as Cassie lay down next to him. In spite of himself he pulled her into his arms. Close never seemed close enough with her. She fit perfectly next to him. Her head lay under his chin. He rubbed her back. Sleepiness began to leave him, and something else poured in. It began as a dull ache in his groin. He inhaled her, and turning her head to him, he began kissing her. The kisses went deeper and the need in him grew stronger. Without a thought to time, place, or tiredness he pulled her under him. She gasped and that made him want her more. In his mind, he was riding through the mountains, loping through the snow-covered peaks. It was dark and the stars sparkled in the sky—suddenly they exploded. Breathing in gasps, he hung onto her. She breathed hard too. It was his last thought as he slipped into an exhausted sleep.

Dusty softly closed the camper door behind him, taking care not to wake Cassie. The sun felt bright and warm for the hour. Squinting, he looked beyond the paddock area at the large red rock mountain formation in the background. It was outstanding, huge and commanding over the landscape. The rays of sunshine lit it up into a fiery red color.

He paused on his walk to the horses and leaned against the paddock, taking it all in. The shadows in front of the hill were dotted with green Saguaro cacti. Dusty had never seen them before. They stood like pale green sentinels around the base of the golden red rock.

"It's a purdy sight, ain't it?" A gravelly voice spoke from behind him.

Dusty jumped. He turned and instantly felt a flush of embarrassment.

"Whoa, sorry, pardner, didn't mean to startle you." The owner of the voice was probably in his seventies. He wore a long gray beard and a brown cowboy hat that had definitely seen some trails.

The old man stuck out a weather-beaten tan hand. "Name's Jim Rice. I hale from Oklahoma."

"Dusty Rose, from Washington."

Jim nodded sagely. "I wondered. I saw you and your wife pull in late last night, but I was too tired to get up and help ya."

"No problem. I'm sorry if we woke you up. The traffic was much worse than we'd anticipated."

*I probably should straighten him out on the wife thing, but heck, let them think what they want.* Dusty pushed the thought aside.

"You're new here. If you'd like to go for a ride later in the week once you get settled, I'd be happy to show you around some." Jim's smile showed a few missing teeth.

"Thanks. That would be great. Love to learn some of the trails." Dusty nodded emphatically. "I'd better feed the horses now, so we can ride today."

"Yeah." Jim nodded at the bright ball of yellow streaming over the mountain. "Looks like she's gonna be another hot one. Riding down here, you want to get an early start."

Dusty whistled as he walked to the horses. This place was getting more interesting all the time.

The furniture truck lumbered down the road. Javier was frustrated. He'd purposefully pulled into the Pahranagat Wildlife Refuge just out of Alamo and waited for Dusty's LQ to pass by. The furniture truck worked well because it blended in, unless you were looking for it. And now he wasn't sure. Why had he tried to take the dogs? Easy money was easy money, he reasoned. Fate had just been unkind to him. Two more minutes! But he must be very careful.

Phoenix traffic had been insane. In the miles and miles of cars he'd lost the truck and living quarters. He felt weak with despair, but chastised himself. "I made a promise, Marisol, my little girl, and I will keep it." He said it with finality, not knowing how he was going to do it.

The cars dropped off and the freeway soon opened up. Javier drove toward the mountains in front of him. The Superstitions, he'd heard them called. It could be lucky.

# Chapter Eleven

Dusty threw the horses hay and filled their water troughs. They tore eagerly into the flakes. It was good to see they were eating well. One of the dangers of traveling with horses was the possibility of them "tying up." A major stomachache could cause at the least discomfort and the worst death. There were still a couple bales of hay left, but they were going to need more soon. Dusty looked around and saw a wheelbarrow and fork nearby. He rolled it into the stalls and began cleaning.

Later, as he opened the door of the horse trailer, fresh coffee filled his nostrils. "Hey." Cassie sat at the dinette table and looked ready to leave. Her long brown hair hung loose over her shoulders, and she wore a light-weight red and black cotton shirt. She smiled, showing perfect white teeth.

"Hey, beautiful." Sometimes he amazed himself at how easily saying things like that came to him when he spoke to her.

"Coffee's ready." She gestured at the pot on the stove.

Dusty poured himself a cup. "The horse pens are cleaned, and they'll be done eating in about an hour."

"Thanks."

"We've only got two bales of hay left."

"That works." Cassie flipped her hair back. "We need groceries, too."

Dusty took a sip of coffee and looked out the window at the

Superstitions. The earlier gold on the mountains had melted off and turned to bright red. "That is some mountain."

"Isn't it beautiful?" Cassie agreed. "This is a great camping spot. She sat back smiling, "I don't think we could get any closer."

"Tonto National Forest, here we come." Dusty grinned.

Cassie smiled. "And you know it's raining in Eagleclaw."

"What's it going to be here today?"

"I saw 80 on my phone."

Dusty stretched back in his seat. "I could get used to this."

In the center of the RV park was a laundry room and a couple hitch rails. Dusty led the horses out and tied them. Cassie brought her brushes over and they began to curry them.

The park buzzed with activity. Most of the occupants appeared to be retired. They parked their huge living quarter trailers for the winter at the Red Rock Stables. The riding looked endless as far as Dusty could tell. He'd looked at maps of the area; not only was the Tonto National Forest right outside the RV park, but across from them sat the Goldfield Mountains, with endless possibilities of their own. The Salt River and more riding yet lay beyond.

Dusty threw his saddle up on Muley. The big roan laid his ears flat against his head. Dusty ignored him and reached underneath to pick up the cinch.

Pulling the bridle on Prince, Cassie watched Dusty deftly put the bit in and pull the headstall over Muley before he could react. "That horse is so nasty."

"It's all a show. The more intimidated you are, the better his day."

"Whatever. Sometimes it's just nice to have a happy horse." She patted Prince affectionately. The gray shook his head and munched on his bit. "I'll get our lunches and lock up if you're ready."

"Sounds good." Dusty buckled the throat latch on Muley's bridle. Having lost the battle, the blue roan stood quietly, occasionally flicking his tail. Dusty was surprised at the lack of interest Muley displayed. He'd never been to Arizona before, but if all the Saguaro cacti didn't faze him, probably nothing would.

Cassie came out wearing her straw cowboy hat. She handed Dusty his lunch and put hers in the saddlebags. In one fluid motion, she mounted Prince.

After tightening the cinch, Dusty got on Muley. As they rode out of the stables, other people were feeding their horses and cleaning stalls. They waved as they rode by. Despite the early hour, Dusty could already feel the warmth of the sun on his back.

A dirt road ran behind the stables and they rode through several spiny cacti. "What kind of a cactus is that?" Cassie pointed at a plant that appeared to be covered in cotton.

"That's a Cholla," said Dusty. "Be really careful of that one. It breaks off in little balls and falls on the trail. It sticks to the horses' fur."

"Ugh." Cassie scrunched her face.

"Worse yet, it has little quills that inject a nasty sting."

"Wait. Is it alive?"

"No, but it sure seems like it." Dusty pulled a comb out of his pocket. "I brought this just in case."

"If your hair gets messed up?"

Dusty replied his voice thick with disgust. "No, not for my hair." He pointed at the little cottony balls on the trail. "If one of those flips onto the horse, we can comb it off."

Cassie giggled. "Sorry, I wasn't thinking about Cholla."

They rode on in silence, huge Saguaro cacti populated either side of the trail.

"It's funny," said Cassie. "A lot of them appear to be in motion. Look over there, they're dancing."

The cacti she pointed at had arms that intertwined and appeared to be frozen in a jig.

"How about that one? He's scared." Dusty pointed at one that had a hole like a mouth and his "arms" up in mock terror.

"How do you think Sammy and Scout are going to do with the cactus?" Cassie asked.

"I'm not sure, but it looks like they'll have plenty opportunity to find out."

"I'm glad we waited to take them," said Cassie. "It was a good idea to at least get the lay of the land first."

"Plus, we don't know about the rattlesnake population around here. We know they're here."

"And they get real big," added Cassie.

Dusty nodded. "That's what I've heard."

The trail was sandy, with vegetation on either side. Trees with huge thorns and other varieties of cactus besides Saguaro and Cholla lay on the ground.

"Everything here has thorns," said Cassie.

"Guess that's how it protects itself."

The trail went in and out through the thorny plants and dropped down to a sandy parking area. Dusty rode through a gate, crossed a dirt road, and they rode into the foothills of the Goldfield Mountains. There wasn't a specific trail, but several different ones weaving through the spiny plants. Occasionally a random dirt road would cross their path.

"What's over there?" Cassie pointed at the group of dark buildings in the distance.

"That's the Goldfield Ghost Town. Let's ride into it. I heard you can stop and tie up at the saloon."

"Really?" Cassie's face brightened.

They wove through the cactus and roads, hitting an occasional wash where an earlier flash flood had rushed through. The sandy bottoms made for soft travel in the otherwise rocky terrain. They found that their routes were eventually cut off by low hanging, thorny trees.

It was noon by the time they rode into Goldfield. The town was alive with tourists. A train pulled out and sounded a shrill whistle. As it chugged around the perimeter of the ghost town, the open-air cars were loaded to capacity with tourists. A loud speaker informed the occupants the history of the area, including the famous Lost Dutchman Mine.

"What is the Lost Dutchman Mine?" Cassie asked.

"That's supposed to be a true story." Dusty reined in Muley. "It's about a German immigrant, Jacob Waltz, who supposedly discovered a huge gold mine in the 19th Century in the Superstition Mountains. He kept its location a secret."

"A German Dutchman?"

"That's what I thought at first too," said Dusty. "But Germans used to be known as Deutschman, so I guess it was turned into Dutchman."

"So what happened?" persisted Cassie.

Dusty shrugged. "Nobody has found it so far."

A group of tourists with cameras snapped pictures of Cassie and Dusty as they rode by. A woman with a stroller hurried in front of them. Dusty had to check Muley to keep him from running into them.

They rode down a hill and in front of them in large letters on a wooden building, the "Mammoth Saloon." All the structures were old west-style clapboard. Several tables sat outside on a wooden deck. Hitch rails ran alongside the building, with a water trough in front. About twenty horses were tied to the rail. Cassie and Dusty looked for an opening. Dusty tied his mount on the outside. He didn't want to risk Muley kicking another horse.

Dusty liked how his spurs jingled as his boots struck the wood planks. He'd forgotten he had his gun on, but he felt it now against his hip. *Nice there is open carry in Arizona.* Passing the tables of tourists and their hamburgers, it was hard to miss the looks. Dusty got the distinct impression that people thought they were the real deal. He smiled. *And maybe we are—at least as close as it gets now.*

Dusty opened the door for Cassie and she passed through. Inside the saloon was dark and smelled like stale beer. Wooden chairs and slab tables sat with napkin dispensers and salt and pepper. Chandeliers made of old wagon wheels hung from the ceiling.

"Good afternoon," a voice called out from the bar.

"Good afternoon." Dusty touched the brim of his hat.

A small black haired, dark-skinned man smiled at them. His

eyes sparkled in the dim light. "What would you like to drink?"

Without hesitating Dusty replied, "How about a couple sarsaparillas?"

"Coming right up. Have a seat and I'll bring them out to you."

Dusty pulled the chair out for Cassie. The bartender stood right behind them, setting down dark brown bottles. Dusty handed the man several bills, and the small man rushed back to the bar.

Country music played in the background. Cassie picked up her bottle and looked at it appraisingly. "I've never had a sarsaparilla before."

Dusty flashed her his white toothed smile. "Guess there's a lot of firsts on this trip."

Sitting at a table in the back of the bar, Javier took a deep drink of his beer, watching the couple intently. He'd lost them once, but he didn't intend to let them slip through his grasp a second time. A lucky guess they'd come here. He reached in his pocket and fingered his cigarettes longingly. There'd be time later to smoke. He chuckled to himself, his lip lifting in a nasty grimace. There'd be plenty of time for lots of things later.

# Chapter Twelve

A country western singer set up on the deck outside and the music floated through the open door into the bar. Dusty settled back in his chair. The smell of old wood and horse sweat mixed with beer filled his senses. Almost as a test, the bar scene at the tavern near the Eagle Cap passed through his mind. He and Mike had been driving down to the Eagle Cap Wilderness to pack in and meet a new outfitter client. It had been late at night and they were both hungry. The small bar with its flickering light had been the only option for food. One short stop had started a deadly series of events and sent Dusty spiraling into a dry drunk. A reactivation of his alcoholism without one drink. He shuddered and checked his emotions. Sitting next to Cassie he felt grounded, maybe for the first time in his life.

"Ahem." Cassie cleared her throat pointedly.

"Sorry." Dusty came back to reality. "Did I miss something?"

"I said, I feel like I'm in a Western movie."

Dusty laughed. "Me too, and I like it."

The bartender rushed up. "Need any refills?"

"I'm good, thank you." Cassie shook her head.

Dusty grinned. "I like to hold it to one drink."

"A wise man." The bartender nodded sagely. "But perhaps you'd like a burger. Everything here is mammoth."

"Do tell." Dusty contemplated the menu.

"That would go with the theme all right." Cassie nodded.

Another couple walked in, catching the dark man's eye. "If you change your mind, you know where to find me." He hurried back to his post behind the big wooden bar.

"Are you hungry?" asked Dusty as an afterthought.

"Not yet, I'm still trying to soak it all in."

Dusty rose and held out his hand. "Would you like to take a turn on the promenade?"

"Love to." Cassie giggled. "Maybe then I can actually find out what a promenade is."

Leaving the horses still tied to the hitch rail, they walked out the other door of the saloon onto the dirt street. A wooden plank sidewalk lined the road on either side abutting several shops.

They casually walked down the planks, window shopping. The road went up a slight incline. At the top of the hill sat a church, its steeple pointing skyward, and a bell underneath to call worshippers to service.

"So accurate," said Cassie. "You just never see a Western town without a church in it."

"That's true."

"We should see if there's a service."

"Really?" Dusty marveled at the idea. Another side to Cassie. "I didn't know you went to church."

"Not a lot, but I am a believer," she said firmly. "Working full time and riding horses keeps me pretty busy."

Dusty didn't say anything, considering what she said.

They walked into a hat store. "Oh, perfect." Cassie grinned.

"Do you need another hat?"

Cassie gave him a deflated look. "A girl can't have too many hats."

"Silly me." Dusty held out his hands, palms up. "Let's see them on you."

She tried on different hats, waiting for Dusty's opinion on each of them.

He sighed. "I have to be honest, you look dynamite in all of them."

"And that's an unbiased opinion?"

"Cross my heart." He made the gesture.

"Whatever. Let's go." She smiled at the shopkeeper. "You have beautiful hats, and I just might be back."

"Thank you, ma'am." The short, stoop-shouldered bespectacled man, wearing an apron, grinned at her.

Walking back out on the sidewalk, a crowd had gathered. In the middle of the street two cowboys were shouting at each other. It was so realistic that the hair on the back of Dusty's neck prickled.

"You're a low life son of a gun," roared a man in a black cowboy hat. He wore a vest, blue jeans, boots and spurs.

A younger man with a striped shirt and a tan cowboy hat squared off with him. "I wouldn't be throwing words like that around, 'less you're planning on dying, pardner."

"Draw, you skinny little coyote!" the large man in the black hat forcefully commanded.

Dusty instinctively put his hand around Cassie's shoulders. Before he could say anything, the air filled with gun smoke. The tan cowboy hat squeezed off several rounds and the black hat lay flat on his back.

Seeing his adversary down, the victor made a big play of twirling his pistol in the air, blowing smoke off the end, then running and jumping in front of the body. He put his boot on the prone man's chest and shouted, "Do I got any other takers?"

A nervous giggle rippled through the crowd as they backed up and began to disperse.

Dusty pulled Cassie along. "Let's check out that church."

"Okay. Dusty, I'm sure that was just a little stunt for the town."

"Oh, I know," he assured her. "But you don't want anybody getting any ideas."

Outside the bar, Javier stood behind a post. His hand convulsed around the gun in his pocket. With all the shooting, it could be a good time to eliminate the large cowboy accompanying the beautiful woman. She would be much easier to pick off if she was forced to travel alone. The thought was alluring to him. The more he watched her, the less he wanted to turn her over to El Patron. True, she would bring a very high price, much higher than he'd ever gotten before, but still, the thought of having her to himself. Involuntarily, his loins burned with the thought. Forgetting for a moment where he was, he watched Cassie's swaying hips, her long brown hair moving silkily over her back, and her small waist.

He licked his lips hungrily.

"Sir," said a voice behind him. "Excuse me, sir," the voice insisted.

Shaking his head to clear his thoughts, he looked behind him. A maintenance man pushed a broom down the sidewalk, and Javier stood directly in his path.

"So sorry, senor." He apologized self-consciously. He was so glad nobody knew what he was thinking.

The maintenance man sneered at him. "Your kind isn't welcome here." The scarecrow-like man jabbed a bony finger at the round Mexican as he pulled a radio from his belt.

Javier looked down at the distinct bulge in the front of his pants. His face burned with embarrassment. He turned and hurried down the street, anxious to put space between himself and the man with the broom, now speaking angrily into the radio.

As he dodged between the spectators, his heart pounded. He had no papers. The fear of deportation made his blood run cold. He darted in and out of people milling on the streets. He hurried down the sidewalk and ducked into a hat shop. Forcing himself to take deep slow breaths, he feigned interest in the shop's wares.

Cassie and Dusty walked up the church steps at the top of the hill. A man in an old-styled suit greeted them and shook hands warmly. "Welcome to the Church at the Mount."

"Thank you." Dusty nodded.

"Service at nine and eleven. Love to see you this Sunday."

The man's eyes were kind, and Dusty found himself thinking about Sunday and the possibility of attending. Something else nagged at him. The preacher looked familiar. He and Cassie walked through the door of the church. The walls were white. The pulpit sat above the pews, a cross high above it on the wall with an American flag and Arizona state flag on either side.

Cassie walked forward, her hand touching the rough-hewn benches. Bibles sat in the small racks at intervals in front of the seats. She picked one up and idly thumbed through it.

Dusty looked around. The two windows on each side of the small church cast an ethereal light in the room, and even Cassie had a slight glow as she bent over the Bible in her hands. He looked up at the wooden beams of the ceiling with the wagon wheel lights. Once again, the old wood smell. A warm, comforting feeling flowed through him, a surprising sense of peace.

The door opened and a small family walked in. A little boy, five or six years old, led the group and related out loud what he was seeing.

The spell was broken. Cassie smiled and put the Bible on the rack. She walked back to Dusty and together they left the church. "We should come here on Sunday," she said.

"Yeah, let's do it." It's always so easy to be with her, all the conversations they didn't need to have. *We're already thinking the same thing.*

The afternoon sun warmed their backs as they walked down the hill. The crowd still flowed through the shops, but it had reduced significantly. "Let's go see if we still have any horses," said Dusty.

"Good idea."

He held the door open to the Mammoth Saloon and Cassie walked in.

As they walked through the dim bar, he nodded at the bartender, who flashed a toothy smile. As they stepped onto the deck, the cowboy singer was taking a break. Muley and Prince stood at the hitch rail; quite a few more spaces were open.

Dusty untied Muley and prepared to mount, his mind still stuck on the preacher's kindly face. *Where have I seen him before?* Then it dawned on him. *Gus from Lonesome Dove.* He smiled and smoothly swung into the saddle.

# Chapter Thirteen

Red Rock stables sat across the road from the ghost town. As they neared the railroad tracks, Cassie and Dusty were held up by the little train, once again piloting its course around Goldfield. The tourists crowded to one side of the open-air cars and furiously snapped photos of them.

"Wow, I guess I know now what it feels like to be famous." Cassie grinned.

"Really? This is the first for you?" Dusty said in mock surprise.

"Oh, I forgot. I'm in the company of the famous Seattle attorney." Cassie checked Prince as he pulled at the bit to go forward. "You've probably been on the front page of the Seattle Times more than you can count."

The train passed and they crossed the tracks. "Oh, no." Dusty gave her a devilish smile. "I can count 'em."

Cassie rolled her eyes. "I knew it."

As they rode back to the stables Dusty noticed more rigs had pulled in. "Looks like new arrivals."

"This place really fills up, doesn't it?"

"Must be the view." Dusty looked at the Superstitions bathed in the now-familiar reddish glow.

"I could get used to this." Cassie dismounted and tied Prince up.

"Yeah, me too. What law practice?" joked Dusty.

After unsaddling, they walked back to the trailer. In the center of the campground, a bonfire flamed out of a barrel in a picnic area, and people gathered around.

Bob waved to them and walked over.

"We are having a get-together at the fire tonight." He gestured behind him. "Come on over and meet everyone." He paused. "Bring small food if you'd like."

Dusty frowned.

"Hors d'oeuvres?" asked Cassie.

"That's it!" The small man pointed at her. "I never can get that word right."

She smiled. "Doesn't make a lot of sense."

"Well, come when you're ready." Bob turned and walked back to the group. A couple more people joined with lawn chairs and drinks in hand.

"Shall we?" asked Dusty as they approached the living quarters.

"The only problem is what to bring," said Cassie. "I don't know that I have any hors d'oeuvres laying around."

Dusty walked into the trailer, pulled open the cabinet under the sink and withdrew a bag of tortilla chips and a jar of salsa. "Voila!"

"Well, aren't you prepared?" Cassie stood back, her eyes shining.

"It's Backcountry Horsemen 101. Always bring something to share. You never know when you're going to run into a potluck or small food situation."

"I'm impressed." Cassie smiled.

Dusty nodded at her. "I'll go get the lawn chairs."

About a dozen couples sat around the fire with Bob. He smiled and nodded vigorously, gesturing for them to sit.

Cassie set the chips and dip on the table next to the other food. She was gratified to see that someone had brought guacamole dip. She opened the salsa and put the tortilla chips beside them. Small plates and napkins sat on one end of the table.

Turning back to the fire, she saw Dusty already talking with a couple. She walked over and joined him, sitting in the chair he'd set up next to him.

The man and woman were in their sixties, gray-haired and sun-tanned. “Hello. I’m Stan and this is my wife, Viola.”

“Nice to meet you,” said Cassie.

“Your husband tells us you’re from Washington,” piped up Viola.

Cassie’s face infused with a reddish blush as she searched for words. Dusty flashed his highest wattage of smile and answered for her. “It sure is beautiful down here. I can see why so many people come.”

Stan nodded. “It’s the place to come in the winter. That’s for sure.”

Viola gave it another shot. “Cassie, there is a fantastic flea market here. Do you like to shop?

Dusty realized he was interested in the answer too. He looked at the still blushing Cassie.

Cassie cleared her throat. “Um, yes, sometimes I do.”

“Well, we should hit it one of these days. It’s open on Friday through Sundays.”

“That sounds like fun.”

Dusty got an odd feeling. A flutter in his throat. A tiny alarm in his head. What was that about? Can I really not let her out of my sight for five minutes to go shopping with a new friend? He fought back a gnawing feeling in his stomach.

Viola wore a lightweight purple and white plaid shirt with blue jeans, her short hair, gray and permed. Her round face wreathed in wrinkles. Her green eyes were lively. Studying her, Dusty thought she looked like an accomplished, capable woman.

Dusty turned back to Cassie and put his arm around her. Conversation buzzed around them. A feeling of contentment filled him. The evening was warm and the sky radiant in reds and golds. *I’ve heard about this place for so long, I can’t believe I’ve never come before.*

“Hey, Jim told me you guys pulled in last night.” A tall man covered in trail dust stuck out his hand. “Name’s Bill.”

Dusty shook his head and focused. “Hello, Bill. Are you from Oklahoma like Jim?”

"Yes, I am." He tipped his well-worn cowboy hat toward them. "In fact we're friends at home."

"You come together?" asked Cassie.

"Oh, no." Bill waved his hand in the air dismissively. "Jim just kept harping on and on about this place. Finally, I decided that's it. I need to get down there and check it out."

"And?" prompted Dusty. "How do you like it?"

Bill winked at him. "I ain't going back to Oklahoma until the snow's gone." He gestured at the mountains around them. "I figured I'll have a big chunk rode by then. We've sure been working on it."

"Do you have any suggestions of trails?" asked Cassie.

Bill eyed her appreciatively. "You're real pretty, but can you ride?"

"Yes, she can ride," answered Dusty evenly.

Bill straightened. "Good. Then you can come with us tomorrow, if you'd like."

"Thanks," said Dusty. "Where are you riding?"

"It's a really good one. One of my favorites. We're going to go down to the marina and have fish and chips for an early dinner. Jim and I are planning on getting up real early and leaving one trailer at the restaurant. We've each got a four-horse so we can fit your horses in too. He'll drop me off at the trailhead to pick up mine on the way back. It's a long one, about a six-hour ride. Bring a lunch." He was taller than Dusty had realized. His jean jacket covered his lightweight snap-button western shirt. Gray hair bristled out of the collar and he held a toothpick in his teeth.

Dusty looked questioningly at Cassie.

She shrugged. "Why not?"

"What time you loading here?"

Bill squinted at an unknown space in the sky. "How about 8 o'clock? Be saddled up and we'll leave."

"Looking forward to it." Dusty nodded.

"I better hit the hay. Daylight comes early." Bill turned to leave.

"Probably a good idea." Dusty yawned, feeling the long drive and the day's ride in his bones.

"Yeah." Cassie stood, shook her long light brown hair back, and folded her chair. Viola and Stan were chattering away with people. Cassie tapped her shoulder. "Nice meeting you, Viola."

"You too, Cassie. Don't forget about our shopping trip," she crooned.

"I wouldn't dream of it."

Dusty picked up the lawn chairs, and they walked back to the trailer. The sun was setting in a fiery glow of red and orange. The Saguaro cactus appeared as a black outline against the colors. He and Cassie stopped to admire at it.

Cassie lifted her face to the sky. "It looks just like the pictures."

The colors changed as the sun lowered, darkness overtook the cactus, and the landscape became black.

Javier folded up his binoculars. She had gone into the trailer now, so there was nothing more to see. The fading light didn't help. He ducked under the rollup door of the furniture truck. It worked out well that Bob had an opening in his dry camp area. It was separate from the horses and hookups for the trailers. Bob had been apologetic. Javier laughed. It couldn't be more perfect.

Driving the truck up and then down a hill, he had backed it in between Saguaro cactus. No one would be able to see it from the camp. He'd checked carefully. Lying on his bedroll, Javier thought about Cassie. Not knowing how long they were going to be here, he'd have to act quickly. He drifted off with the thought of that beautiful woman in his care. *Oh, the things I can show her.* He shivered with excitement and fell asleep with a smile on his face.

# Chapter Fourteen

Dusty felt like he had just lain down when his alarm sounded. He quickly turned it off. Cassie was still breathing evenly. The sun streamed through the edges of the shades in the trailer. He lay still for a minute. A strange feeling washed over him. Contentment. Warmth in the pit of his stomach. There was something else, too. He looked forward to their ride today. Optimism. It had been a long time since he'd felt that way about anything. He looked over at the sleeping form with the shiny brown hair on the pillow next to him. Fear of commitment now just seemed like an abstract thought. It had nothing to do with him.

Easing himself carefully out of the bed, he slid down to the floor and went into the bathroom. Dressing quickly, he grabbed his hat, crown down on the table, and went outside. Walking to the back of the trailer, he opened the door and let out Sammy and Scout. Shaking the sawdust from their coats, they ran among the cacti and did their business. When Dusty turned toward the stables Scout followed him, with Sammy right behind.

Early morning was a busy time at the stables. Wheelbarrows were rolling by with boarders cleaning their stalls. Dusty greeted them as he grabbed a couple flakes of hay for Prince and Muley and threw them into the feeders. The water looked about gone, so he turned on the hose to fill Muley's tub; apparently, he wasn't the only one noticing the warmer temperatures. The big roan tore greedily at the hay in his feeder. Dusty was glad they had come before the winter in Washington had really kicked in. Muley didn't have a thick winter coat yet. It made it a lot easier for him to adapt to the heat without all that extra hair.

Scout watched Dusty expectantly.

"Come on, boy, it's your turn." He went back to the trailer to feed the dogs.

Dusty hesitated. Go back and clean the stalls, or put the coffee on? He carefully opened the door. The smell of coffee filled his nostrils, and Cassie sat at the dinette, fully dressed and ready to go.

"Good morning," she said cheerfully.

"I could have sworn I left you sleeping."

"Really?" Cassie frowned, fine lines between cool blue eyes. "Maybe that was someone else?"

Dusty didn't miss a beat. He sat down on the other side of the table. "Huh, possibly. I have a lot of traffic in this trailer. Especially going to Arizona. What did you say your name was?"

Cassie grabbed a magazine from the table and threw it at him. "Why do I believe you?"

Laughing, Dusty threw his hands up in mock terror. "Just kidding. Honest."

"Fine," Cassie said. "The coffee's almost done."

They cleaned the stalls while the horses ate. Cassie just finished putting her lunch in the saddlebag when Bill and Jim pulled up in Jim's four horse trailer. Jim jumped out. "Looks like yer all ready."

"You said 8 o'clock, right?" said Cassie.

Bill nodded. "On the button."

Dusty untied Muley's lead rope and led him to the back of the trailer, where Jim took the rope and loaded him. Prince followed Cassie and stepped in the trailer right behind Muley.

"We've got the other trailer down at the marina waitin' for us when we get done," said Bill.

"What time did you get up?" asked Dusty.

"Probably about 4."

"Wow, I'm impressed."

"Well, don't be, I haven't really got sleeping down very well since I got here." Bill rocked back on his heels. "In fact, I find it a lot easier to stay awake than trying to sleep."

Jim slammed the trailer door shut and locked it.

Cassie and Dusty climbed into the back seat of Jim's older model Ford truck. Assorted trailer hitches and tools littered the floorboards. Coats lay on the seat with bits of hay and mud on them.

"Just move my stuff over," Jim said. "Been a while since I've had passengers."

Dusty was glad Cassie had agreed about not bringing the dogs. It was just too difficult when they were riding with new people. They had no idea how their horses would react to a dog and neither one of them wanted to see a dog or horse get hurt.

The truck's engine roared, so talking was difficult. Bill and Jim had their windows down and the morning fresh air felt good on Dusty's face. He was almost chilled by it. He glanced over at the Superstition Mountains. The sun shone on top and the rocks gleamed gold, the shadows more pronounced in the early morning. A few cars passed them. Disoriented for a minute, he asked, "What day is today?"

Cassie smiled. "It's Tuesday, Dusty."

"Oh," he said sheepishly.

She squeezed his hand. "It's okay. On vacation all days are the same."

Before Dusty could respond, Bill turned to the back seat. "Here we are. First Water Trailhead."

Jim turned into a large gravel parking area. A couple of horse trailers and a half dozen passenger cars occupied the lot.

"It's a popular hiking area too," Bill explained.

They bridled their horses and rode down the trail.

The horses' shoes clicked on an occasional rock in the sandy soil. Saguaro and Cholla dominated the landscape along with other thorny groundcovers. Jim set a good pace. By the look of his horse

Dusty figured it was a Tennessee Walker. A lot of people favored the gaited horses. No bias whatsoever, he assured himself, but he liked Muley's compact form and versatility better. His appaloosa could climb rocks, slide down snow banks, and walk fast enough to keep up with the other horses. And despite Muley's dominant personality, he wasn't high strung in the least. If something happened, the big roan bucked, shied or planted. And then he was done. It wasn't something that continued on. Past images of friends on docile horses that in one second turned into bucking broncos made him wince. He shook his head and continued to look around.

Rows and rows of Saguaro stood like sentinels in the early morning, in some places intermittent, on other hillsides hundreds.

"I wonder what the horses think of all this cactus," said Cassie.

"I know, it's way different from Douglas Fir trees." Dusty turned in his saddle. "I was wondering that myself."

"Have you ever taken Muley to the ocean?"

He shook his head. "No, never wanted to."

"Really?"

"There's only two trails." Dusty grinned. "Up and back."

"I guess." Cassie tossed her head. "Some places have more variety. Like if you go to Oregon, I heard they have woods to ride in as well."

"Huh," grunted Dusty, uninterested.

Cassie continued on, ignoring him. "My point being that Prince never reacted to the roaring of the surf either. I'd wondered what he'd do about it when he got there, but it didn't faze him."

"I never considered that."

"Yeah, he still didn't like getting his feet wet, but that's just him."

"We don't have any beaches in Oklahoma," chimed in Bill. "The girls have to take them down to the Gulf and it's quite a drive."

"The girls?" asked Cassie.

"Well, yeah, isn't it a girlie thing to ride on the beach?"

"Sure 'nuff," said Jim.

The men laughed. Dusty turned to look at Cassie, her cheeks pink. He mouthed at her, "It's okay" and winked.

She gave him a withering look, and he quickly turned back around in his saddle.

"I feel outnumbered. We need to ride with more girls," she said in a small voice.

Javier woke late. The darkness inside the furniture truck made it difficult to tell time. He turned on his flashlight. 9 o'clock. He froze in panic. What if they'd left? He rolled the backdoor open and stepped outside. The sun was already climbing in the sky. He blinked and rubbed his eyes in the bright light.

Walking to the restroom from his camp, he had to pass through the parked living quarter horse trailers. Nonchalantly he glanced over at Dusty and Cassie's trailer. It was dark. People were walking back and forth from living quarters to the horse stalls behind the restrooms. A few were seated outside in lawn chairs having coffee. He smiled and waved at them and they returned the greeting.

At least they weren't gone yet. *I'm going to have to move faster*. A plan began to form in Javier's mind. Deep in thought, he opened the door to the restroom/laundry room and almost ran into Bob.

"Oh, good morning." The owner nodded. "You're just the man I wanted to talk to."

Javier's blood ran cold. He felt the cool steel of his knife, a six-inch blade resting against his back. "Yes?"

# Chapter Fifteen

Bob's face lit up in a big smile. "We meet out here most nights." He waved toward an empty awning with a burn barrel and a few empty tables. "People come to meet and share food." Bob faced Javier. "You should come and meet people. Very fun."

This was not what he expected. Javier took a moment to think about it. That wasn't a bad idea, get to know people and show them what a great person he was. That way, later on when the woman went missing, they wouldn't be so quick to think of him.

Bob appeared to misinterpret Javier's quietness as hesitation. "It's fun," he urged.

"It sounds okay," said Javier. "I would like to come."

Bob clasped his hands together. "Great. I will let you know when the next one is." He began to walk toward the stables. "I work now. Never stops."

Javier smiled warmly. "No, work never does."

Walking back to his furniture truck, Javier pulled out a cigarette and lit it. The smoke coursed through his lungs and relaxed him. This was going to be a good day after all. Things happened for a reason. He'd heard that so often growing up. A bad thing can turn into a good thing; it was all how you looked at it.

It was mid-morning now, and a lot of the snowbirds were riding horses down the trail out of camp. Superstition Mountain, previously in silent repose, now swarmed with brightly colored little specks—

horsemen and hikers. Some of the little bits of color seemed to actually be climbing up the mountain. Fascinating. People in this country had time to walk and explore things. In the village where he grew up there was a lot of walking, but to and from the fields. Digging and planting and harvesting. Hard work in hot sun. No time for fun, like these people seemed to enjoy. His wife and daughter flashed through his mind. They would be working hard now, harder yet because it had been some time since he had sent them any money.

He took a deep inhale of smoke to calm himself. It was hard. The United States wasn't what everyone had said, that money grew on trees. The old anxiety rose in him. Yes, there was work, but for a pittance. He snorted. *A man like me could make so much more money and so much easier*. He felt the familiar cloak of superiority settle over him. Being of such high intellect, no one really had a chance around him. He would make more money than all of them.

Flicking his cigarette butt into the sand, he turned back to the furniture truck. Maria and the girl did not need to worry at all; lots of money would be coming their way. He felt the tingle of thrill rise in the pit of his stomach and branch into his chest. They would be so proud of him. He straightened up, swaggered to the truck and threw open the door. Time to get ready.

As he drove toward town, Javier kept an eye open for horse outfitters. There were several along the road, but he wanted one run by someone he could relate to, another Hispanic. He pulled into a lot with a handwritten sign, "Horses by the hour–or the day. Guided rides." Several saddled horses stood tied to the hitch rail. A makeshift shelter stood close by, and Javier saw that his approach was being monitored.

"Hello, senor, are you looking for a ride today? These are the best horses in the area." The gray-haired, small man approached him.

Javier couldn't tell his age, but he looked to be well in his sixties. The outfitter's skin a golden brown and looked leathery tough, only years in the sun could do to a person. He wore cowboy boots and a snap western shirt. The outfit was completed by a dirty gray Stetson and wild rag around his neck. Javier heard the jingling of spurs as the older man walked. He glanced down and saw large rowels adorning dusty, well-worn cowboy boots.

"Name's Pedro Ortega." The older man thrust out a brown wrinkled hand.

Javier quickly shook it. "Javier Mendoza." He looked around. "Very nice-looking horses."

Pride flashed in Pedro's face. He switched to Spanish. "Been doing this a long time. I learned early on the best stock is worth its weight in gold."

Javier smiled and nodded. "I'm sorry to say, I haven't ridden much. Do you have a horse that someone like me could ride? Maybe take off by myself?"

Pedro frowned at him. "Why? Why would you want to ride off by yourself?"

Heat flushed through Javier's face. *Maybe that was the wrong thing to say. I know nothing of horses.* "I'm staying down at Redrock Stables right now. I would like to rent a horse for a few days and ride it from there."

Frowning, Pedro stroked his chin. "Down at Bob's place, huh?"

"Yes," Javier said encouragingly.

"I dunno." The outfitter shrugged. "What do you know about horses?"

"We used them in the fields down in Michoacán when I was young."

"Field horses are different."

Javier swallowed hard, his plan was slipping through his fingers. He needed a horse. It was far too hot for him to walk. "How about we go on a trail ride? Then you can see I can handle the horse?"

A smile touched the edges of the outfitter's mouth. "Okay. When?"

"Right now." Javier didn't want to lose his chance.

The outfitter stepped back. "You going to ride like that?"

Following his gaze, Javier realized he was still wearing his sweat pants and flip-flops.

"I can change, I have my clothes in there." He pointed at the old furniture truck.

Pedro shook his head. "How long do you want to go for?"

"I will go all day." If he wanted to take the horse back to the stables, that would give him ample time to show Pedro he knew what he was doing.

"You're going to need a long-sleeved shirt or light jacket, some food for a lunch and plenty of water. And boots." Pedro looked down at the flip flops.

Javier hurried to his truck, threw open the door, and got in back to change. He'd seen a little convenience store nearby so he could go over there when he got done. Pulling on his jeans, he changed belts and kept the knife in its sheath secure behind his back. You never knew when you would be needing it. Next, he pulled on his cowboy boots. Lucky for him he had them. Not being very tall, he'd always appreciated the extra height they gave him.

Grabbing a long-sleeved shirt, he jumped out of the truck and slammed the door shut. Pedro was on his cell phone. If he found it unusual for a man to be changing clothes in the back of a furniture truck, he gave no indication of it.

Javier pointed at the small convenience store across the lot and headed over there at a fast pace. He'd get the rest of the things he needed.

Pedro was just finishing bridling the last horse when Javier came back. "My nephew is on his way. He'll watch the place while we're gone."

"Where are we going?"

"I've got a favorite spot I'd like to go." Pedro checked the cinches on both horses and gave the second one a couple of pulls. "I don't get out very much anymore, I'm always here." He gestured at the lot and saddle horses. "But if I'm going to see you ride, that's just what we're going to need to do."

A small weather-beaten red Toyota pickup pulled into the lot. A young Hispanic boy got out. Javier didn't place him for more than sixteen, but he was probably older than that. "This is Carlos, my nephew."

"Senor." The boy nodded at Javier.

Javier nodded back.

"I guess we're ready," said Pedro. "I'll pull the truck and trailer around."

"Truck and trailer?" Javier was confused.

"It's the best way to get out of here. The trailhead is quite a ways down the road." The outfitter walked to the back of the lot to get his rig.

Moments later he drove up in a beat-up blue truck pulling an ancient horse trailer. The sides of the trailer were wooden slats and the top was missing. Pedro jumped out and opened the back. "Grab Chester and I'll take Ki." He gestured at the chestnut brown horse with a white blaze and then the white spotted Appaloosa horse.

Trying to look as experienced as possible, Javier untied the lead rope and lead Chester to the back of the trailer. He was thankful the big brown horse didn't step on his foot. Those big clodhoppers looked like they would hurt.

Once the horses were loaded, Javier jumped into the truck. Pedro ground it into gear and they drove off. Javier enjoyed being a passenger. He looked around at the cactus on either side of the road. As they came up to Redrock Stable, he looked across the street at the Goldfield Ghost Town. Pretty realistic for a tourist town—although as rude as they had been to him, he didn't feel like ever going back.

Pedro seemed perfectly content driving in silence and Javier didn't push it. A lot of men didn't like to talk. After about twenty minutes, Pedro said, "This is it." He pulled the truck into a trailhead called "The Bulldog."

Javier noticed quite a few cars and one other horse trailer. "Is this pretty popular?"

"Not to horsemen so much, but then most of them don't know where to go." He winked.

A tingle of excitement ran through Javier. "I can't wait."

The trailhead was filled with Saguaro cactus and large rocks. They rode down sandy trails and through empty streambeds. The cactus flowers and vines were particularly beautiful. For an area that was so dry, Javier was surprised at the amount of growth.

After about an hour when Pedro picked a steep trail that switchbacked down into another empty ravine. The bottom was full of sand and huge boulders. Javier was impressed with Chester's ability to clamber over the top of rocks and then slide down the other side. Some of them looked so slick he clenched his teeth until it was over. But the big brown horse plodded on. He knew his job.

They rode for quite a while in the dry river bottom which held occasional pools of water so the horses were able to drink. Huge rocks towered over them on either side and the shade cooled the breeze.

"Here it is." Pedro stopped.

Behind him, Javier rounded the corner and what he saw in front of him made his mouth drop open. This was it! Exactly what he'd been looking for.

# Chapter Sixteen

Prince walked down the trail with methodical steps, rocking Cassie from side to side. The murmur of voices wafted ahead of her as Dusty spoke to the other men. The only other sound was the thudding of hooves, with an occasional clink from horseshoe hitting rock. Cassie was in her favorite place, the smell of horses and dirt, the sun warm on her back.

The hills were dotted with Saguaro cactus. In some places stands took up entire hillsides, and in others just a few lone cacti. The ground was sandy and rocky, with spiny vines spreading their thorns outward. The old "bones" of Saguaros scattered on the ground. Small animal skulls and teeth would turn up at intervals. Cassie shivered. Such a place of rugged survival and death. She had seen barrel cactus at home in stores for in-home plants. But nothing like these barrels, huge and thick. More than ten inches across and standing over a foot high. They could only grow so large before they toppled over from their own weight. She imagined it wasn't long before another desert creature would find a use for it once it lay helpless.

For all its attraction of warmth in winter months, the Arizona desert held an underlying toughness. She gazed up at the sun. The Pacific Northwest was experiencing freezing temperatures and frost, and of course rain. This felt so much better, right now anyway. It was probably going to reach 80 today, in October of all things. But without the right equipment a person could end up in bad shape quickly out here. Water was its own kind of gold. She looked at the bottle in her pommel bag, in easy reach, hanging off her saddle horn. Even with two more bottles in her saddlebags, her mouth felt dry and parched.

In the short time they'd been here Cassie had learned a lot about cactus and animals. The Cholla with its cottony covering was probably the worst. Dusty had mentioned them earlier, but she'd now experienced it for herself. It dropped little balls on the ground and looked harmless with just a few spines on them. But when a horse walked by, the tiniest breeze would flip them in the air and they would affix to the horse's leg, immediately causing the animal to limp. Dusty's idea to carry a small comb and flick them off was the best method. If you tried to use your hand, the plant ball would affix itself to you, even penetrating through the leather of your glove. Cassie rubbed her hand where the spines had pierced. It had glommed on immediately and the pain felt like a bee sting, but had lasted much longer. It only needed to happen once, that was enough.

Prince stopped abruptly just short of ramming Muley.

"Cassie, do you want to stop for lunch?" Dusty said in a voice that didn't sound like it was the first time he'd asked.

"Sure. Whatever you guys want to do."

Jim turned around in his saddle. "It's gonna get pretty rough after this part, so we probably better stop here."

Cassie glanced ahead. The hill dropped off into a gully. Bushes rose high on either side, and the trail disappeared below in a wash.

Jim reined his big black horse down a draw and the rest of them followed. To Cassie's surprise it was a small campsite. A large rock stood to one side with the remains of a campfire ring a few feet from it. The ground was sandy and free from spiny cactus in the immediate area. Velvet Mesquite grew at the edges, and Cassie walked up to one to tie her horse. She pulled her lead rope across a limb and yelped when a thorn pierced her glove.

"Be careful," Dusty cautioned.

"Yeah, thanks." She murmured as pain shot through her finger. "Sooner or later I'll hopefully get used to being attacked by plants."

"I guess the rain mellows them out up our way." Dusty stood waiting for her.

Cassie pulled her lunch out of the saddlebag. "I like that. Another point for rain."

Jim and Bill perched on a rock around the dismantled fire ring. Cassie squatted down on the sand, and Dusty sat beside her.

"This gully drops off quickly and then we start picking our way up through the rocks and cactus." Jim took a bite of sandwich. "It's a long ride, but the views from the saddle are worth it."

"Yeah," agreed Bill. "I was pretty surprised my first time through here."

"It ends up at a marina?" Dusty leaned back.

"Yeah, it's Canyon Lake Marina," said Jim.

"It seems so odd to have a lake in the middle of the desert," Cassie took a bite of her sandwich.

"The lake is actually a reservoir made from damming the Salt River." Jim said reaching into his saddle bag.

"Really? I didn't realize that," said Dusty with raised eyebrows.

Jim smiled. "Yeah, I wondered too, so I checked it out. They made four reservoirs and Canyon Lake is the smallest; of the four lakes on the Salt River, Roosevelt Lake is the biggest."

"What are the other ones?" asked Cassie.

"Can't remember right now," said Jim.

Bill poked him. "That's because we're not riding to them."

Jim laughed. "True, true. Ain't no point in learning 'bout it, if I ain't riding it."

"Makes sense." Dusty nodded sagely.

Cassie glanced at Dusty. He was so handsome. His deeply tanned face creased in a grin. Crinkles around his eyes. The light blue work shirt made his eyes even bluer. He was relaxed in his chinks, cowboy boots and spurs. His holstered gun lying against his belt, western style. He looked perfectly natural.

Downtown Seattle and the courtroom flashed through her mind, such a contradiction. Dusty was a good chameleon, that's for sure—or maybe he wasn't. Cassie took a bite of her sandwich thoughtfully. *I was in that courtroom too, but it doesn't make me that person either.* Making money is necessary and sometimes circumstance drove the end more than desire.

"Hey," Dusty said softly. "You're being quiet. Hope the thorns aren't getting you down?"

The concern in his voice, the flash of white in his smile struck Cassie as funny. She stifled a laugh. "No, I think I'm going to make it."

He smiled. "That's good news. I'd hate to have to tie you to Prince and bring you out."

Cassie feigned concern. "Yeah, I'm not sure. Prince has never packed. It might be tough starting with a body."

Dusty put his hand on her knee. "Good point. You better ride him out." He looked over at Jim and Bill. "That reminds me of a story."

Both men perked up. A story around a campfire was as good as it gets, even if it was an empty fire ring.

"I've got a buddy back in Washington, he's an outfitter by the name of Paul Webster. He used to be a sheriff's deputy."

"There's a good combo," said Bill, "Outfitter/Deputy Sheriff."

"Yeah." Dusty nodded. "Can come in handy."

"They had a guy that died up in the Cascade Mountains, and they needed the body packed out, so Paul got the job." Dusty dug into his potato chips. "Paul mantied him up and tied him onto the pack saddle. The problem was the guy was stiff as a board, and darned if he didn't bounce off every rock on the way down."

"You always gotta bend them over a log for easy transport." Jim nodded with a grave expression.

Bill looked at his friend sideways. "Oh, yeah, Jim? And how many dead bodies have you packed out?"

Jim ignored him. "I've heard tell."

Dusty continued, "After they got him down, the medical examiner told him to never do that again. With all the bruises he couldn't tell what had happened to the guy, pre and post mortem."

Jim slapped his leg. He and Bill broke into loud guffaws. "That's a good one, Dusty."

Cassie looked at him. "Is that really true?"

Dusty winked at her. "Of course."

She smiled, not knowing whether to believe him or not.

Jim stood up. "We better hit the trail. We got a long ride ahead of us still."

Picking up his lunch bag, Bill followed.

Dusty got to his feet and held out his hand to Cassie. She took it and stood. Always the gentleman, downtown Seattle or the middle of nowhere.

The afternoon heat beat down on them as the trail began to climb. Prince's coat was slick with sweat. Cassie felt bad she had no water for him. She knew horses were adaptable and strong. Still, Cassie hoped the lake was coming soon.

They finally wound up a steep switchback and came to a flat spot. Jim pointed behind them. "This is it."

Cassie turned in her saddle and gasped. Behind her lay a valley, rugged and beautiful, in a way she had never seen. The greens of the Saguaro and other flora dotted the bottom, with huge jagged rocks of bright red and dark brown. With the azure sky frame, it looked prehistoric. Cassie felt like she was in Jurassic Park and wouldn't have been surprised to see a Pterodactyl fly by.

Dusty sat on Muley grinning. "Wow, Jim, this is really something."

Jim smiled. "Makes the ride worth it, don't it?" He reined his horse over to the other side of the rock platform. "Check this out."

Cassie and Dusty followed him. Below them a deep blue lake sparkled in the hot afternoon sun.

"Canyon Lake," he said simply.

The contrast was striking: brown dirt and rock dotted with desert plants up to the shore of the blue lake.

"That's beautiful," Cassie breathed.

The small marina and paved parking area lay at the bottom of a windy switchbacked trail.

Jim turned his mount. “Let's get us some fish and chips.”

“Yeah, let's do it.” Bill urged his horse forward.

“And water for the horses.” Cassie followed.

One by one they dropped off the rock platform and headed down the trail.

# Chapter Seventeen

Javier could not take his eyes off the deep caves set in the hillside. They were deceptive. At first he thought he was only looking at shadows from the rocks, but at this angle when the sun hit them just right, he could see an entrance.

"What do you know about those caves up there?" he asked Pedro rubbing his hands together.

The older man flinched. These were the first words spoken since they left the trailhead. He obviously wasn't expecting it. Pedro turned his dirty brown cowboy hat to study the dark opening.

Javier stood rigid He wanted to go up there and check them out. The old man seemed to take forever to answer. Finally, when Javier felt he could wait no longer, the outfitter spoke.

"They are deep. People have been lost in them," he said simply.

His heart beat in his throat. "What are they from?"

Pedro lapsed into another long silence.

Javier's mind raced ahead. This was perfect. A place to keep her until it was time to do the transfer. He tingled with excitement. He would take Cassie here and hold her prisoner. His prisoner. He would negotiate the highest price for her and then he would sell her. But what if it took a while? He felt a large smile creasing his face. Well, maybe he would have to sample her. After all, that cowboy she was with had. It's not like it would make any difference to the buyers. Javier snorted. Besides, her life expectancy may not be that long in trafficking. He'd heard that ISIS was still in the market for wives and would pay a good price for them. Their women didn't last long.

Pulling on his reins, he directed Chester over to a Mesquite tree. "I want to stop here and check the caves out."

"The Lost Dutchman," said Pedro quietly.

"Wha-a-at?" asked Javier, confused.

Pedro motioned at the caves. "You asked me who made them. It was the people looking for the Dutchman's gold."

"Oh." Javier hastily tied his big chestnut horse to the brushy tree, being careful not to snag his gloves on the thorns. He bounded across the dry river bed and climbed up the short embankment into the darkness of the cave.

It took a few minutes for Javier's eyes to adjust to the darkness. The damp chill flowed over his skin, even though it was past noon on a hot day. He shivered, then shook it off. Lowering his head, he trudged on into the darkness. The entrance narrowed and then it opened into a large cavern. Reaching into his shirt pocket, he pulled out a lighter. Flipping it on, Javier saw a labyrinth of other darkened tunnels. *I'm going to have to be very careful.* A man could get easily lost in here. But that could be a good thing too—for those who tried to follow.

Taking care to flash his light around the main cave to check for snakes or other venomous creatures, he proceeded around the perimeter of the main room. True to what Pedro had said, a few old shovels and broken picks lay on the ground. With a sense of relief, Javier noticed nothing skittering around. He picked a tunnel closest to the outside and walked into it. Coming around the first corner, he saw a small sliver of sunlight about twenty feet from him. The bottom was sandy, and the walls were rock. He bit his lip. Hopefully they'd shored it up when they dug it.

An occasional small rock fell, the echo bouncing off the cavern walls. The tunnel was empty except for him. Pedro had apparently elected to stay with the horses. As Javier made it closer to the light, he heard dripping. Water? In here? Rounding another bend, he found a pool filled with dark algae. Water splashed on the smooth rocks behind it. He shined his lighter on it and a few small fish flicked by the surface. Javier was transfixed. Who would have thought? He was so intent on the water, at first he didn't hear the high-pitched sound. His mind dismissed it as an electrical wire. He just stared at the fish.

Suddenly, he jolted back to the present. There was no electricity in here. A movement by the pool caught his eye. Then he saw it! Coiled not three feet from him was the largest rattlesnake he'd ever seen. It had to have been eight feet long and thick as a man's forearm. Javier licked his lips, his mouth dry. He wasn't sure what to do. All he had was his knife. His pistol lay deep in the saddlebag on his horse. He stood perfectly still. The snake didn't seem to notice. It coiled tighter and rattled louder. The narrow red tongue flicked furiously in and out of its mouth. Javier was certain it was going to strike. He flexed his fingers tentatively. Sweat trickled down his back. He had to at least get his knife. He could try jumping to one side and cutting off its head as it struck. Anything was better than just waiting for death. Slowly, he inched his hand towards his belt, his eyes glued to the pulsing, massive length of reptile.

Time seemed to stand still—his hand finally closed around the hilt of his knife. He slowly pulled. Before he could completely pull it free, the monstrous snake went airborne. Javier saw long, spiny fangs, and a gigantic open mouth barreling across the room at him. A blood-curdling scream tore through the air, followed instantaneously by a deafening roar.

Javier opened his eyes. He lay flat on his back with the large snake draped over him. Blood soaked the front of his chest. He was dying. He thought of Maria and his beautiful daughter. He drew in a ragged sob, knowing he would never see them again on this earth. He waited. Nothing happened. Was this how death was supposed to be? Another sure sign of being dead was he didn't hurt. He felt pain free. Whatever injury the snake had inflicted upon him was gone. "Thank you, Jesus," he murmured reverently. Still nothing.

A wrinkled tan hand grabbed his arm. "Hang on for a minute, I'll get one of those shovels and get that snake off you." Pedro flashed a pen light on him briefly, then disappeared. In a few minutes he came back. Javier still lay flat on his back. A rotting smell filled his nostrils. The snake's body lay inches from his face. He wrinkled his nose in disgust. "I never realized they smell so bad."

Pedro carefully inserted the shovel under the snake and lifted it off Javier. Pulling out a large knife he sliced its head off. Having completed his task, he stood back and admired the reptile. "That is the biggest one I have ever seen." He shook his head. "I've heard they could grow up to eight feet, and this one is all of that – if not more." He turned to Javier. "You're lucky I decided to walk up here, senor. One more second and you would have been dead."

Javier sat up slowly. His hands were shaking. Pedro's words fell over him, but he was having a hard time picking them up. The black shadow of death had been so close, he thought he had died. Finally, he said, "Gracias, amigo. I am forever in your debt."

A wave of urgency flowed over him. "Let's go." He wanted out of the caves and away from the snakes. Where there's one, there's probably more. Javier stood up and turned to leave.

Pedro stood unmoving, in front of the snake. "What shall we do with it?"

"Nothing," snapped Javier. "I've had enough."

"Well, perhaps you have, but I'm not going to waste this skin." Pedro took out a knife and bent to begin his work. "This will bring a lot of money."

Shaking his head, Javier left Pedro and the snake behind and walked into the warm sun. He slid down the short hill and walked over to Chester. His horse stood lazily in the sun, eyes half-closed, tail flicking at flies. If anyone had almost died, it hadn't caused the horse any concern. Javier pulled his water bottle out and sat down on a flat rock in the shade. Taking a large drink, he felt the adrenaline surge began to leave his body. His heart now beating at its normal rate. His palms were no longer sweaty. Javier felt a bone-weary tiredness replacing the excitement.

He glanced at the cave speculatively. It still was a good place. No one would find them there. He would have to find out how to get rid of those monster snakes. Perhaps another cave would be better though. If that was a female snake, there might be baby snakes in there. Javier shuddered. He'd heard the babies are supposed to be more poisonous than the adults, because they don't know how to control their venom when they bite. He drank deeply. Maybe not a cave.

Pedro walked out of the entrance with a long pattern-back skin hanging over his shoulders and a big grin on his face. Javier noticed it draped over his back, almost hitting the ground in the front as he walked. He felt his stomach convulse. "How are you going to pack that thing out?"

"Very easy." Pedro took the slicker off the back of his saddle and opened it up. He carefully laid the fresh hide on it and loosely wrapped it up. He tied it back on his saddle making sure to keep all the ends inside.

"That's going to make your slicker stink. That snake smells really bad."

"My slicker will wash." Pedro finished tying off the bundle behind his saddle. "Snakes do that when they are frightened."

"The snake was frightened?" Javier looked at him in disbelief. "He didn't act frightened."

Pedro nodded seriously. "All animals have their ways. That's just his."

"Was just his," corrected Javier. He mounted Chester. "I'm ready to head back."

"Yes," agreed Pedro. "I'd like to take care of this hide before the desert does it for me."

They rode in silence through the dry rocks and occasional Saguaro cactus for a while, then Pedro spoke. "There are worse things out here than rattlesnakes."

Still thinking about the close call with the snake, Javier frowned. "Like what?"

"Killer bees," the old outfitter said mysteriously.

"Honey bees?" asked Javier.

"Sort of." Pedro turned in the saddle and checked his load. "They cross bred them with African bees and came out with a mistake. A very angry bee that repeatedly stings its prey until it's dead."

Javier shuddered. "I don't want to see any of them."

The old man chuckled. "Don't worry, senor. They are very, very rare."

Later, as Javier drove back to Red Rock Stable, he turned over in his mind whether he'd been successful in showing Pedro he could handle a horse by himself. The snake had seemed to overshadow everything else.

Pulling the furniture truck into the main entrance, Javier saw a plume of smoke and several people gathering around the fire ring. A man waved to him, gesturing for Javier to come and join them, Javier guessed that was Bob. He waved back. What could it hurt to go over there? He smiled. *I've probably got the best story to tell today.*

Stiff from his long ride, he approached the fire ring. A few more people had arrived. Bob was in the middle of a tale; laughter rang out as he hit the punch line.

"Hello," Bob greeted him enthusiastically. "Sit down and meet everyone."

Javier felt self-conscious, but forcing a smile on his face, he nodded to the group. They smiled and made introductions.

"Where are you from, Javier?" A lanky cowboy asked. He'd just introduced himself as Bill.

Javier racked his brain. Where did his cousins live? "Yakima."

"Oh," said Bill. "Another Washingtonian. Do you know Cassie and Dusty?"

"It's a big state," Javier quickly responded.

"Yeah," agreed the cowboy in his Oklahoma drawl, "but horses make the community a lot smaller."

"Cassie, how was your ride?" A stocky woman with iron-gray curly hair called out to the approaching couple.

Eagerly, Javier followed her gaze. Cassie carried a Tupperware bowl and a box of crackers. He looked at her tanned face, her silky light-brown hair blew in the slight evening breeze. Her small waist was accentuated by the belt with silver buckle. Her supple hips and long legs strode toward them. Javier's loins tightened at the sight of her, the craving, the need becoming a wild animal trapped inside of him. He felt himself losing his grip with each passing day. What had once been a random thought, a way to make money to send home, now was growing into something much different. Desire passed through him with such intensity he shook and a small stream of spittle dripped out of the corner of his mouth.

Desperately he pulled himself back from the emotional edge he teetered on. He wiped the corner of his mouth with his handkerchief. Repositioning his now tight jeans, he surreptitiously glanced around, hoping no one had noticed. All eyes seemed to be greeting the newcomers. He forced himself to relax and tore his eyes away from Cassie. He felt something else. Next to Cassie, Dusty carried their lawn chairs. His eyes bored holes into Javier. He'd seen! Looking back at Dusty, his insides turned to ice. All desire left him like a cold shower. Anger was evident on the large man's face. The icy blue eyes fixed on him in a murderous rage. For the second time in one day, Javier felt death was near.

# Chapter Eighteen

Bob quickly rose to greet Dusty and Cassie. Javier wasn't sure whether it was because he'd caught the expression on the man's face or he was just being hospitable. Dusty flicked his eyes from Javier and nodded to Bob, who pointed where to sit down.

The explosion came from nowhere, a cracking inside the blaze which shot out a fiery ember. Long afterward, Javier believed it must have been an act of God, because nothing else could have caused it to happen at exactly that moment. The ash popped, the short, iron-gray haired woman screamed, and threw her hands over her face.

"Viola." Cassie ran over to her.

The woman's husband leaned over and said gently, "Move your hand, honey. Did it get you in the eye?"

"Ye—yes," she stammered. "It hurts, Stan. Bad."

"Let me take a look," her husband urged.

Javier quietly folded up his lawn chair and walked off into the gathering dusk. He kept thinking he would hear heavy footsteps behind him, but no one followed.

The furniture truck sat alone at the end of the dry camp area. He threw the chair into the truck, got in and slammed down the heavy door. Damn it! This was enough. Anger and frustration flowed white-hot through his veins. He lay down on his sleeping bag in the darkness. He couldn't sleep. *When dawn comes, I'm leaving. Dusty knows. All my plans are ruined.* A vile taste arose in his mouth. Defeat.

Sleep was elusive. Maria's face rose in his mind, and his daughter, pleading.

"Please Papi, don't leave us."

"It will be good," he said, "I will be back soon, with lots of money."

Her little eyes sparkled with excitement. "Really, Papi?" She put her arms around him and hugged him tightly.

"Yes, Marisol, my beautiful one." He patted her on the head and continued. "We will move from here and buy a wonderful home."

She knelt in the dirt. "With real floors, Papi?"

"Oh, yes, wood floors."

"Oh, Papi!" She jumped in the air and clapped her hands.

He felt so powerful and loved. He was a good father and he provided well for his family. All the people would see this when he returned. The old rumors of "Javier the worthless" would be put to rest. Instead, "Javier the best provider" would take its place.

Javier felt a surge of pride as he envisioned his homecoming. And then Dusty's face appeared and it all vanished into mist. He groaned and flipped over on his sleeping bag.

The heavy darkness pressed down on him, and the air tasted stuffy and stagnant. Javier could barely breathe. Sweating, he sat up and pushed the button on his watch, 4 a.m. He stood and walked over to the door. With a huge heave he threw it open. The cool desert air struck him in the face and he felt better. Staring into the distance, the Saguaro cacti stood in silence, the Superstition Mountains loomed large and black. A slight breeze riffled the air, cool against his skin. Javier sat down on the truck tailgate and lit a cigarette. He drew in deeply and the smoke soothed his lungs. His shoulders relaxed. The desert was still. Ever so slowly, the sky changed in front of him. A reddish-yellow outline slowly became a fire-orange background against the black silhouette of the mountains.

He still felt uneasy from the lack of sleep and something more. It tore at his stomach in an angry knot—failure. He hung his head and rubbed his temples. *I can't take it anymore.* He jumped down and decided to walk it off. He would make a new plan. There were other women. He could talk to El Patron and make him understand.

She was not the only one. As he walked, he felt better. He hadn't even realized that his steps were taking him back to the stables.

Dusty's breathing was even and deep, his handsome features in repose. Cassie stole a look at him. *Maybe for once I can beat him to feeding the horses.* She slowly lifted his hand off her thigh and scooted carefully away from him. He groaned, and she froze. He rolled over and she was free. She slid to the end of the bed and soundlessly let herself down. Her clothes lay on the floor.

As she slipped into her jeans, she thought about last night. Dusty had been different. He'd never said what it was, but after Viola got the spark in her eye and Stan finally took her to emergency after washing it out didn't help—Dusty seemed distant. Figuring out his moods sometimes was difficult. Seeing Javier had been an unpleasant shock.

"There's something about that guy, I just don't trust him," Dusty had said.

She'd replied. "He tried to steal our dogs, that's bad enough."

"No, besides that," Dusty said slowly, "I have a really bad feeling about him." He pulled Cassie into his arms, "Just be careful, okay?" He kissed the top of her head. "I don't want to lose you."

She'd laughed. "Don't worry, I'm not getting lost."

They'd gone and checked on the horses, and then walked back to the trailer. Once they'd shut the door, she'd turned to go change for bed.

Dusty pulled her into an embrace and kissed her so deeply she felt it down to her toes. After that, their clothes had flown across the trailer and the night was filled with passionate lovemaking.

Passing by his sleeping form, Cassie felt a longing in the pit of her stomach. Maybe she'd surprise him with more than just feeding the horses when she got back. She silently opened the trailer door and slipped into the cool dawn.

As she walked to the barn, the camp was cloaked in darkness. Nobody had risen yet. That was pretty good as it seemed like these people consistently got up at dawn. She approached Prince's stall and he nickered to her. She grabbed a flake of hay and threw it into the feeder. Muley gave an insistent full-throated reminder from the stall next door and kicked the wall.

"Easy boy," she cooed to him. "I'll be right there."

She walked over and fed him from the bale in front of his stall. The barn lights were always on, so she could see the water container was empty. She turned on the hose, and with a whoosh, the half barrel quickly filled. The dry air was so different than Washington State, and the horses went through a lot of water. Made sense, because they also sweated a lot on the trail. Muley ripped into the hay and upon hearing the water, turned and thrust his muzzle in, sucking it up almost as quickly as it filled.

Cassie felt a chill as she turned and filled Prince's water. She hadn't brought the dogs because she was afraid they'd bark and wake everyone up. But something felt off. She hung the hose up and strode quickly back toward the trailer.

She passed by a large stack of hay, which blocked the stable light. Suddenly, she was engulfed in darkness. Powerful arms closed around her, pinning her own to her sides. Foul breath struck her cheek and a voice soothed, "Be calm, Senorita, it will go easier for you that way."

As a screamed ripped from her throat, it was silenced before escaping her lips by a sweaty rag covering her nose. Her gut contracted in revulsion and she kicked backwards as hard as she could. Laughing, the assailant wrenched hard up on her arm behind her back. She felt dizzy. Taking another gulp of air through the rag, a faint realization the rag was doused with something flitted through her mind. Her vision shrank to a pinpoint and then darkness.

Javier worked quickly. He chuckled, the part-time job at the vet clinic had paid off in stolen chloroform. Well worth it. He zip-tied Cassie's hands behind her back and picked her up. Avoiding camp, he took a long trail around the RVs. A few lights were just beginning to flick on, and he heard a trailer door shut as someone got up to feed. He quickened his steps to the furniture truck. The mountains now glowed reddish gold as they reflected the early morning light. Javier forced himself to concentrate on one foot in front of the other. He wanted to shout for joy, claim final victory, reap the spoils of his work. A thousand thoughts passed through his mind. *I did it.* Never underestimate the power of Javier. Sometimes things took time to be done right. The surge of excitement and accomplishment built in his stomach and flowed through his limbs. Cassie was a tall woman by his standards, but now in his victory march, she was weightless. He was Javier! The respected. The man to be feared.

Walking into his camp, he set her down by the door. Her sedated form slumped in a pile on the ground. He rolled up the door. Rope lay in one corner. He pulled his large buck knife from the sheath behind his back, sliced off several lengths, and tied her feet together. Cassie's breathing was labored. Not now. He looked at her beautiful face, clear skin and perfectly formed lips. He stopped. Those lips—he couldn't take his eyes off them. He felt the ever-present desire rise in him. Like a drug addict forcing himself away from the next fix, he tore his gaze off her and stiffly walked to the door. Later, he told himself. There would be much time later.

The sun began its climb above the Superstitions as he slipped the truck into gear. Instead of taking the road that led through the main camp, he backed up and took an old two-track he'd walked on before. Seeing no one, he drove through the cactus. A series of gravel backroads wound out to the street. Leaving the gravel, the engine groaned as he geared it up and turned south. He wound find the perfect spot where no one would ever find them. He drove with a mixture of desire, triumph and then finally, visions of little Marisol's face when she moved into her new home.

# Chapter Nineteen

Dusty turned over. A sound had woken him. Lying still, he listened. Silence. Reaching over, he felt for Cassie. Nothing. The bed was cold. He smiled. She must have gone to feed. *She is so self-sufficient. I love that about her*. Then, he heard it again. A low whine coming from the back of the trailer. The dogs. Puzzled, he sat up. Why would she have left the dogs in? He rubbed his eyes, and looked at his watch: 7 a.m. *I must have been tired.* Sliding down from the bed, naked, Dusty looked for his clothes. They lay strewn on the floor, and he smiled again as he dressed, thinking about their night. *No wonder I'm tired.*

Pulling on his boots, he picked his hat off the hook by the door, and stepped out into the morning sun. People were walking to and from the stalls, feeding and visiting. Jim and Bill stood with cups of coffee by Jim's rig. Dusty waved and walked to the back of the trailer to let the dogs out. Scout and Sammy bounded by and leaped into the dry drainage ditch behind the trailers to do their business. Dusty waited. Cassie must be cleaning out the stalls. He called to the dogs and headed to the stable area.

Muley and Prince were finishing up their hay. The water troughs were half full. Dusty looked around. The stalls were dirty. He felt a twinge in the pit of his stomach, but he willed himself to be calm. Walking like a robot, he circled the stables, the arenas, and the wash rack. Nothing. The two Aussies ran in front. Dusty looked carefully at Sammy. Her nose to the ground, she seemed to be looking for Cassie as intently as he was. Finally, he went into the laundry/bathroom area. He called out, “Cassie, are you in here?” All he heard was the washer and dryer hummed with early morning laundry.

Shutting the door behind him, he walked over to Jim’s trailer. The two old cowboys were drinking coffee and talking quietly.

“Mornin’ Dusty.” Jim saluted him with his cup.

“Morning.” Dusty tipped his head.

Bill looked at him sharply. “Somethin’ wrong?”

Speaking through the cardboard in his throat, he replied, “Have you seen Cassie?”

Bill frowned. “Not since yesterday.”

Jim pushing back his hat. “Nope. Not since we got back.”

A cold lump of dread was forming in his stomach. Dusty croaked, “I can’t find her.”

“She’s probably just dumping manure or something,” Jim drawled.

Bill turned to look over the area. “I’m sure she’s around here somewhere.”

“I’ve looked.” Dusty’s voice came out flat.

Jim raised his bushy eyebrows and set his coffee cup down. “Let’s go have us a look.” “I’ll go around this way and you go that way.” He pointed at the stables.

Bill stopped. “Isn’t she friends with Viola? Mebbe she’s there.”

A faint spring of hope flashed through Dusty. “Good idea, I’ll go check.”

Taking long strides with the dogs next to him, Dusty cleared the distance to the living quarters quickly. He knocked on the door.

Stan pulled it open. “Good morning.”

“Hi Stan. Hey, I was wondering if you’d seen Cassie?”

His white brows drew together in a frown. “No, I haven’t. Not since last night at the fire.”

The spark in Viola’s eye. “I’m sorry,” Dusty said absently. “How is she?”

"She's going to be okay. Just a slight burn, it's not going to affect her sight."

"I'm just gonna look like a pirate for a few days is all." Viola came up behind Stan with a black patch over one eye.

Dusty tried to smile, but his face felt frozen. "I'm glad you're going to be okay." He wiped his face. "Have you seen Cassie this morning?"

Frowning, Viola said, "No, I haven't. Why? Can't you find her?"

"Not so far." Dusty shook his head.

"How long has she been missing?" asked Stan with concern.

*Missing*. Dusty's insides clenched at the word. He hadn't allowed himself to go that far. "I don't know. I woke up late and she was gone."

"Oh, she's probably just feeding or cleaning the stalls," offered Stan.

"No, I checked."

"Maybe she went to the store and she's going to surprise you with a nice breakfast," suggested Viola.

Dusty rubbed his eyes. "Truck's still here."

Viola nodded her gray head. The elastic of the eyepatch created a band, her puffy curls pouring out above and below. "We'll come out and help you look. Come on, Stan." She pushed around him and stepped out of the trailer.

"Shouldn't you take it easy?" asked Stan.

"I still got one good eye." She stumped toward the stables.

Stan came out of the trailer. "Cassie's going to turn up." He put a hand on Dusty's shoulder. "It will be okay." He followed his wife's retreating figure. "Viola knows everyone here. She'll get to the bottom of it."

Later, as Dusty walked up, the group stood in front of the stables. "We can't find her," said Jim.

"I've asked everyone here," agreed Viola, "Nobody has seen anything."

Dusty felt the dark thoughts he'd pushed down inside him

explode. Javier! His leering stare at Cassie last night at the fire hit him like a brick. *Why didn't I think of it right away?* Dusty spun around and quickly walked toward the dry camp area.

"Where ya going, Dusty?" called out Bill.

Dusty didn't answer. The words bounced off his brain. They buffeted by him like a wind. He broke into a run, the dogs with him. The sand slipped under his boots and he almost pitched forward. He righted himself and the physical exertion felt good. He was doing something. As he rounded the corner of the road, a hill obscured the camping area. The remote location provided no amenities. Dry was exactly what it was, just a flat place to park your rig. He'd seen Javier's truck when they'd ridden back from Goldfield Ghost Town; it hadn't registered then, but it did now. The elevation of the Goldfield Mountains had given them a birds-eye view of the camp.

Sweat stung his face. The hill seemed neverending. Finally, he made it to the top. His breath was ragged and sweat trickled into his eyes. The dogs ran ahead of him, Sammy in front. Cresting the hill, they stopped and looked back at him. Dusty's heart fell. His eyes bored into the now empty camping spot. A piece of trash skittered across the sand in a slight breeze. The hill afforded him a 360-degree view. The cactus and dirt roads stretched out ahead of him a vast, flat expanse as far as he could see—all empty.

Dusty stopped and bent over to catch his breath. He felt a physical punch to his chest. The reality knocked him backwards. He heard running behind him, but it was far away. Scout pushed against him, leaning into him and licking his face. Sammy paced and whined.

Trying hard to focus, Dusty looked up at Jim. The older man was talking, but the words weren't making sense. Rubbing a hand over his face, Dusty stood and tried to focus. Panic had settled, cold ice in his veins. Jim's face was a mask of concern and he was talking slowly and purposefully. "We're going to have to get some help, Dusty. We'll get the police out here."

Bill joined in. "They ain't gonna get that far, they've probably only just left."

"Good point, Bill." Jim studied his watch, "It's only 7:45 now. They probably don't got that big of a lead."

"'Sides," Bill added, "That big ol' furniture truck is gonna stick out anywhere."

"Let's get back and make the call," said Jim. "No time to waste."

As they half walked and half slipped down the hill back to camp, Viola, Stan, and Bob hurried toward them. Viola held firmly onto Stan's arm. Dusty couldn't tell if she was pulling him or dragging him.

"What'd you find?" Her voice boomed across the distance.

Jim answered, "He's gone."

"Bob, have you got the license plate number for the furniture truck?" Bill asked.

Bob nodded his head vigorously. "Oh, yeah. Always required."

"Let's go call," Jim said.

The whole group turned and headed back to the main camp. Dusty walked slowly at first, and then picked up speed, the Aussies running with him. The furniture truck. He had to find it. Leaving the rest of the group far behind him, he got to his Ford and unhitched it from the trailer. Opening the door, he slid behind the wheel and both dogs jumped in. Later, Dusty couldn't remember clearly where he'd gone, but he'd driven up and down streets, hitting the surrounding highways. Nothing.

When he finally came back, Viola offered him a hot cup of coffee as they stood around the now-cold firepit. Dusty accepted it gratefully, remembering he hadn't had any this morning. The liquid burned as he swallowed it. His throat was so dry, he wouldn't have been able to talk without it.

"Thanks, Viola," he croaked.

She patted his arm reassuringly. "I'm glad I could do something, Dusty." Then brightening, "This is going to work out. I'm sure of it."

Dusty desperately wanted to believe her.

They were still gathered when a dirty white Ford Explorer pulled into the campground. A dark-skinned man with sunglasses and a black uniform got out. His gold badge glinted in the sun. The group walked over to him, Viola leading the way.

"Officer, A woman's been abducted."

Dusty again felt the battering ram to his stomach. He wondered nonsensically if people would just stop saying it, that the whole thing would go away.

Viola introduced Bob, and the deputy sheriff directed him to gather the information on Javier Mendoza. She motioned emphatically at Dusty to come forward and tell what he knew.

Later, as they watched the sheriff's car driving out of the stables, a plume of dust followed it. Dusty wasn't sure what to do next. Jim said sympathetically, "It's just a waiting game for the next little bit, Dusty. We need to see if they can find that truck."

He nodded woodenly. Waiting. How could he do that when every second that went by that hideous little man was taking Cassie farther away from him?

Turning from the small crowd, he walked back to Muley. He slipped the halter over his horse's head. The big blue roan looked at him skeptically, head high. Grief and agony coursed through Dusty and made his movements stiff. A slight flicker passed across the horse's eyes. He then did something he'd never done; lowering his big furry face, he nuzzled the man on the side of the neck. Stroking his nose, Dusty absent-mindedly assumed he would move his head. He did not. Muley leaned into him, as if attempting to transfer to Dusty the strength that he needed.

The musky equine smell filled his nostrils. Dusty, eyes half closed, leaned against his horse. He murmured into the gray neck. "Come on, let's go for a ride."

# Chapter Twenty

Dusty rode Muley back to Javier's campsite. The deep ruts of tire tracks still lay in the sand. Looking behind the camp area, he saw more fresh wheel marks. Being careful to stay off them, Dusty reined Muley to follow alongside the road, avoiding the cottony Teddy Bear Cholla. There was more than one dirt road. Luckily the tracks were easy to see. Hope bloomed in his chest. He rounded a corner and the two-track ran up a small hill and onto asphalt. Dusty felt sucker-punched again. Riding to the street, he looked down the road and saw it connected eventually into the Apache Trail main highway. The other way was a residential area with lots of homes stretching up to the base of the Tonto Wilderness at the foot of the Superstition Mountains. There was no way to track it from here.

Reining Muley back to the stables, Dusty turned over the events in his mind. The pain and loss made it difficult, but he pushed himself forward. *I've got to call Mike.* If anyone could figure this out, he could. Making his mind up gave him purpose. He let out Muley and the horse sprang forward in powerful lunges. The sand flew from Muley's hooves and the wind burned Dusty's eyes as they ran faster and faster down the trail. He felt almost free sitting astride the powerful horse plunging beneath him. The pain lifted and floated somewhere above him.

Slowing Muley just outside the campground, they walked in. The big roan snorted and jigged, and Dusty pulled him to a stop at the hitch rail. The pain returned, settling on his shoulders and stomach like lead. Sliding off, he quickly tied his horse and went to call Mike.

Lying in bed, Mike heard his cell phone chirp. Gray light filtered from behind the closed blinds. Terri lay sleeping next to him, her hair wild in a curly mop. He glanced at the clock, after nine. They were up late last night watching *Lonesome Dove*. Terri hadn't seen it before and he was getting his yearly fix. The phone buzzed again. He picked it up. As quietly as he could, he got out of bed and whispered, "This is Mike." He walked out of the room and pulled the door shut behind him.

At first there was just breathing. But Mike had seen the number flash and knew who it was. "Dusty? What's up?"

Finally, a choked voice came across the airwaves. "She's gone."

Assuming it was an argument, Mike replied calmly, "I'm sure she'll be back."

Louder this time, an anguished "No."

Mike was puzzled. Why was Dusty calling him because they had a fight?

His question was quickly answered.

"K-k-k-kidnapped. He took her…" Dusty's voice trailed off, and then Mike heard something he'd never heard in all the years he'd known Dusty. Visceral sobs filled the line, like a wounded animal.

Mike's insides froze. "Just calm down, buddy. We'll get her back." He wasn't sure Dusty had heard him.

Then there was a large intake of breath and a strangled, "Can you come?"

"I'll be on the next plane. I'll text you my flight number."

"I'll be there," came the hollow response.

Mike clicked his phone off and turned to get his clothes in Terri's room. He almost bumped into her. She stood behind him, wild auburn hair, pink terrycloth robe, her eyebrows drawn together.

"What's going on? What's wrong?"

"I have to go to Arizona." Then hating to say the last part, "Cassie's gone."

"What? Gone?"

Pulling her into his arms, Mike said into her hair, "Dusty thinks she's been kidnapped."

"No." She hugged him harder and then gathered herself. "You've got to go right away."

"I hate to leave you with all the horses."

"It's fine. Terri's eyes were wide. "I'll just get the trailer and pick up the ones from your place and bring them over here. That way everybody will be in one place to feed."

Mike had taken Dusty's packhorse to his house to feed while Dusty was gone. "I can help you do that."

"No. Go." Terri shooed him toward the door. "Every minute counts."

Mike kissed her, remembering all over again why he was crazy about her. Reluctantly letting her go, he went to the bedroom to get his clothes. He stopped to rub his eyes. A mist clouded his vision.

Blue sky and bright sunshine reflected off the plane as it taxied into Sky Harbor Airport. The vacation feel of sunny skies would normally lift Mike's spirits after the gloom of the late fall in the Pacific Northwest; this time it had a different effect on him. Mike had been going mentally over the steps he would take to find Cassie. Upon landing, he looked at the landscape merely as the place to get to work.

Walking off the plane with his carry-on, he saw people in flip-flops, shorts and T-shirts greeting others. Mike scanned the crowd and saw his friend. Dusty stood in the back, against the wall. His height made him stand out. Mike immediately saw the change in Dusty. Usually fluid in his movements, Dusty stepped rigidly toward Mike. He wore blue jeans, a light blue work shirt with the sleeves rolled up, and dark glasses. His normally tan face looked pale and tight.

Mike walked up to him and engulfed the larger man in a bear hug.

Dusty gave Mike a half-hearted slap on the back. "Thanks for coming."

"Let's get to work." Mike released him.

As they drove back to the stables, Dusty filled Mike in on the events so far leading to the disappearance. "We first started seeing this little guy, Javier Mendoza, outside of Alamo."

"That's a pretty common name, what did he look like?"

"He's short, dark hair, dark complexion; he looks Hispanic and speaks with a Spanish accent." Dusty hesitated. "He smokes. And he also drives a furniture truck."

Mike frowned. "A furniture truck?"

"Yeah, it's not real big, but one of those trucks they load up from the store to your house."

"That's different." Mike stroked his chin.

"Yeah, but probably convenient if you're into transporting women…for the sex trade," he finished raggedly.

"Dusty, don't even go there." Mike stopped him. "We're not going to let that happen. If you focus on what could be, you're going to miss the details we're looking for now."

"Sorry. Yeah, I know better." He smiled wryly. "I guess it's true. When it's personal, objectivity goes out the window."

"We'll try to make this as brief a personal experience as possible." Mike looked out the window as the Goldfield Ghost Town approached on their left. Dusty turned the truck into the Red Rock Stables. The Superstitions glowed in the late afternoon sun.

"Wow," said Mike.

Dusty said nothing as he drove by the stable area and pulled in to park in front of his trailer.

As they slid out of the truck, Viola hurried up. "Dusty, any news?"

"No," said Dusty wearily. "This is my friend Mike. He's a private investigator."

"Oh. I'm glad to see you." She held her hand out to Mike.

"Viola. If I can do anything to help at all, please let me know." She touched her eyepatch self-consciously. "A campfire spark got me in the eye last night. It's just temporary."

Mike nodded. "I need to talk to Dusty some more and walk around the site, but later on, I'd like to talk to you, too."

Viola nodded, her gray perm bounced emphatically. "Oh, yes. I'd be happy to help in any way I can."

Then in an apparent attempt to support Dusty she said, "He was a vile little man." Seeing Dusty visibly slump she realized her error. "I'd better get dinner going for Stan. Stop by any time, we're right over there." She pointed a pudgy finger at a living quarters horse trailer a short distance away. Without waiting for a response, she wheeled around and hurried off.

Dusty said nothing, and Mike followed him into the trailer.

# Chapter Twenty-One

The late afternoon sun was warm as Dusty drove his pickup along the highway with the window down. Mike glanced over at his friend who looked gaunt and tired, his usual vitality gone. It was a testament of how much his friend cared for Cassie. Another first, Mike reflected. Gazing out at the sandy terrain dotted with Saguaro cactus, it struck him how different life was here. Rugged and barren. Plants armed with sharp thorns. Where would someone take Cassie? He scanned the Goldfield Mountains. Caves? He'd heard there were lots of those down here. And mines, plenty of those from prospecting. But where else? He pushed down the concern that rose in his stomach, threatening to choke him—the skin trade. Mike quickly glanced sideways at Dusty. It was so prevalent in Washington State, he could only imagine how it would be here, so much closer to the Mexican border. And true, Cassie was older than the usual women taken, but her beauty was heart stopping. He shifted uncomfortably in his seat.

Dusty and Mike didn't talk a lot in general, but now they spoke even less. Dusty appeared robotic as he piloted the truck down the highway.

"What did they say when you called?" Dusty asked in a flat tone.

Mike was pulled back from his thoughts. He refocused on the question. "They said they have a detective that would be in the office at 4 o' clock." Mike cleared his throat. "He specializes in missing persons."

Dusty nodded his head curtly. His dark sunglasses made his eyes unreadable.

They finished the drive in silence. Dusty pulled into the parking lot. The sandstone, one-story building sat on the newly asphalted development. An American flag and Arizona State flag fluttered on a pole in front, reflecting off the many windows on the building. The words "Maricopa Sheriff's Department" adorned the glass front door. They got out and slammed the truck doors behind them.

A petite Hispanic woman at the receptionist desk greeted them. Mike surmised she was bilingual by her quick glance at Dusty and then a hesitation as she looked at him. He felt the corners of his mouth turn up. They never could quite figure out what he was—he loved it.

Having olive skin made him be mistaken for Hispanic more often than not, including by Hispanics. He hoped she wouldn't opt for Spanish, because he didn't understand it.

The nameplate on her desk said "Rosa." She nodded quickly at Dusty, her ponytail bobbed, and her long earrings sparkled. Turning her dark eyes to Mike, she smiled. "Can I help you, Senor?"

Mike grinned. A combination of the two. She was good. "Yes. My name is Mike Dracopoulos." He gestured at his friend. "And Dusty Rose. "We're here to see your missing persons detective."

Starting to rise, she hesitated.

Seeing the frown cross her brow, he added quickly, "Mike is fine."

Rosa brightened. "Please have a seat. I'll let Roberto know you're here."

"Thank you." Mike and Dusty had no sooner sat down when a Hispanic man in his thirties pushed through the side door in the lobby. He was dressed in tan suit pants and a white short-sleeved shirt with a royal blue necktie.

Since Mike and Dusty were the only two people in the waiting area, he approached them. "Roberto Aguilar."

Grinning, Mike stood and extended his hand, recognition spreading across his face. "Roberto, long time, no see."

"Mike Dracopoulos. Well, this is a surprise. I had no idea it was you." A wide smile split the detective's face. He shook Mike's hand enthusiastically.

"Yes. Last I heard you were moving to Phoenix." Mike grinned, equally pleased.

"True. It rains far too much for me in Seattle."

"It rains far too much for all of us in Seattle, but most of us just don't understand we can leave."

The two men shared a chuckle.

Mike gestured toward Dusty, who remained unusually silent. "Roberto, this is my friend, Dusty Rose."

"Pleased to meet you, Dusty."

The larger man nodded.

Not waiting for a further response, Roberto gestured towards the interior door. "Let's go back to my office."

He pulled open the door to a small cubicle with white walls, a solitary window, and pictures of a woman with children on his desk. More photos on the walls of Roberto and a young boy on a soccer field. By the resemblance, Mike assumed it was his son.

As they pulled up the chairs, Mike said to Dusty, "Roberto and I met years ago at a detectives training at Highline Community College in Federal Way.

"My favorite part was the mock trial." Roberto laughed.

Mike put his hand to his forehead. "Don't remind me. That was the worst testimony I've ever given in court."

"Don't take it so hard, Mike. The lawyers were law students."

His face sobering, Roberto turned to Dusty. "Why don't you tell me about why you're here?" He pulled out a notepad. "Be as detailed as possible, please."

Mike pulled out his own notepad and waited for his friend to speak.

Dusty visibly pulled himself together. "We first ran into this man in Alamo. We had just put the horses out when he pulled up in a furniture truck."

Roberto stopped him. "A furniture truck. Can you remember what it said on the side?"

Learning forward, Dusty rubbed his eyes. "It was pretty weather beaten, wooden siding. It looked like a big green arrow, maybe a foot or so wide. It ran about six feet on the side of the truck." He sat back in his chair. "The paint was peeling. I saw the word 'furniture' on the bottom of the arrow, but I couldn't make out what the top said."

Roberto nodded, writing on his pad. "Go on."

Dusty outlined the events of his and Cassie's encounters over the last few days with Javier. The final one being his leering look at Cassie at the RV park campfire.

"When I saw him look at her like that, I just lost it. I wanted to pulverize the little creep. Before I could do anything, a woman got a spark in her eye from the campfire. After that, pandemonium broke out. They had to take her to emergency." Dusty dropped his head and rubbed his eyes. "When everything cleared, he was gone."

Seeing the emotional toll on his friend, Mike put a hand on his shoulder. "It's okay, Dusty, you did what anyone would have done."

"Don't blame yourself," Roberto said, "There are things that happen. That's just how it is. The worst thing is to get stuck blaming yourself. It blocks your mind on other thoughts and possible evidence that could be helpful to us." He sat back and leveled brown eyes at Dusty. "We need you here in the present and working this case with us."

Dusty nodded slowly. "You're right. I'm sorry."

The detective waved his hand in the air dismissively. "No problem. It's what we all do. But now things are different. We are solving a disappearance."

Roberto's statement seemed to focus Dusty, and a strength

appeared under the pale skin. Mike was encouraged. He remembered Roberto from those trainings. The young Hispanic detective was a standout. If Mike could have personally requested someone to help him, never in a million years could he have hoped to have a guy like Roberto. He was the absolute best.

"Tell me about Cassie." Roberto held his pen poised over the notepad.

"She's a lawyer," Dusty said. "Works in private practice."

"A lawyer." Roberto said nodding.

Dusty filled him in on everything he knew about Cassie, including the last morning. "When I went out to feed the horses, they had been fed." He swiped an eye. "I usually feed them. I think she was trying to beat me there on purpose. Maybe to surprise me." The lines in Dusty's face tightened. He stopped and looked down for a moment.

Roberto carefully checked his notepad, giving Dusty a minute. "Can you give me a description of the suspect?"

Looking up, Dusty responded. "Said his name was Javier Mendoza. He's short, about 5'5", black hair, Hispanic. He's probably packing an extra fifty pounds."

Roberto took notes. "Okay, anything else?"

Dusty volunteered, "He smokes."

"I'll run that name." Roberto looked at Dusty sympathetically. "I don't want to get your hopes up. Javier Mendoza is a very common name, but I'll see what I can do." He closed his notebook. "I'm going to need pictures of Cassie. Good ones. Close-ups and full body. I need to get this out on missing persons ASAP." Roberto looked at Mike. "Including at all the border checkpoints."

Dusty nodded. "I've got some photos."

"If you send them to me digitally that would be best." Roberto stood.

Mike and Dusty rose to their feet. "Dusty, why don't you meet me out at the truck? I want to talk to Roberto for a minute."

Dusty picked up a business card. "I'll send the pictures over to you as soon as I get back."

"Thank you," Roberto said. "I'll keep you updated."

Mike watched the door close behind Dusty and then turned to Roberto. "So what do you think?"

"This guy Javier is different." Roberto scratched his head. "Kidnapping a lawyer. Honestly, unless there was some specific monetary purpose, like, say a ransom, a woman that age and that educated would be a very poor choice."

"That's what I wondered," said Mike. "Aren't the victims of the sex trade usually in their twenties as opposed to their early thirties?

"Yes." Roberto nodded. "They drug the women and make them pliable to sell for sex."

Mike touched his phone and brought up some photos. "Would this complicate that theory?"

Roberto held out his hand and looked casually at the phone. Startled, he took a closer look. He exhaled loudly. "That is a beautiful woman."

"Exactly."

The detective stared at the phone picture. "I think this would drop the age requirement. This woman looks like she's in her twenties anyway."

"I was afraid of that." Mike took his phone back and put it in his pocket.

"We'll do everything we can, Mike." Roberto opened his office door, signifying the end of the meeting.

"Thanks, Roberto, I know you will." Mike stopped. "I couldn't have asked for a better detective."

"Thank you, my friend. I will do my best not to disappoint you."

His mind reeling, Mike walked out to the truck.

Roberto thoughtfully watched Mike get into the pickup. He turned from the window and picked up his phone.

# Chapter Twenty-Two

Dusty pushed his fork into the manure and pitched another load into the wheelbarrow. Muley flattened his ears and moved out of the way. Normally that would bring a smile to his face, but right now Dusty didn't feel like smiling. He finished up his horse's stall and then moved over to Prince's. The big gray eyed him speculatively, as if to confirm he was not Cassie. Dusty shook his head. It had been a long couple of days.

Mike had left early to drive around and see what he could find out in town. Dusty didn't know exactly what detectives did, but he wished Mike would hurry up. His life had taken such a nosedive in the last couple of days, and emotionally he was having a hard time keeping up. Feeling eyes boring into him, he looked down and saw two pairs: the dogs.

Scout had not been letting Dusty out of his sight lately. Every time he turned around, he stumbled over a 75-pound-Aussie. Sammy was different; she seemed lost. Every person that would come by, or noise that occurred, she looked up hopefully. Occasionally a low moan would issue in the back of her throat. Dusty understood that perfectly. It was exactly how he felt. It had been long enough–where was Cassie?

Trying to stifle his fears, Dusty dug harder into the ground with the pitchfork. Images of that disgusting little Javier leering at Cassie replayed in his mind. And what would he do with her once he got her? Dusty's stomach roiled. He'd promised himself he wasn't going to think about this anymore. Then stealthily it would creep back into his thoughts.

"Hey, boss."

The familiar greeting startled Dusty.

Mike smiled at him as he walked up to the pen.

"Find anything out?" asked Dusty, rubbing the back of his neck.

"Not sure." Mike said, swiping his cheek.

"Oh, yeah?" Dusty set down the manure fork and leaned against the stall wall, eyeing Mike intently.

"I decided to hit all the horse rental places." Mike reached down and scratched Scout's head. "I heard talk around here that Javier had been seen out on the trail."

"Really?" Dusty was surprised.

"Yeah, far out from the RV park. They must have trailered out there. It's a place called the Bulldog Trailhead."

Dusty's brow wrinkled. "Yeah, I know that place. I think we may have been out there with Bill and Jim. And if not that, we passed it and they told us about it."

Mike nodded. "So I figured he had to get the horse from somewhere."

"So you hit the outfitters," finished Dusty.

"Yeah, it seemed like a good place to start." Mike leaned back, "I went down the Apache Trail and looked at the different vendors. I was thinking that Javier would probably go for a Spanish speaking outfitter."

"So how were you going to talk to him?"

"And therein lies the problem." He got on one knee and tried to coax Sammy to him, but she was having none of it. She looked at him mournfully and held her distance.

"Most of the vendors are bilingual, at least to a good extent. So that helped." Mike flashed a big grin. "Plus they like me."

Dusty smiled back. "Yeah, I bet they do. Right until you open up your big Greek English-speaking mouth."

"Touché." Mike stood. "I might have done okay though. I was almost through when I came upon an outfit with several horses tied to hitch rails already saddled. Signs were out saying horses for rent. There was a small concessionaire shed on the property. I went up and knocked and an older Hispanic gentleman answered."

"Did he invite you in?" Dusty took a breath.

"No, he tried to talk me into a rental horse. He came outside and showed me his stock, quite the salesman. We talked for a while. I wanted to build a little bit of a rapport."

"Good idea. What happened?" asked Dusty, fascinated, but anxious to get to the end of the story.

"I finally asked him if he'd run into a friend of mine. I was going to describe what he looked like when the outfitter's nephew came in. He was a young kid, maybe fifteen. He said, 'Hi' and kind of hung back patting the horses."

"Once again, I began to describe what Javier looked like." Mike shook his head. "That's when I definitely got a weird vibe from the old man. His face seemed to go blank and he clammed up. When I told him the person drove a furniture truck, Carlos piped up: 'Uncle, the furniture truck.' The old man barked, '*Callate*' and the kid clammed up."

Mike brushed his hands off. "And that was it."

"That was it?" asked Dusty, eyes widened.

Mike looked at him intently. "They know something. That's the good part. And we're going to get it from them."

"Great," said Dusty. "When are we going to do that?"

"As soon as possible."

"Can't we just make him tell us?" Dusty paced.

"Dusty, last time I checked, waterboarding was out. I'm going to investigate the guy a little more and see what kind of leverage we have. I stopped by to see Roberto, but he was out until later this afternoon."

Dusty swallowed hard. This was the first time he'd been involved at a personal level with any of Mike's business dealings. It just seemed like it should go faster.

Mike looked out at the late morning sun. “You want to go for a ride?”

“A ride? Now?”

“It would be a good time to check the place out. There’s not much more I can do until I can talk to Roberto.”

“What are you going to ride?” asked Dusty.

“Well, Prince, if you don’t think Cassie would mind.”

Dusty’s mouth turned up at the corners. “What are you going to do about the stirrups?”

Mike gave him a disgusted look. “I’m sure they’ll raise up, Dusty.”

“Okay.” Dusty sighed. “I’ll go get the saddles.”

Mike led the two horses out to the hitch rail by the laundry room. The area was a hub of activity, campers visiting by the burn barrel, new rigs pulling in and unloading horses.

Prince moved nervously as Mike brushed him. Speaking in a low voice, he stroked the large gray horse, calming him. “He seems pretty amped up today.”

“That’s strange. Muley’s pretty mellow. The warm weather seems to relax him.”

“Huh,” grunted Mike. He picked up Cassie’s saddle and threw it on the horse’s back. The second the saddle touched his back, Prince blew up, leaving the saddle in a pile of dust.

Dusty held himself back, laughter threatening to erupt.

Mike spoke calmly to the horse and laid a quiet hand on him. Picking up the saddle, he stretched to the upper limit of his 5’9” frame and carefully set it down on Prince’s back. This went over a lot better and the horse stood quietly. Mike tightened everything and put the bridle on. Surveying his work, he pulled a bandana out of his pocket and wiped his brow. “It’s hot out.”

Dusty was already seated on Muley. He wore an Old West beige shirt with the sleeves rolled up, a silk copper colored jacquard scarf knotted loosely around his neck. His worn silver belly Stetson and sunglasses protected him from the glare.

Taking a deep breath, Mike untied Prince and led him a little way from the hitch rail.

"There's a mounting block over there." Dusty pointed, the corners of his mouth lifting.

Mike shot him a dark look. Putting the reins in his left hand and grabbing the pommel, he put his left foot in the stirrup and swung his leg up. He never made it to the saddle. Prince exploded like a rocket, and Mike ended up in a spin; one foot in the stirrup, the other half-way across the saddle. His head out at an angle and the horse in a tight twirl, Mike was plastered to the side, unable to move. Prince was operating in full panic mode, and he spun through the center of the common area. Campers near the fire barrel fled out of harm's way, knocking over their chairs.

Dusty's eyes were riveted on Mike. Certainly, from that position he was not going to regain his seat. Prince spun perilously close to the metal awning in the picnic area. It looked certain to slice Mike's head off. At the last instant Prince dipped and it just knocked Mike's hat off as the mad spin continued.

Hearing the ruckus, Bob came out of the laundry. Although he'd said he didn't ride horses himself, he apparently could see that something wasn't right. He ran back inside and came out waving a towel. "No, no," he shouted, running toward the spinning horse and rider.

Before Dusty could tell him not to do that, Prince saw the flapping towel and shouting Bob running at him. That was all he needed. He switched from a mad spin to rodeo bucking. When Dusty thought about it later, he couldn't decide if Mike had flown fifteen or twenty feet through the air before he hit the ground. Either way, it was the highest and longest bucking dismount he could ever remember seeing.

Mike lay inert on the ground. He was hatless and face down. Dusty bounded off Muley and ran over to his friend. "Mike, buddy, are you okay?"

Painful silence ensued. At last, Mike groaned and slowly sat up. "I don't know."

Seeing Mike was okay, Dusty doubled over and burst into laughter so hard, he couldn't talk. Finally, he managed, "You... You should have seen yourself, Mike. I thought you were gonna fly to the moon."

Mike said dryly, "Yeah? Well, I think next time I'll use a real rocketship."

Dusty couldn't stop laughing. "You looked like a spinning top."

Bob had taken Prince back to the hitch rail and tied him up. He rushed over to Mike. "You okay? Need ambulance?"

Stiffly, Mike got up. "I'm good."

Viola trotted up, Mike's hat in hand. "Oh, you poor guy, are you okay?" She clucked worriedly.

"I'll be fine, thank you."

Mike put his hat on and turned to Dusty. "You think you could hold him while I get on this time? Prince seems to be a one-woman horse."

"Apparently." Dusty smirked.

"I would like to at least be sitting in the saddle when we discuss it this time." Mike gave him a wry grin.

Dusty followed Mike to the hitch rail, leading Muley. This time the mounting process went smoothly.

They took the trail behind the Red Rock Stables. The sun was warm, and the horses were glad to be out; they picked up a good pace.

Mike glanced at all the Saguaro cactus. "Have you seen any snakes around here?"

"No, I haven't personally, but I hear they're around."

The trails were well-defined and lined again on either side by the Saguaros in many poses.

They rode for a couple of hours, the great rocks of the Superstition Mountains guiding them on their right. The trail ran into the dirt road of the Apache Trail; they followed that for a short distance and came to the parking lot and trailhead of First Water.

"That's different." Mike pointed at the stone outhouse.

"Yeah." Dusty nodded. "That's what happens when there are no trees to hide behind. I'll hold Prince for you." He dismounted and held the reins of both horses while Mike went into the bathroom. The area around the outhouse was busy with tourist cars coming in and out of the parking area. Lots of backpackers, several of them coming up and wanting to pet the horses. Dusty accommodated the best he could. Muley was okay as long as he saw you coming. And Dusty didn't really know about Prince, other than so far so good.

Preoccupied with the young hikers petting the horses, Dusty didn't see the outfit enter the parking lot. Mike walked out of the bathroom; without hesitation he walked over to the outfitter and nodded. "Good afternoon, Pedro."

The older man's brown leathery face broke into a grin under his weather-beaten straw hat. "Senor Mike, we meet again."

Mike smiled and nodded. "Yes."

As they spoke, Pedro's group waited in turn to use the concrete restroom.

Dusty's curiosity got the best of him. Leading the two horses, he walked over, dogs trotting along next to him. He tipped his head at the outfitter.

"Pedro, this is my friend, Dusty."

Nodding enthusiastically, the older man greeted him. "Pleased to meet you, Senor Dusty."

Pedro went into an animated explanation of the trails around them, and as he spoke, his riders filed back. He dismounted and helped his guests remount. When he finished, he turned back to get on his horse.

Mike mounted Prince, and he and Dusty stood next to the group. Dusty asked, "So have you run across a short, dark-haired Hispanic guy driving a furniture truck?"

The question seemed to catch Pedro off guard. He turned pale and then shook his head vigorously. "No, Senor, I never saw any furniture truck." Then he added quickly, "No one named Javier." He kicked his horse into a fast walk. "We must be leaving now." He nodded back at his riders. "You know, we're on a time schedule."

Dusty and Mike nodded at him and stood silently watching the dust swirl as the horses walked down the trail.

After the last rider disappeared from sight, Dusty looked at Mike. "Where to?"

His friend's eyes narrowed and his brows were drawn together.

It was a look that Dusty had only seen on Mike when they worked a case and he was puzzling through something. What could have happened that he missed in that short conversation? "What's wrong, Mike?"

Mike stroked his chin thoughtfully with his leather-gloved hand. "I never told him the name of the man I'm looking for is Javier."

# Chapter Twenty-Three

The afternoon sun hung low in the sky, the Superstition Mountains golden, as Dusty and Mike silently drove into town. Traffic was light and Dusty easily swung into the sheriff's office parking lot. He turned off the engine and turned to look at Mike.

Without hearing a question Mike said, "Yeah, come on in with me. Let's see what he says."

As they walked toward the door, Mike was careful, seeming to favor his left side.

"You okay?" Dusty asked.

"Yeah, the ground gets harder every year." He pulled the door open and they walked into the office.

The young receptionist smiled at them, a spark of recognition in her eyes.

Mike asked, "Is Roberto back yet?"

"Yes, he is." She gestured at the couches. "Please have a seat and I'll let him know you're here."

Mike sat down and Dusty dropped heavily into the seat beside him.

Within minutes Roberto opened the reception door. "Mike, Dusty, come on back." He opened the door wider and stepped to one side to allow the men entrance, his face unreadable.

Silently they followed the detective down the hall.

Dusty was dying to hear what he had to say, but at the same

time he didn't want to hear any of it. Something told him that it was going to be bad news. If it wasn't spoken, maybe he could pretend it never happened.

They entered Roberto's small cubicle and were once again greeted by photos of his family on the bookshelves, framed by stark white walls.

Roberto closed his office door. He went back to his desk and sat down. A manila folder lay in the center, and Roberto's fingers curled around the outside edge.

Mike and Dusty watched him intently, neither one speaking. The tension was palpable.

Finally, Roberto spoke, his handsome face, closely cropped moustache and fine brows knit together. "I'm not going to lie, it's not good news."

Dusty exhaled.

Mike watched Roberto even more closely. "Go on."

"The furniture truck was spotted."

A spring of hope bloomed in Dusty's chest. "Where?"

"That's the problem." Roberto grimaced. "It was on the freeway cams, around three this morning. No one actually saw him, just the film."

"Where was he headed?" asked Mike.

"Where he probably is now." Roberto tapped the folder on the desk. "Mexico."

For the second time in as many days Dusty felt the wind knocked out of him. Mexico. *How are we going to get her out of there?*

The bewilderment slowly turned into resolve. *We will get her out of there.*

Mike persisted. "Wouldn't you know for certain if he crossed the border?"

Roberto hung onto the file and shook his head. "We should, but we don't. If you've been watching lately you'd probably notice the U.S./Mexico border is porous. Whether he entered legally or illegally, he's probably across now."

"What do you suggest we do?" asked Mike.

Roberto looked weary. "On the record or off?"

Mike said, "Let's try off the record first."

"Go down there and bring her back."

Mike considered the information. "And what's on the record?"

"Go home and I will call you when any new information comes in." He put his elbows on the desk and rubbed his face. "We'll begin the process."

"I see." Mike leaned back.

"It's not really a choice, is it?" Dusty stared at his hands.

"Could you help us look for her?" Mike's piercing dark eyes were questioning.

Roberto's smile deepened. "You will probably need someone along who can speak Spanish."

Mike smiled. "Yes, as opposed to someone who looks like they should."

All three men laughed.

Roberto clapped his hands together. "It's a deal. I will go home, pack and tell my wife I will be gone for a few days."

Dusty and Mike rose. "Great," said Mike. "We'll find someone to feed the horses while we're gone."

"I really appreciate this, Roberto." Dusty looked earnestly at the smaller man.

Roberto waved his hand in the air. "It's nothing. All in the line of duty." He winked at Mike, and they walked out.

Cassie slowly came to, lying in darkness. Her hands were tied behind her back and her ankles were bound. She tried to sort through the fog in her mind. *How did I end up here?* Cassie remembered waking up that morning and planning to surprise Dusty by feeding the horses while he slept. She had fed them; she could remember that much. Everything else was blank. She couldn't see, so she tried to smell. Wrinkling her nose in disgust, the odor was dirty socks. Her stomach muscles tightened and bile rose in her throat. *Where am I?*

Her insides turned to ice as she guessed where she was—the furniture truck, which rattled and bumped along. Horror sank in and she shivered, her limbs numb. She rolled slightly forward. Then, a muffled screech of machinery. Truck brakes. Lots of talking, but not anything she could understand—it was all in Spanish. One voice and then the deeper voice of the driver, back and forth. Laughter from the driver. A chuckle from the other man. Finally, the voice sounded like they agreed, more laughing. The truck ground into gear and the roaring kicked back in. They were moving ahead. It felt like a freeway, but there were a lot more bumps.

Cassie's head throbbed as the enormity of the situation overwhelmed her. She closed her eyes and fell into a dozing stupor. Her body bouncing against the hard bed of the truck.

Javier hummed to himself. *I've done it!* Javier the respected was on his way home with the spoils. The border patrol had been easy. Nothing was so great that a little money wouldn't grease the way. He had been careful not to mention the existence of the woman in his truck. Had they known, that would have been the end of her. One look at her face and body, and she would be on her way to prostitution. Javier puffed his chest up at the thought. He had saved her. Then the familiar ache lodged in his groin. *I saved her from them, but what about me?* The argument resumed in his mind. *Would it matter if I sampled the merchandise? I'm going to sell her to sex trafficking anyway.* How would they even know?

The need became so great that he almost pulled the truck over right there. His hands were sweaty on the steering wheel. He thought of Cassie's silky hair, large breasts and small waist. Her long legs, how they could wrap around him as he pushed himself into her. Feeling himself get hard with desire, he wondered desperately what to do. Fatigue flowed through his shoulders. He should pull over. It had been a long drive and he didn't want to get in an accident. Perhaps if he took a short nap, things would be much clearer for him. Seeing the small dirt road, he turned off. It wound through rocky hills, with an occasional dead-looking Mesquite tree and dots of Cholla cactus and green scrub.

Another small road veered to the right and Javier quickly turned the wheel, hand over hand to make the sharp corner. The old truck groaned and raised on two wheels. For a second it felt like it could go either way, then it thumped back on the dirt road. Javier wiped the sweat off his forehead with the back of his hand and continued more slowly on the bumpy road. One more large hill and then a grove of Russian Olive trees. Javier's stomach relaxed. The perfect place. No one would see the truck behind the hills and stones. Leaning back in the seat he stretched his arms and felt the kinks go out of his back. The late afternoon sun felt warm and satisfaction filled him. He closed his eyes briefly, and then out of the darkness another feeling engulfed him–lust. It was like a large dark monster grabbing him by the genitals and demanding release. *Her long legs wrapped around him. Those perfect breasts with hard nipples rubbing against his chest.* The small man gasped with the intensity of his thoughts. He opened the cab door and hurried around to the back of the furniture truck. Fumbling with the latch, he finally managed to throw the door open. Cassie lay there, her beautiful long light brown hair strewn about, and her hands and feet tied—waiting for him.

"*Amorcita*, I'm here," he whispered thickly and crawled into the truck.

# Chapter Twenty-Four

Dusty stepped out of his trailer and locked the door. He wore a tan khaki shirt and jean jacket, bleached by many washings. A faded green ball cap and Aviator sunglasses hid his face. All his major credit cards but one, locked in his trailer. He carried a couple hundred in cash, his driver's license, passport, and one American Express card. A lot had been going on in Mexico lately, and he had no idea where he was going to end up.

Mike stood a short distance away, wearing a natural colored frontier shirt and jeans, topped off with a brown vintage double-breasted vest and his silver belly cowboy hat. He greeted Dusty. "All ready for this?"

"Yes." He nodded. "I can't wait to be on our way back."

Mike touched his arm. "We'll get her, Dusty."

"Damn right we will," Dusty replied with more conviction than he felt.

An older model green Ford Explorer pulled up. Roberto rolled down the window. "Ready?" Although it had only been a day since they'd seen him, his chin was dark with 5 o'clock shadow. Deeply tanned muscles bulged in his white T-shirt, cut off at the sleeves. The familiar smile with white teeth split his handsome face. "Let's go to Mexico."

"Let's." Mike climbed in the passenger seat. "New ride?"

Roberto laughed. "It's my wife's. She was kind enough to let us borrow it."

When Dusty got in the back, he pushed aside a couple toy trucks and a dinosaur.

"Sorry about the mess back there," said Roberto. "I didn't have time to get everything out."

"No problem at all." Dusty replied in a flat voice and buckled his seatbelt. "I really appreciate you helping us."

"I like Mexico," said Roberto evenly. "Despite all the problems in recent years, I have family there. It is a beautiful country."

"So I've heard." Mike sat back in his seat. "And I have good news."

"Oh?" asked Roberto.

"I've got Javier's home address in Morelia." Mike grinned. "And it was no easy feat."

"Morelia?" Roberto raised his eyebrows.

"Yup. I've got a friend out of Seattle. With the furniture license plate and driver's license I got from Bob at Red Rock Stables, my friend was able to come up with an exact address." He cleared his throat. "I hope."

"Is that so." Frowning, Roberto stroked his chin. He looked up quickly. "Oh, but of course. I had just thought something a little different. Morelia it is."

Dusty sat in silence, watching the cactus pass by. It was hard to think of any place where Cassie was being held against her will as beautiful. He sighed and stared out the window. Mike and Roberto talked in the front seat. The morning sky was a perfect blue with white wispy clouds. He couldn't believe this was almost November. He also couldn't believe how something so wonderful had turned bad so quickly. He fell into a troubled sleep.

*The campfire popped and crackled. It was one of those rare times when he and Uncle Bob were in camp alone. The dudes had left that morning and the hands had ridden out to get the next group. The cook had joined them to resupply. Dusty watched the blue flames lick the edges of the logs and the bright red embers glow in the center. He was fourteen years old and spending the summer with Uncle Bob on the outfit. Dusty loved the calm after everybody left. On this night the sky was clear, the stars sparkling like small diamonds. Occasionally one streamed downward. A warmth glowed in the pit of his stomach and he felt completely relaxed. The woods had a way of doing that to him. It took him away from thoughts of his father's affairs with different women and continued absence. Dusty loved his mother and was constantly torn between protecting her and finding a way to love his father. His home life was difficult–until he got up here in the Pasayten Wilderness; then everything fell in order.*

*Uncle Bob sat next to him, his brown Stetson tipped back on his head as he sipped a cup of coffee and stared thoughtfully into the fire. "Dusty, I really appreciate your help this summer."*

*Dusty's cheeks grew warm, compliments did that to him. He quickly tried to brush it off. "I'm not doing that much." He moved his foot to step on a spark that flew onto the dirt next to him.*

*"No, Dusty," Bob said forcefully. "You're a man now. You've been doing the work of one and you deserve the respect."*

*Uncertain of what to say, Dusty mumbled, "Th—thank you, Uncle Bob."*

*The old outfitter took a drink of coffee and stared hard into the fire. "Respect is an important thing, Dusty. Don't ever sell yourself short on it."*

*"No, sir."*

*Silence followed for so long Dusty was sure Bob was done talking.*

*His uncle turned and looked at him. The campfire glow cast dark hollows around his eyes, but Dusty knew they were a piercing blue. "There's going to be some men that claim to be your friends. Some that don't. The ones to be careful of are the ones that want what you have." He shook his head sadly. "They will do anything they can to get it."*

*Dusty held his breath, wondering who these men were and the new dangers that came with being an adult.*

*Uncle Bob turned back to the fire and shook his head. "But they won't get nothin' from you. You are strong, and you are good. In the end that's what wins."*

"Dusty, are you awake?" Mike's voice was insistent.

"I am now." Dusty slowly sat up, rubbing his eyes.

"Good, we're coming up to the border."

Dusty looked around. They were driving into a small town with weather-beaten houses in various stages of disrepair. Chickens walked freely about, pecking the ground. Young children played barefoot in the dirt.

Roberto slowed and honked as a cow shuffled, unconcerned, across the road in front of the Explorer. "We're almost there." He pulled over to the side of the road. "You guys are going to need to put your guns out of sight. They are not allowed in Mexico."

"A lot of good that seems to do," commented Mike.

Roberto shrugged. "I don't make the laws. I just know what they are."

"What kind of a border crossing is this?" Dusty frowned.

"An easy one," said Roberto. "And, by the way, Mike is mute, so don't try to talk to him."

"Why?"

"You must have been asleep. I told him that since he could be mistaken for Hispanic, it may anger someone if he refuses to speak the language of the people. It's best not to speak at all."

"Oh." The realization that they were going into a foreign country was quickly becoming a reality.

They rounded a corner in the village and a border blockade appeared in front of them. Roberto rolled down the window and nodded at the border patrol. He handed his ID to the agent. Dusty wasn't sure what it was, if it was a police ID or private citizen. As the man scanned it, Roberto handed him a thick packet. The officer smiled widely, nodded, and handed Roberto back his paperwork.

He waved them through.

As the patrol station became smaller in the rearview mirror Dusty asked, "What just happened there? Nobody asked for my ID."

"Yes." Roberto nodded, his handsome face dismissive. "Sometimes it's not necessary."

"Where to now?" asked Mike.

"Michoacán. With Javier's address, if he goes home, we've got him."

Dusty felt hope surge in his chest. They were on the road to getting Cassie back. Then apprehension flooded through his veins. Would Javier take another woman home? Surely if he had a wife, how would he explain another woman?

The Explorer bumped along the dirt road between small hills, cactus and scrub. An occasional car rolled past.

"Don't look at the occupants in the other cars," warned Roberto. "Lots of gang activity around here. Try for invisibility as best you can. Keep your head down." He hesitated. "Especially you, Dusty. Gringos are the best targets in these areas."

Dusty pulled his ball cap down and sat lower in the seat. Skin color, it worked both ways.

Roberto re-entered the main highway after a couple hours of backroads and they drove on. It was dark as they approached the city. Lights blinked in the distance and residences popped up thickly around them.

Dusty peered out the window. "What city is this?"

"Sinoloa. It's about halfway there," said Roberto. "I'm going to have to pull over and get some sleep."

"Where are you thinking?" asked Mike.

"I have a cousin who lives on the outskirts of town. I called him and he expects us late."

As they wove through residential streets, the darkness made it hard to see. The houses were whitewashed with no yards. The roads were paved. The new construction in town didn't look much different than in the U.S. As they continued, the houses appeared smaller and closer together. A less affluent area.

"Oh, no," murmured Roberto. "I told him to keep it to himself."

He pulled the Explorer into a driveway crowded with cars, barely enough room to squeeze in. The windows were brightly lit. Mariachi music and laughter filled the night air. Dusty couldn't tell for sure, but it looked like people were dancing in the living room.

"What's going on?" asked Mike.

Roberto rubbed his face with his hands. "My family is very close." He sighed. "They don't get to see me often, so it looks like they're celebrating."

"Really?" Mike shook his head. "I went back to Illinois one time to see my family and my mom couldn't even take time off from her part-time job for my visit."

"There's benefits to that, my friend," Roberto replied wearily. "Let's go in." He opened the door. "At least there will be plenty of food."

# Chapter Twenty-Five

The truck had come to a stop. Cassie lay still, listening. Her throat was dry and her mouth felt like cotton. She tried to think. *How long has it been since I've eaten or drank?* Her brain foggy, the drugs distorted her sense of time. She heard no movement and relaxed. Maybe he'd abandon the truck and leave. *If I have enough time I can get out of the ties.* They were moderately tight, not nearly what they were when Javier first put them on.

Suddenly the truck door rolled open such force that it slammed against the ceiling. The chubby man pulled himself into the back of the truck, murmuring something Cassie couldn't understand. He paused at the door and carefully pulled it back into place. Fear pulsated through her body. She knew not to give into it; anger was much better than fear. Rage motivated her, and with fear she froze. She willed her mind to be calm and calculated.

After pulling the door shut, Javier threw himself on her body. The foul stench of stale cigarettes and armpit filled her nose. His dirty hair fell in her face as he stroked her breasts, muttering what she was sure were endearments. She heard the ripping of her shirt and felt the air exposing her bare breasts as he greedily took her nipple in his mouth. Groaning, he fumbled at her belt to pull her pants down. Cassie writhed in a nightmare. Never had she felt such revulsion. Bile rose in her throat. *He's going to rape me!*

*I'm powerless to stop it. Where is my gun?* She felt the heat of rage course through her body. Her head felt ready to explode.

Having moved her pants down to her ankles, Javier stood above her and pulled his own off. "Oh, senorita, you are so beautiful," he crooned. "Look what Javier has for you!" He proudly exposed himself above her. "I have waited for this for so long."

In the dim light Cassie could see him standing over her. She looked away so she couldn't see anything else. The muggy air felt cool on her exposed damp nipples. Her hands were still tied behind her back and her pants bunched around her ankles. Feeling helpless increased her anger.

Javier crawled on her again, kissing, rubbing and murmuring. His hand forced itself between her legs, prying them open. She was having none of it and fought to keep them together.

Javier laughed. He reached up with his mouth and bit her nipple. Pain seared through her breast. "Fighting a little is okay, but it's now time for Javier to take what's his." He pulled himself on top and began to force himself inside her.

Cassie gasped and bucked, trying to get him off.

More laughter issued from Javier as he stubbornly hung on and continued thrusting against her. His breathing was so loud and foul against her face, at first she didn't hear the sound. But there it was again; gunfire outside of the truck.

Javier lay still. More gunshots ricocheted off rocks very close by. Pinging sounded as pieces hit the truck. He frantically grabbed for his pants and shirt. Quickly he picked up Cassie, still half naked, and put her in the front of the cargo box. He covered her with old moving blankets. As he pulled his shirt on, he put his finger to his lips in a sign of silence. "We'll finish this later, *amorcita.*" He turned and hurried out the door.

"Hola," he yelled as he opened the roll up door. "I am here."

Three young boys stood nearby, guns pointed at him.

Javier gave them his most conciliatory smile. "I was sleeping," he said apologetically. "I didn't realize anyone was there."

Three sets of dark eyes focused on him. Finally, one stepped forward. Javier guessed him to be the leader. "What are you doing with the truck?" he asked in Spanish.

"I deliver furniture," said Javier. "Right now, I am on my way home. I became tired, so I stopped to sleep."

"Where do you live?" asked the leader.

"In Michoacán. I have been working in the United States and I wanted to go home to see my family." He smiled. "I have a beautiful little girl that I miss very much."

The leader frowned. His pants rode low on his hips. Holding AK-47s, the three boys talked to each other in rapid Spanish.

Javier followed what they were saying. Kill the old man, take the truck—or not. The shorter one argued if they took the truck they were going to be sent on another load across the border. They had just gotten back. They were supposed to have some time off.

The one in the middle argued, but if they brought back this truck, wouldn't Juan be happy? Maybe he would put in a good word for them, maybe they would receive more money?

The shorter one argued, but maybe not. And then they would be stuck again on another haul with this truck. And what if this time they made it across the border, but they were arrested? With the new American president, he'd heard that people got arrested. That they were put in jail and didn't get to come back—for years. What about that?

The one in charge frowned. His dark features drew together. His gold chain glinted in the sun. He walked up to Javier. He pointed the AK-47 directly at the older man's head. His young eyes bored holes into Javier's skull.

Much to his shame, Javier could feel the wet running down his legs.

The other two gang members pointed and laughed. The shorter one said, "Paco, look, you made him wet his pants."

"What?" In disbelief the boy lowered his gun. "Coward. You are disgusting." He shook his head. "Get out of my sight."

Without hesitating, Javier scurried around and jumped into the cab of the truck. He turned over the engine and floored the accelerator, driving away without taking the time to warm it up. His heart beat against his chest. He was lucky to be alive. He needed to get home and see Maria. He would drive, if it took all night.

The sun was just rising as the furniture truck putted into the outskirts of Michoacán. The fear had been so strong that Javier ran on adrenaline and drove all night long, stopping twice to re-fuel. At the second stop he remembered to get water and food for Cassie. He made his purchases at the small gas station and pulled the truck over to a parking spot away from the pumps. He rolled open the door and climbed up in the back. Cassie's hair was the only thing that appeared from under the blankets.

"Oh, *amorcita,* I'm so sorry, I had to hurry us away," he murmured.

Pulling aside the covers, he pulled her into an upright position. Cassie's head flopped to one side. Oh my God, have I killed her? He panicked. Sitting down next to her, he pulled her head into his lap. Hurriedly he uncapped the water bottle. Her lips were dry and cracked as he poured small amounts of water into her mouth. Slowly she came around, coughing. Her eyes flickered, and she drank.

Javier felt joy pulse through his body. She was alive! She finished one bottle of water and he gave her a second one. He liked holding her in his lap. Her hair fell in her face and he tenderly pushed it back. Her shirt was wide open, her breasts exposed. He couldn't take his eyes off her body. *I should take her now*. He felt himself becoming aroused. *I'm too close to home.* Control. He forced himself to pull her pants up and fix her ripped shirt the best he could. "I will find you some more clothes, *amorcita.* Please forgive me, but you are so beautiful." Unwrapping a cheeseburger, he carefully fed her, wiping her mouth with a napkin.

As he drove down the highway toward Michoacán his thoughts were full of Cassie. And it finally dawned on him. *I love her.*

His small bungalow stood in front of him. A few chickens pecked in the yard. Javier hurried to the unlocked door, threw it open and walked in.

The house was dark in the early dawn. Javier walked quietly to the bedroom he shared with Maria. She was sleeping soundly as he took off his clothes and slid in beside her. Putting his arms around her, he pulled her to him.

Wakening, she said, "Javier, is that you, or am I dreaming?"

"It's me, Maria. *Mi Amor*, you are not dreaming."

He peeled her nightgown off and was finally able to finish what he'd started hours earlier with Cassie. Although it was a different body, Javier could see Cassie's image as he satiated himself with his wife.

Javier was not sure how long he'd slept. He was tired, but he felt relaxed. A little voice said, "Papi, is that you?"

Little Marisol had come into the room.

"Yes, baby, I've come home."

"Oh, Papi, I missed you so much." She squealed and jumped onto the bed, hugging him.

"Calm down, little one. Let me get dressed and we will visit." He laughed and hugged her back.

# Chapter Twenty-Six

Javier took a shower, using the buckets of water outside. He slicked back his wet hair and entered the kitchen. Maria kneaded dough, humming, with her back to him. Marisol smiled at him with a big toothy grin. Javier held a finger to his lips and crept up behind his wife. He suddenly threw his arms around her in a big bear hug.

Maria screamed and threw the ball of dough into the air. It landed with a plop on the dirt floor. In a split second she realized it was Javier. "Oh, now, see what you made me do with the conchas I was preparing for you," she scolded. Bending over, she quickly scooped it up and set it back on the counter. Turning to Javier she embraced him and kissed him soundly on the lips.

"Am I forgiven?" he asked in a small voice.

"Javier, you home again has me forgiving you for everything."

Marisol clapped her small hands together. "Papi, you made a joke." Still laughing, she ran over to her mother and father and hugged both their legs, echoing, "You arc homc again."

Savoring the moment with his family, Javier took a clay cup, poured himself coffee, and sat down at the table. "What are you making for breakfast?"

"Your favorite, huevos rancheros with conchas." Maria continued to knead the bread despite its collision with the kitchen floor.

He beamed. “I am a very lucky man.”

“And we are lucky, too, to finally have you home.” His wife gave him a wide smile.

A small nerve pinged in his neck. *I’m not staying, Maria.* Trying to push the thought from his mind, he felt little hands hanging onto his thigh, pushing past his coffee cup and crawling into his lap.

“Papi, you have come home. Finally. I am so happy.” Marisol pushed her dark curly head against Javier’s chest and gave him her best hug.

“Oh, my beautiful little girl, I am so happy to be here.” He hugged her back.

The breakfast was delicious and when he finished, Javier was stuffed. “That was the best food I’ve eaten in months,” he proclaimed happily.

Maria’s round face shone with happiness.

As he stepped out to the backyard, Javier lit a cigarette. He blew out a line of smoke and considered the surroundings. Inside the house he didn’t notice it, but out here the abject poverty was blatant. The chicken coop in the backyard was barely standing and it certainly didn’t keep the few chickens they had inside. Hens milled about pecking at the dirt. The large red rooster with his scraggly comb threw his head back and cockadoodled.

Javier smiled. “I know how you feel, my friend. So many women to choose from.” His thoughts went out to the moving truck and its treasured contents. The morning breakfast and his family had distracted him for a while, but his mind determinedly made its way back to Cassie. The thought of her beautiful body in his hands quickened his heartbeat. He took a drag of his cigarette to calm himself down.

*I can’t stay here. I don’t want to sell Cassie anymore, I want to keep her*. He would need to take her somewhere safe. His mind searched all the places he’d been or heard of that would be secure. *I can leave her there and come down and visit her from time to time.* Excitement pulsed through his body at the thought of Cassie at his beck and call. *Oh, the things we could do…*

"Papi," a little voice interrupted his thoughts.

"Yes, my sweet little girl."

Ignoring his smoldering cigarette, Marisol once again pulled herself into his lap and laid her head against his chest. "I am so happy you are home." Her voice muffled from the material.

"So am I," said Javier, in what he hoped was a convincing voice.

"Papi?"

"*Si, mi vida.*"

"I am going to start school next year. Will you walk with me there on my first day?" She sat up and looked him straight in the eye.

Practiced in deception himself, he still found it difficult to lie to her. "Of course, Marisol." He hugged her. "It would be my honor." Guilt gnawed at him. He set her down and patted her on the bottom. "Go play now. I must visit with your mother."

Her dark eyes danced. "Yes, Papi." Marisol rushed back into the house yelling, "Papi said yes! He will walk me to school!"

Maria pushed through the screen door. She dried her hands on her apron. "Is that true?" Her eyes were bright and hope etched across her face. "You really will stay this time?"

Javier felt evil. He didn't like being made to feel that way. Anger seeped through his veins. *Aren't I the one who sends all the money from the United States to you? Where would you be without me? How dare you criticize me for all that I do?* Indignation filled his chest, and he stood up, shaking with rage.

Maria quickly stepped back. "Javier, no, I'm sorry. I didn't mean to say that—"

Javier slapped her across the face so hard she lost her footing and fell back against the stucco wall of the house. A small whimper escaped her lips, and she sat on the ground by the house, holding her face in her hands.

"How do you think you live in this house?" he roared. "It is because I sacrifice for you. I live alone in that horrible country just so I can make money for you."

"I—I'm sorry, Javier. I am so selfish," she cried out in a small voice. "Please forgive me."

Lighting another cigarette, Javier took a deep pull, feeling the anger began to leave his body. "You know I cannot take stress," he barked.

"Yes. Yes, I know that. Please forgive me."

Feeling himself relax, Javier took another drag on his cigarette. He contemplated Maria still cowering on the ground, holding her cheek. He felt himself becoming aroused. Violence did that to him. It felt like a completion of the act. He flicked the rest of his cigarette onto the ground.

A couple hens rushed over to peck it and just as quickly left. Raising his hands above his head, Javier stretched and yawned. "That good breakfast has me wanting a nap."

"You have traveled a long way," Maria said hopefully.

"Yes. Come with me." He snapped his fingers at her. "We will nap together." His laugh hollow and humorless.

Maria got up obediently and followed him into the bedroom.

Javier locked the door behind her.

After he finished with his wife, Javier completely relaxed. He was tired, but his mind still turning. Maria fulfilled a need, but all he could think of was Cassie. Her beautiful long light brown hair, her legs, and her breasts. He felt his breath catch in his throat. He glanced over at Maria. She had fallen asleep, her breathing slow and steady.

He'd take a short nap and then he would be leaving. Cassie would need to eat and use the bathroom. He must take care of her. He would find a safe place for them to be together forever.

Smiling, he turned on his side to doze.

# Chapter Twenty-Seven

When Dusty awoke it was mid-morning. He lay cramped in the back seat of the Explorer. Sitting up and rubbing his eyes, he looked around. There was no sign of Roberto and Mike. The many cars blocking the driveway the night before were gone; just one left parked in front of the garage.

Opening the car door, Dusty got out and stretched. Another warm day, at least in the 70s. Foggily, Dusty remembered how he'd got in the back seat of the car. He rubbed his neck and squinted into the bright sun. A mental pat on the back, certainly better than the old days.

The party had been in full swing when they arrived. Roberto was the guest of honor and a wild celebration broke loose when he walked in the door. Roberto introduced Mike and Dusty and then was swept off in the crowd of family and friends. Mike and Dusty stood back for a while, and some young girls came up and asked them to dance.

Dusty wasn't interested in dancing and was firm. The beautiful young girl with the dark braid pouted, but after several tries, she finally walked away. He couldn't think of anyone but Cassie.

Mike, on the other hand, had an equally pretty young girl asking him to dance. Dusty noticed Mike had a drink of some kind, and it looked to be a Margarita in a large cocktail glass and a salty rim. Dusty clicked his lips. "Oh-oh, Mike," he said softly, knowing

Mike almost never drank. When Dusty went out to the car a short time later, Mike was dancing and busting out some moves that Dusty had never seen before. He grinned to himself.

Walking to the house that morning, Dusty wondered where he would find Mike. The screen and wooden door of the house were closed. Not bothering to knock, he pushed them open and walked into the living room. No one had yet cleaned up from the party. Popcorn, drink glasses and pieces of confetti were all over the floor. As he glanced around, he saw a blanket on the couch, with a deep snore rumbling under it. Dusty smiled. He'd know that snore anywhere—it belonged to Mike Dracopoulos.

And the good part was no girls around, so Mike wouldn't have anything to say to Terri and nothing to feel bad about. Except maybe a hangover, Dusty corrected himself.

But where was Roberto? Dusty walked over and laid a hand on Mike's shoulder. "Hey, buddy, are you awake?"

The snoring came to an abrupt halt. An annoyed voice answered, "And you would ask me that, why?"

"Sorry to interrupt, Sleeping Beauty, but I want to get going to Michoacán." He leaned over Mike. "I'm afraid if we're here too long, he's going to get an even bigger lead on us."

"Okay," Mike groaned. "I'll be with you in a minute."

"Where's Roberto?"

Mike sat up. "Is he missing?"

"Well, I don't know where to look." Dusty shrugged. "I don't exactly want to start pushing doors open."

Mike rubbed his eyes. "There were so many people last night, I'm not sure what happened to him. But he's got to be around here somewhere."

"Unless he walked," said Dusty. "I slept in the car last night."

"Bummer." Mike yawned.

"No, it wasn't bad, I put the seats down and I could lay out all the way."

Dusty walked toward the first bedroom door. "Time's a wasting." Knocking on the door, he called out, "Roberto, are you in there?"

No sound came from the room. Dusty looked uncertainly at Mike. Mike shrugged. Making up his mind, Dusty shouldered into the door, opening it, and walked into the bedroom. The curtains were pulled shut and the dim light revealed no one in the bed. Dusty walked out.

Mike stared at him intently.

"That takes care of door number one," said Dusty. "Two more to go."

The rambler had a long hall with a bathroom at the end and doors on the right and the left. Mike followed Dusty into the hall, and the two of them stood in indecision. Dusty pointed at the one on their right. Dusty knocked sharply on the door. *Did I just hear something? Was that a groan?* He hesitated, looking again at Mike. He nodded. Dusty put his shoulder into the door and pushed it open. He instantly wished he hadn't.

Sunlight filtered around the curtains. Roberto lay on the bed sound asleep. Dusty recognized the young girl with him, the same one who'd tried to get him to dance. Dusty and Mike stood uncertainly. Not wanting to feel like a voyeur, Dusty cleared his throat loudly. "Roberto, are you awake?"

"Dusty, you need to find another line. He obviously isn't awake, and neither was I." Mike sounded annoyed.

"Here nor there," Dusty replied. "Hey, we need to get going," he tried in a louder voice.

Roberto stirred in the bed. He opened his eyes, and it seemed to take him a second to focus. The girl lying next to him awoke, squeaked, and pulled the sheet up around her. Her hair was no longer in a braid, but streaming over the sheets. It reminded him of Cassie. Dusty felt a lump in his throat. "Get dressed." He ordered. "We'll meet you in the living room."

Dusty and Mike sat waiting, neither speaking. Low voices murmured from the bedroom, and then the door clicked shut. The water in the bathroom ran. In a few minutes Roberto appeared, his hair wet and slicked back. He flashed them a wide grin. “Ready to go to Michoacán?”

“Been ready.” Dusty stood.

“Let’s do it.” Mike headed for the door.

They had been driving for some time when Mike finally spoke, “So what time do you think we’re going to get there?”

Roberto frowned. “It’s about a seventeen-hour drive, so if we keep up the way we’re going we should get there by about 1 a.m.” He paused. “Provided nothing happens.”

Mike looked at him. “Like what?”

“Oh, I was just thinking about banditos or something like that; it’s not how it used to be around here anymore.”

Mike considered it. Involuntarily he reached on his side and felt his gun, exactly where it should be on his side holster. Staring out the window for a while, Mike finally asked what he’d been wondering. “So…you and your wife have an open marriage or something?” He tried to keep the disappointment out of his voice. He’d held Roberto in high esteem ever since they’d met, had looked up to him, and hoped that he’d become half the investigator that Roberto was. He felt the burn of disappointment collect in the back of his throat. *I hope I’m wrong.*

Roberto laughed. “No, we actually don’t.” He waved behind him. “That’s just what’s in Sinaloa stays in Sinaloa.” He winked at Mike and continued driving.

Mike looked out the window. He found no humor in the situation. He sighed and felt sorry for his friend. Laying his head against the window, he shut his eyes.

# Chapter Twenty-Eight

Javier turned over in bed. He wasn't sure what woke him up, maybe it was the quiet. The dark night sky filled the window. Dios Mio!

Maria slept next to him, now wearing her night clothes.

"Maria," he demanded angrily.

"Wha-what's wrong, *mi amor*?" she said sleepily.

"Why didn't you wake me up?"

She sat up in bed surprised. "You didn't say?"

He jumped out of bed and picked up his clothes. "I must leave."

Maria sat up. "No, you just got here."

"I told you I couldn't stay," he barked. "I must go now."

Thoughts of Cassie lying hungry and thirsty in the dark furniture truck spurred him on. He had to hurry. Another thought nagged in the back of his mind. *What if someone knew who I was? They would have time to follow me.* He pushed it out of his mind. The odds were slim, he lied to himself.

Sitting up in bed, Maria rubbed her small hands together. "Must you go?" she tried again in a small voice. "We will miss you."

Javier looked at her, now seeing her for the first time. "Oh, *amorcita*, I will be back." He walked around the bed to hug her.

"Stay safe," she said, resigned.

"I have to make money to send you." He started to walk away and stopped. "The next time I come, it will be for longer, I promise.

I am going to make a lot of money." He puffed up his chest. "You will see."

"Javier, I don't care about the money."

He waved her off. "It will be good. Give Marisol a hug for me and tell her how much I love her." He couldn't bear to say good-bye to his daughter. Her crying was one thing he couldn't abide, it tore his heart to pieces.

"Si, Javier."

He paused on his way out the bedroom door. "Maria?"

"Si?"

"I'm running a little low on money, give me some to help me get back to the United States." He said it as more of a command than a question.

Maria got up and walked to the beat-up dresser. She dug into the top drawer and pulled out a sock. Her shoulders were bony, the skin under her upper arms jiggled. Her hair fell into her face as she concentrated pulling bills from the tattered sock.

Holding it in her fist she walked over to Javier and placed it into his outstretched hand. Closing his fingers over it she looked up at him. "I would do anything for you, my Javier."

Javier's face was blank. He felt revulsion in the pit of his stomach. She was pathetic. *What had I ever seen in this old woman?* "Gracias," he said coldly. Walking out the bedroom door, he left her standing, watching him leave.

"Hey, Roberto, what is this big city? Is this Morelia?" Mike peered out the windows. Hundreds of lights cut into the black sky.

"Yes, it is."

"Wow," said Mike. "It's a lot larger than I thought."

"How much further to Javier's house?" Dusty sat erect.

Roberto looked at his phone's GPS. "It's only about fifteen minutes. We're close."

Dusty double checked his shoulder holster for his gun. It was there and loaded. He fidgeted. So close now. *Cassie, we're coming.*

Javier crossed the living room to the front door. As he reached for the handle, a small voice said, "Papi, where are you going?"

He froze. He turned to face his young daughter. She stood with her hair mussed from sleep, holding her favorite doll under one arm. Her big dark eyes were questioning. "Papi, why are you going outside in the dark?"

Getting down on one knee, Javier pulled her close. "I must go for a little while, *mija*."

"But Papi, you just got home." She began to cry.

Javier felt his heart breaking. "Remember the house I'm going to buy for you?"

She hesitated. "Yes, Papi. I remember. No more dirt floors."

"Yes," Javier said excitedly. "I must go so I can get money to buy the house for you and mama." He hugged her in his best bear hug and growled. "Do you understand?"

In spite of herself Marisol giggled. "Are you a bear, Papi?"

"Yes." He growled again and pulled her into another hug.

"When will you be back, Papi Bear?"

"Very, very soon," he said seriously. "Will you take care of your mama?"

"Yes, for you Papi Bear, I will."

"Okay, then." He stood up quickly. "Until we meet again." Javier patted her on the bottom. "And off to bed you go."

"Yes, Papi." Marisol obediently turned away.

Javier watched her tousled long curly hair swaying, pulling her doll by one arm, the rest of it dragging on the floor down the hall to her room. As she walked away, Javier's chest felt tight. She was his sunlight. *I won't let you down, my bebe, it might just take a little longer*. His mind flicked back to the precious cargo in the back of the furniture truck. Sighing heavily, he turned to go out the door. Sometimes a man had to make a decision. It wasn't always easy. Cassie's face appeared in his mind, and his heart quickened. *I'm doing the right thing*. He felt absolutely no doubt.

Javier went out the door and shut it behind him. The night air was cool as it brushed against his cheeks. He took a deep breath.

Of everywhere he would go, this would always be his home. He loved the smell of it. Such happy memories. He went straight to the truck cab and climbed in. He would check on Cassie, but he needed to leave first. He couldn't risk having Marisol or Maria coming out and asking him what he was doing.

He turned the key over, the starter ground and stopped. A faint panic tightened his chest. *What? Not now.* Javier willed himself to be calm. Don't flood it. Give it a minute.

Roberto slowed down and turned a corner. Dusty leaned forward from the back seat and drummed his fingers on the headrest. "How much further?"

"According to my phone, it's just a couple of blocks," Roberto replied.

"The town looks different than I envisioned it," said Mike. "I thought it would be more rural."

With a sweaty palm, Javier put the key in the ignition again and slowly turned it over. It sputtered, died. One more time, he told himself. Please God. Perspiration dripped from his armpits. Come on! Maria is going to be out here in a minute. He turned the key again. He thought it would sputter, but it didn't. The old motor engaged with a grinding sound and turned over.

He flinched. Nothing like letting the entire neighborhood know I'm leaving. Uneasiness made him not wait more than a matter of seconds to warm up the big truck. Pushing it into gear, he drove, turning down the next road behind a wall of shrubbery.

Within minutes, Roberto pulled up in front of the small bungalow.

"Are you sure this is it?" Mike peered through the windshield.

"That's the address you gave me," said Roberto.

"No truck," said Dusty flatly.

Roberto opened his car door. "Let's find out."

The three men went up to the front door. Hesitating only slightly, Roberto knocked. The door opened wide within a short time. A middle-aged woman in a nightgown threw the door open, a huge welcoming smile on her face. The partial name "Jav—" froze on her lips.

Dusty watched her intently. Confusion, fear, and finally resolution passed over her countenance. She stood solidly in the doorway.

Roberto hadn't missed any of it. Already knowing the answer, he asked in Spanish, "Is Javier home?"

She shook her head furiously.

"Mama?" A beautiful little girl with large dark eyes appeared in the doorway next to her mother. "Who is here?" She looked questioningly at the three men.

Roberto didn't miss a beat. "Hello sweetheart, is your papi at home?"

"No," the little girl answered sadly in Spanish. "He just left."

The women sharply said something to the little girl. The child looked puzzled, staring at her mother.

"How long ago, my little one?" Roberto continued.

The woman interjected. "She is confused. There was no one here."

"No, Mama. Papi just left," the little girl insisted.

Dusty couldn't stand it anymore. "How long?"

The girl looked up at Dusty. Her little chin set, she said definitively. "Three minutes."

"Which way?" asked Mike.

Apparently enjoying the attention, she pointed a pudgy finger down the road in the direction the truck had just taken. "That way." And then added, "Papi thought I went to bed, but I got back up and watched him drive away."

Roberto nodded. "We'll be back." The three men turned and ran to the Explorer. Dusty jumped in the front and Mike climbed into the back seat. Roberto slammed it into gear and took off before the doors were shut. Gravel sprayed as they sped down the road.

# Chapter Twenty-Nine

Cassie felt the engine groan as the big truck vibrated and lurched forward. She'd slept hours in a semi awake state. Her head burned. The smell of moldy moving blankets, along with the dust of the old truck turned her stomach. It had been a long time since she felt her hands. The pain from the zip-ties had given way to a faint buzzing sensation. She had to go to the bathroom and she had no idea if Javier was coming back. She shook her head in revulsion, *I hope he never comes back.* Finally, she sat up. Her pants were not secured from Javier's ravaging earlier. Rolling to the side of the truck, she pushed her pants down in the back and relieved herself on some blankets. Much better. Whatever happened to his blankets was probably a move up—*he's truly a disgusting little worm.*

Rolling and inching away from the wet blankets to where she had been before, she was able to move her jeans back up. Thirst and hunger overwhelmed her. She shut her eyes. The darkness made it difficult to see what was in the truck, but he was living in it, so there must be something she could use to cut the ties. And maybe there was something to drink. She swallowed. The dry lump caught in her throat. Inching to the front wall, she sat up, ignoring the searing pain in her arms. Beside the pile of moldy blankets, she couldn't see much else. Despair pierced her stomach, maybe he was keeping sharp things in the cab of the truck. Weak and shaky, she lay down. She would think more about it later. Her lids were heavy with fatigue and fever. She closed them and descended into darkness.

The sun rose in bright red, orange, and yellow streaks through the palm trees. Javier sighed. *How I miss this. Once I take care of everything, I'll bring Cassie back here.* Maria would surely understand. Javier wiped his forehead. If she doesn't, she'll have to leave—one way or the other.

Morning traffic was becoming thick, a car sliced in front of him and he honked, barely missing it. He needed to go somewhere and get lost. Get back to the United States, Mexico was too dangerous. He shook his head remembering the close call a couple days ago at the border. There are just too many gangsters now. Another car cut in front of him. Some things never change.

Dusty kept his eyes peeled for the outline of the old furniture truck. Traffic congested the road. Driving was free form with cars cutting in and out, old buses mixed with new, bicycles and pedestrians crossing haphazardly. Suddenly, up in the distance he saw it. The wooden roof of the truck.

"Right up there, Roberto," he shouted, pointing at the truck.

Taking his eyes off the melee in front of him Roberto glanced ahead. "Yes, that might be it."

Dusty sat up in the seat at full alert. The traffic made it impossible for them to go any faster. He looked ahead, to the barely moving truck. Making up his mind in a split second, he grabbed the door handle.

Mike reached forward to pat his friend on the back and instead his hand fell to the empty car seat. "What?"

In one fluid motion Dusty flung the door open and ran down the street, jumping between the slow-moving vehicles. He rapidly closed the distance to the truck.

"Oh, man." Mike grabbed the back door handle and followed his friend down the street.

Glancing in his rear-view mirror, Javier didn't immediately notice anything amiss. Then he did a double take. A big white man was running down the street behind his truck. Javier slowly moved forward. He looked back again. The face, now contorted in rage. He'd seen it before. Then it struck him. Dusty! A smaller man ran close behind. Javier was stymied, what could he do? He wasn't going to just leave the truck and Cassie in the middle of the road. But what? Before he could come up with an answer, the large man ripped his door open and grabbed him by the shirt. Javier didn't have a chance to say anything before a large fist crashed into his face.

The red-hot anger was in control, not Dusty. He grabbed the small man. He wanted to kill him and he began to do just that, methodically beating him. He wasn't even aware of Mike, jumping on his back, pulling him off. A huge cacophony of noise ensued, with police cars appearing out of nowhere, lights flashing as they roared down the median. Uniformed officers jumped out and struck Dusty with batons. He faltered under the blows. Before he could collect himself, they handcuffed him. Howling in despair he yelled, "Mike, get her! Get Cassie!"

"I can't, said Mike. "I'm cuffed too."

Other officers picked up Javier and helped him to his feet. Javier spoke in Spanish to them, waving at Dusty and Mike. "Banditos" was all Dusty could understand. Sympathetically the officers nodded to Javier. They waved him on. He got in his truck and drove away.

"Nooooo!" screamed Dusty.

The officer pushed Dusty to the back of the police car. Holding the top of his head he loaded him into the back seat. Mike was pushed in behind him.

The Ford Explorer screeched to a stop on the median, just as they were leaving. Roberto jumped out, ran to the driver's window. "No, wait," he implored in rapid Spanish. The officer stopped, Roberto explained the situation, or at least Dusty assumed he did.

He pulled out his badge and showed it to the officers and pointed at Dusty and Mike. Roberto said, "Mike, show him your license."

"I need my hands free, so I can get my wallet."

More Spanish. The police officer walked around to the back and removed Mike's cuffs. After rubbing his wrists for a few seconds, he pulled out his wallet. Taking the investigator's badge, he handed it to the policeman. The man carefully looked it over so long, Dusty assumed he thought it was fake. Finally, the officer handed it back to Mike. Walking to the front of the car, he spoke to Roberto some more. From what Dusty could tell, he seemed to have a hard time making up his mind. Roberto was very persuasive, and Dusty thanked God that he had come with them. Shaking his head, the officer got in the car and called on his radio. Dusty didn't know how long it took, everything ran in slow motion. After another long discussion, the officer seemed to come to a conclusion. He hung up the handheld and got out of the patrol car. Once more, talking to Roberto, he gestured towards Mike and Dusty. Finally, he came over to the door on the rear part of the cruiser. Pulling Dusty out, he uncuffed him. Walking around to the other side, he gestured at Mike to get out of the car. A few more words to Roberto, to which the detective nodded his head vigorously. The policeman nodded, got in his car and merged back into traffic.

"So what was that all about?" asked Mike.

"You guys are lucky. You barely stayed out of jail."

"I got that feeling." Mike shook his head.

Roberto turned to Dusty. "You need to get a grip on yourself, Dusty. We could have had them."

Dusty hung his head. His face felt tight. The realization of what he'd done hit him hard.

Roberto spoke in a softer voice. "Beating up people is a crime here. Luckily, I was able to convince the officer that it was a domestic. If he'd taken you in, I don't know when you'd get out." He turned to Mike. "You either."

Dusty demanded, "Why didn't you tell him the truth: that Javier stole Cassie?"

"Because you're in a different country now, Dusty. If I told him that, if he knew there was a woman in the back of that truck, or anywhere, I have no idea if we'd get her back again." He shook his head. "There are good cops and bad cops. Beautiful women bring money." Roberto rubbed the back of his neck, "The less they know, the safer Cassie will be." He paused. "It looks like our little friend is keeping her all to himself for the moment."

Dusty groaned inwardly.

"It's okay, in this case that is the best outcome." Roberto got into the Explorer.

Mike jumped in the back. "Dusty, we'll get her. They're not going to be that far ahead."

Dusty sat. "How do we know that? They could be anywhere. It's a big country."

"Just relax," Roberto said calmly. "We'll get them, but this time don't beat on him, okay?"

Dusty didn't answer. He stared ahead, willing his eyes to see the dark brown outline of the furniture truck.

# Chapter Thirty

Javier's heart pounded in his chest. He could not believe how lucky he had been. The adrenaline was pumping so fast through his veins that he didn't feel any pain. Glancing in the rearview mirror, he gasped. One eye was swollen almost shut and his jaw puffy. Poking his tongue tentatively over his teeth he felt a couple loose ones. Still lucky. His hands were slick on the steering wheel; one at a time he wiped them on his jeans. Sometimes the police took hours to arrive at the scene. Since murders were so rampant, Javier just figured something like this would be low on the priority list. Thank God it wasn't. He giggled. That's the first time the police actually worked to his benefit. Who would have known?

The traffic thinned out. The honking and swerving vehicles now became few and far between. As relief flooded through his body, Javier felt sensation flow back into his feet and hands. *I may make it out of here after all.* A crossroad appeared ahead, he signaled and turned off the freeway. He was going to have to take side roads for a while. One encounter with Dusty was enough! A shudder ran down his spine, the large man had been in a blind rage. Javier had seen that enough with his own father. The difference was Dusty, he was sure, would have killed him. And all over a woman. Sure, Cassie is beautiful, no doubt. And he wanted her, but she was not the only one on the earth. *I wouldn't beat someone to death over her*. The familiar dark longing filled him. *Would I?*

A gas station appeared on his right. The houses were farther apart and the countryside was becoming more desolate. Russian Olive trees grew in groves, with intermittent sagebrush. An occasional farm appeared with irrigated green fields, but most of it was dry. Javier put the truck in low gear and pulled into the gas station. He took cash out of his pocket, and as the truck fueled, he hurried into the store. Grabbing orange juice and a six pack of water, he looked around trying to think what would be good for Cassie to eat. He finally bought a dozen warm burritos. Those are always good, he reasoned, hot or cold.

Javier set his purchases on the front seat of the truck and pulled the hose out of the gas tank. He put the key in and waited. Being warmed up, the engine only ground once. It started on the second try, and warm relief flooded through him. He pulled over to a parking space near the dumpster in the far end of the lot. There was activity by the pumps, but the rest of the parking area was vacant. Making sure no one was watching him, Javier took his bags and went to the back of the truck. He walked slowly with a loose gait and acted like he didn't have a care in the world.

Throwing the door up halfway, he set the bags down and pulled himself into the truck. He was not prepared for what he saw.

The smell of urine, so strong it burned his eyes. The closeness of the truck and lack of ventilation, combined with the heat and humidity made the smell more intense. He had to look hard to distinguish Cassie from the blankets, but he saw her hair first. She lay on her back. Javier walked over to her and set down his grocery bags.

"Cassie, I'm here."

Her eyes were closed, he could feel the heat coming from her before he even touched her face. She was burning up. He pulled his knife from his belt. Carefully turning her on her side, he cut the ties that held her wrists together.

Cassie moaned.

*I left it on too long. What was I thinking?* He slapped his forehead with his hand. The gashes on her wrists oozed pus and blood. *I'm going to have to get some bandages.*

"Cassie, can you wake up?" When she didn't respond, he shook her arm. Her eyelids fluttered open, but didn't focus. He tried again. "Would you like some orange juice?"

She opened her cracked parched lips. "Water." It came out in a raspy whisper.

Panic rose in his chest. *Oh my God, what have I done?*

He pulled the lid off the orange juice. Sitting next to her he pulled her into his lap and cradled her head. Slowly he poured juice into her mouth. Most of it spilled out of the sides, but a bit went in. Cassie swallowed, uncoordinated at first, and then drank greedily. "I'm so sorry, *amorcita.* Javier was bad," he crooned, stroking her hair. "I should have come back to you sooner."

He took the orange juice away. "Not so fast, you are going to make yourself sick."

The drink seemed to revitalize her enough that she was able to speak. "More."

Javier obliged, mesmerized by how beautiful she was even now. Her hair was in wild disarray, her clothes barely covering her. He felt himself responding to her. In spite of her fever, he wanted her.

Cassie stopped drinking. She burped and then the orange juice came up. She vomited partially on the truck floor and some on Javier.

Javier jumped up. "Dios Mio." He felt as if someone had thrown a cold bucket of water on him.

She flopped back onto her side and groaned.

Javier carefully removed the blankets she'd vomited on. Using those, he cleaned up the floor next to her.

"I'll be right back," he said to her inert form.

Crossing the parking lot, Javier re-entered the convenience store. He walked back to the frozen food, found peas, and bought two bags. They were cheap and would do the trick, he hoped. Stopping in the front of the truck, he pulled out a small first aid kit he'd found in the glove compartment. He walked back to the rear of the truck and slid the door up.

Cassie lay pretty much as he'd left her, flat on her back drawing shallow breaths. The truck now smelled pungently of vomit as well as urine. He took the frozen vegetables and lifted her arm. She was flaccid as he placed the frozen bag under her armpit. She flinched at the cold, then lay still. Lifting her other arm, Javier did the same thing.

"That will help with your fever," he said gently.

Opening up the first aid kit that he'd seen in the truck's glove compartment, he tended to the gashes on her wrists. He cleaned them with antiseptic and then carefully wrapped gauze around them. "You'll feel better shortly."

Packing up the rest of his kit, he walked out the door and pulled it down. He slid the small hook in place. Even if she wakes up, she won't be getting out of there. A smile etched his face—unless I let her. Still staring at the door, he lit a cigarette, thinking about Maria digging in her sock to give him money. So pathetic. A broken woman. He snorted in contempt. But in there is a real woman. A spirited beauty. *I will break her to me, but I must be gentle. She's like a wild mustang, who soon will only respond to my touch.* He took a drag of his cigarette, and swaggered back to the truck cab. "El Patron will have to make other arrangements. This woman is mine." He smiled.

This time the engine turned right over. Javier pulled out of the driveway and pointed the truck back toward the United States. *I'll stay on backroads until we get close, then I'll risk it to cross the border.* And after that? He thought hard about where to go, then suddenly it came to him. Such a perfect idea, why hadn't he thought of it before? Whistling, Javier drove into the warm afternoon sun.

"He must have turned off," said Dusty. "I'm not seeing anything."

Roberto nodded. "I'm thinking the same thing."

"There's a lot of backroads?" Mike peered out the window.

"There are," confirmed Roberto. "And even more if you're from here."

"That's what I was afraid of," said Dusty with an empty stare.

"I've pulled in every favor I've got down here," said Roberto. "There are a lot of people looking for that furniture truck."

Mike leaned forward in the back seat. "Hey, could you pull over at that gas station? I need to use the bathroom."

Wordlessly, Roberto pulled in. Mike jumped out of the back and walked into the store.

He came back a few minutes later with a big smile on his face.

"What's up?" Roberto turned to look at him.

Mike slammed the door. "A furniture truck was here a few minutes ago." He pointed north. "They went that way."

"The United States?" Dusty jerked his head back.

"That would be my guess." Mike nodded.

Roberto stroked his chin. "It's a possibility."

"Sure," said Mike. "He went home and he knows we're right behind him. It's not safe in Mexico anymore."

Slumping back in the seat, Dusty laid his head on the window.

Mike reached forward and patted his friend on the back. "If nothing else, we'll grab him at the border."

"It's a big border, Mike," Dusty said dejectedly. "God, she was so close. If only I could have gotten in the back of that truck."

"We'll get her." Mike's voice held a firm note. "You've got to stop beating yourself up and stay focused. This could be good news. He turned in his seat. "If he's headed back to the U.S., it means he's not selling her."

"He's keeping her then and that's good news?" Dusty said with his eyebrows raised.

"It's a known evil," said Mike.

Dusty shut his eyes, exhaustion taking over. His thoughts took him to another time many years ago. He was young then and nothing was impossible…

*"I'm going to find that elk."*

*The old man's deep blue eyes stared at Dusty. "Son, that's a wily old elk. Grown men haven't been able to find him. How's a boy like you gonna do it?"*

*"I can do it, Uncle Bob." He stood up straight. "Besides, I'm not a boy anymore, I'm fourteen years old now."*

*"Is that right?" The old packer nodded. "Well, then, you'd best be on your way. Saddle your horse. You can bring along Blue for a packhorse" He nodded at the camp kitchen, "And pack yourself a couple of days' worth of food. You never know, you might need it."*

*Dusty was thrilled. He almost broke into a run, but stopped himself short; he was a man now, and men didn't run; or not much anyway. He got his saddlebags and packed a sandwich, apples, and beef jerky. Grabbing his bedroll, he went down to catch his horses. He liked to call Dan his horse. His for the summer anyway. Good old Dan, the sorrel quarter horse with a white blaze and four white socks. Dusty had heard that referred to as a lot of chrome. He liked that, made his horse sound like a fancy car.*

*Dan was easy to catch in the small log corral below the outfit. Dusty brushed him, saddled up, and was ready to go in minutes. Blue was easy, too. Dusty had the packsaddle and panniers on him in no time. Saddling and unsaddling for Uncle Bob's outfit for years came in handy. He was just tying on his bedroll and slicker when Bob came up to him.*

*"Ready to head out?"*

*"I think so," said Dusty.*

*"Got your rifle?"*

*"Yup, right here." Dusty touched the stock of his rifle in the holster on the side of his horse.*

*"Okay, then," said Bob. "I expect to see you back with your elk in a couple of days."*

*"You will." Dusty nodded.*

*Bob raised an eyebrow and waved good-bye.*

*Dusty picked up the lead rope to his pack horse and rode away from camp. How difficult it might be to find the elk, or any possibility of failure never entered his mind. Instead, he took a deep breath of mountain air. It smelled and tasted like fresh snow with a hint of pine. The shrill squeal of a hawk trilled overhead. Dusty watched the bird take a sharp turn and then drop suddenly into the alpine meadow below him. Just as quickly it shot up into the sky, the only difference Dusty could see was the little bundle squirming in his talons.*

*He followed the main trail for a short way and then dropped off and rode through the trees. Trails and trees probably didn't make that much of a difference up here, he reasoned. To find the biggest elk possible, Dusty figured he'd be holed up in a remote spot. The trees were thick, but nothing like the West side of the Cascade Mountains around Eagleclaw. In that area it was dark from the big Douglas Firs. These pines allowed light through them.*

*A small creek splashed through a valley in front of him. Dusty studied it carefully. A good spot for a camp in the trees at the edge. Lots of grass for his stock. And if he took the camp at the head of the valley, he'd have a full view of everything that came and left. Making a decision, Dusty rode to the spot he thought would be best. And sure enough, as always seemed to happen, someone had camped there before him. Passing under the perimeter trees, Dusty saw the telltale campfire ring. A pile of chopped wood lay next to it and a few large logs. Score! He wouldn't even need to cut anything tonight for a fire.*

*Dusty unloaded his pack horse and stripped the saddle off Dan. Strapping the hobbles on the horses, he turned them loose in the meadow. The livestock wouldn't be a problem if any deer or elk came in, it never stopped them from sharing the meadow. Dusty threw his bedroll out and set to make a small fire. He didn't need to cook anything, but a camp always felt more like home with a fire in it.*

*As the night sky darkened, silver stars twinkled above the mountain peaks. The horses had long stopped eating and now stood quietly together in the meadow. Soundlessly, Dusty got up and walked out to them. He unfastened the hobbles, looped them around their necks, and brought the horses back to his highline in the trees. After securing the animals, he went back to his quickly dying fire.*

*The meadow lay still. He wasn't sure where, but tomorrow morning would be his hunt. He banked his fire and crawled into his bedroll. Uncle Bob had told him before, things happen the way they're meant to. Just go with it. Dusty had no idea why he had ridden to this spot, but he knew it was right.*

*The bellow went off like a foghorn, and it sounded like it was in his face. Without moving, Dusty slowly opened his eyes. In the early dawn light, no more than twenty feet away from him stood the largest bull elk he had ever seen. The antlers were enormous. Dusty guessed them at seven points. The elk bellowed again and pawed at the ground. Steam blew from his nostrils, white puffs in the early morning air.*

*Turning slightly, Dusty rose on one elbow to look down the meadow. He saw a couple of cows, but there on the edge, a young bull stood. That had to be the problem. The bull moved forward aggressively, then froze in the torrent of bellowing. Dusty slowly reached for his gun. He had one shot, that would be it.*

*His heart hammering in his chest, he pulled himself along the ground and rested the rifle barrel on the fallen logs in front of him. It gave him a perfect shot. The big elk wasn't paying any attention to him, he was focused totally on the young bull. Dusty didn't want to hit him in the back. He focused instead on the large bull's head, dropping his aim to behind the right shoulder. He waited, his hand sweaty on the trigger. Giving a last blood curdling blast, the bull put his head down and then threw it straight into the air, readying for a charge. Dusty eased back on the trigger and the bullet cut through the air. The elk screamed and leaped forward. At first Dusty thought he'd missed, but the animals' legs crumpled from under him and its mighty head fell to one side. Stillness enshrouded the meadow.*

*The young bull planted himself in stunned silence. After a few minutes he rounded up the cows and they left the meadow. Dusty went to get his blood sacks and skinning knife. This would take a while. Keeping his gun close and eyes alert for cougar or bear, Dusty set about preparing the meat for transport.*

*When he came into camp, Bob hurried out to meet him. To this day, Dusty would never forget the look on his face. Shock, disbelief, followed by intense pride. "You got him all right, Dusty." He shook his head, "I can't believe you pulled it off yourself, let alone got him out of there." Bob stared at Dusty's pack horse, heavily loaded with game bags stuffed with meat, topped with the head and horns. "That there is the biggest head and horns mount I can ever remember seeing. You done yourself proud." Admiration poured out of the older man's eyes, they glistened as he looked at Dusty. "I'm mighty proud to know you, son. You get what you go after, that's for dang sure."*

*Dusty felt like his insides might explode. Uncle Bob was good to him, but he didn't freely throw around compliments. And he'd just done it at least three times in the last few minutes.*

*"Being a man's not so bad," observed Dusty.*

*"No, not the way you do it, son." Bob turned, "Come on now, let me help you with that meat before it spoils."*

# Chapter Thirty-One

Late the next day, Javier approached the border. Not wanting to run into any more cartels, he picked his spot carefully. He'd checked on Cassie once. The frozen peas seemed to be helping, she didn't feel as hot as she had. He'd picked up some Motrin, the clerk at the last grocery had said to keep that up every four hours.

The roads were dirty and lined by scrub on either side—low-growing cactus and scraggly Russian Olive trees. Javier shook his head, more than once he'd felt the prick of those branches, nothing in Mexico was hospitable. Beautiful, yes. But you better be able to take care of yourself, nothing was easy here.

He rolled up to the remote border station. A lone guard sat watching him from inside the rickety old booth. As Javier put the truck in gear to stop, black smoke billowed from the exhaust pipes in protest. Waving his hand to clear the air, the guard came out and stood by Javier's window.

"Paperwork?" The man requested, holding out his hand. He wore a dark olive-green uniform with yellow official patches on the shoulder and chest. The buttons on his uniform strained to contain his stomach—a possible tribute to the inactivity of his station. Hatless, his hair was cropped close to his skull.

Javier's palms oozed sweat and a trickle ran down his armpits. "It's in here." Slowly leaning forward, Javier dug in the glove compartment of his truck. Just be calm, he told himself, *I have the phony paperwork in here—they assured me it was good.* Nervousness paralyzed his grip, the papers slipped out of his hand and fluttered to the floor.

The border patrol wore an amused expression. "What's in the back?"

"F-furniture, Senor, that is all."

The guard threw his head back and laughed. "I doubt it."

"Oh, no, it is so," insisted Javier.

"Then show me," the border patrol agent commanded.

Javier felt like all the wind had been punched out of him. "But my papers, they're right here."

The man waved dismissively. "Show me what's in back."

Javier's shoulders were heavy, but he had no choice. "Follow me then." Slowly he exited the truck and walked around to the rear. In the distance the engine of an approaching vehicle sounded.

"Be quick," barked the border patrol.

Javier threw the hook from the door and rolled it up halfway. Cassie was not immediately discernable, but the smell of urine and vomit was.

"Ewwee. Shut it now." The guard turned back to the booth. "Whatever you've got in there is very, very sick. Get them out of here before they're dead—if they're not already." He stopped just short of the guard station. "How much money do you have?

"W-what?" asked Javier.

"For your crossing," the guard insisted, glancing quickly at the approaching truck.

Javier wanted out of there as quickly as possible, he reached in his pocket and grabbed the rest of the money Maria had given to him. Throwing it at the guard he said, "That is all I have."

The guard caught it in one swipe. "Go."

Not looking back, Javier slammed into gear and rumbled away. The old truck negotiated the next couple of curves at breakneck speed. Javier wanted as much space between himself and the guard as quickly as possible. Coming to a straightaway, he wiped the sweat from his forehead. The truck was at a low roar. Javier wasn't sure, but he could have sworn he heard machine gun fire in the distance.

Not looking back, he pushed the old truck as fast as he dared. It bounced down the rutted dirt road.

After having driven for what seemed like hours, a rest area appeared on his left. Turning on the signal, he pulled into it. A few cars dotted the parking spaces, a couple of big trucks and a few RVs in the oversized lot.

Hurrying, Javier hopped down from the truck and walked briskly into the men's bathroom. A kindly-looking white man was at the sink. The man appeared to be in his late sixties, wore a light-blue polo shirt, tan safari shorts and Birkenstocks. He nodded at him.

Javier gave the man a quick nod and hurried over to the urinal.

"A hot one today, isn't it?" Birkenstocks offered.

Taken a little aback, Javier gave a quick look around to see who the man was talking to. They were the only ones in there. "Si—yes—yes." *I'm in the United States now, it's English.*

Javier walked to the sink. The man seemed in no hurry to leave. He still stood there.

"The missus and I have been on the road for a couple months now. We've seen some amazing places."

"Really." Javier feigned interest, wishing the man would leave.

Birkenstocks listed the places they'd been. "Tombstone was every bit as good as the movie. Except of course, Kurt Russell and the boys weren't there." He smiled.

Javier wasn't sure what he was talking about, but he nodded anyway. He walked out the door with his new friend following.

"We just left Cochise's Stronghold."

"Oh," Javier said lamely.

"Yeah." Birkenstocks pulled himself up to his full height. "And you know what? I gotta say, that was one impressive place." He gestured in the air expansively.

Javier pulled out a cigarette. This may take a few minutes, might as well put them to good use. "How so?"

"Because he hid his entire village in there. Women, children, livestock, all of them."

Javier perked up. "It's big then?"

"Very, very big," affirmed the man. "And it's beautiful. Thick grass, trees, rocks, and lots of water. All kinds of hiding spots." He winked.

A little unnerved by the wink, Javier blew out a stream of smoke. "Were there lots of people there, um, looking at it?"

"Naaaw, it was pretty empty. Especially out in dispersed camping. That's where we always go," he confided. "It's free."

"Where is this place?"

"You just go out to Highway 10, head for Cochise. It's right out of there. There's plenty of signs," Birkenstocks said, apparently eager to aid his fellow traveler.

Javier threw down his cigarette butt and ground it out with his shoe. "Thank you for the information." He smiled. "It sounds beautiful."

"Oh, it is." They walked down the concrete path to their vehicles, "Well, I better go find out what the missus has planned for us now." He nodded conspiratorially to Javier. "After going on our trips for a while, I always enjoy a little male company." He slapped Javier on the shoulder. "Enjoy Cochise's Stronghold." Birkenstocks turned toward the RV in the parking lot.

Walking back to the furniture truck, Javier mulled it over. He had been considering the caves out of Apache Junction, but this was much closer. And, he shuddered, there were snakes there. Perhaps there would be no snakes here. He walked to the back of the truck. Surely if Cochise brought his tribe, he would not want snakes to bite them.

Throwing open the back door of the truck partway, he pulled himself in. "*Amorcita*, how are you doing?" He crawled up alongside her and put a sweaty palm on her head. She felt a little cooler. He hoped it wasn't just because he wanted her to.

Cassie moaned and pulled her head away. Her hair was plastered to her head in strands from sweat and dirt, her lips dry and cracked. Her shirt stuck to her skin, her breathing was short and shallow.

Consulting his watch, Javier saw it had been four hours since her last dose of Motrin. Carefully he got behind her and cradled her head in his lap. She moaned again, and Javier spoke to her, reassuringly, stroking her head. He took a bottle of water and dribbled a little over her lips. She drank it and he gave her some more. "Careful, *amorcita*," he crooned, "Just a little at a time." He opened the Motrin bottle and took out two of them. Dropping them in her mouth, he poured more water in.

She coughed. He held her, watching to make sure none of the Motrin came out. He checked her frozen pea icepacks. They weren't frozen anymore, but still cold. Finally, her wrists. The wounds had stopped oozing, which was a good sign. He put on more Neosporin.

Javier carefully laid her head down and got out from under her. She seemed comfortable. He found a blanket that was unsoiled, laid it on the floor next to her, and carefully moved her onto it. He straightened her pants, pulled them up and snapped them. Feeling almost fatherly, he pulled her shirt down and smoothed it. His hands lingered on the outline of her breasts, his thumbs dragging across her nipples, as he ostensibly fixed her shirt. Not fatherly at all, he admitted, as he felt the familiar surge of lust course through his body. He hesitated. *No, Javier, she's sick. There'll be plenty of time when we get to Cochise's Stronghold.*

# Chapter Thirty-Two

Roberto, Dusty and Mike rolled down the dirt road in the dust-caked Explorer.

"Where are we, anyway?" asked Mike.

"I'm not exactly sure, but I do know that there's a border crossing coming up." Roberto pointed through the scrub and parched trunks of long-dead Ironwood trees.

"Do we need paperwork this time?"

"Always good to have it on hand," replied Roberto.

Mike dug through the glove compartment until he found what he wanted. "This it?" He held up a packet of papers.

"Good as any." Roberto looked intently down the road.

The guardhouse had just come into view. It looked desolate sitting in the middle of nowhere.

Mike leaned forward. "They left a big sack of garbage in the middle of the road."

"Something's not right," said Roberto warily.

Dusty sat up in the back seat, his hand closed around his gun.

As they pulled closer, Mike exclaimed, "That's not a sack of garbage." He grabbed the door handle and hopped out.

The guard lay face down in the dirt, his back riddled with bullets. Mike quickly flipped him over. The man's eyes stared blankly at the sky.

"He's gone," Mike said quietly, the color draining from his face.

Dusty and Roberto stood next to him looking around the area. It was silent except for the slight breath of wind on the surrounding vegetation.

"You think it was a robbery?" asked Mike finally.

Roberto sighed. "Most probably. Everything seems to be about money."

Dusty silently scanned the rocks and hills around them, his mouth in a tight line.

Mike straightened up. "There's not much else we can do."

"No. They'll find him shortly when he doesn't answer his radio." Roberto sighed. "This is all too commonplace. Human life goes far too cheaply." He turned to the car. "Let's go, we don't want them to get any farther ahead of us than they already are."

"Wherever they are," said Mike.

They climbed in the SUV and left.

Dusty wasn't sure how long they'd been driving, but he needed to make a stop. "Hey, could you pull over at the next opportunity, Roberto?"

"No problem." He turned the corner and a blue "Rest Area" sign appeared on the right. "We'll be there in two miles."

"Thanks." Dusty stared out the window and tried to imagine what Cassie was doing right now. Was she all right? His mind was working so slowly lately, it seemed like months ago that they teased and joked on their trip to Arizona. Now it had become a time trap of bad feelings, a bubble with no way out. It was as if all the emotion had been painfully wrung from his body. He was just a shell, going through the motions of life.

Roberto pulled into the rest area. "As you ordered." He waved.

"Thanks," Dusty grunted as he got out.

Watching him walk away Roberto asked Mike, "Is he okay?"

Mike's brows drew together. "Honestly? This is the worst I've ever seen him. Almost getting Cassie and then being trapped in the police car while she was driven away really took a toll on him." He slumped back in the seat. "And he already felt bad."

"I get that," said Roberto. "I just wish there was something I could do for him."

"So that's it?"

Roberto held his hands up. "I'm a detective, not a magician, Mike. You of all people should know that."

Mike's cheeks flushed. "I get that, but I was hoping there was still something we could do. Somewhere we could look?"

"I'll call the office and see if anything has come up on the all points for the truck, but other than that, I don't know what we can do. We can't just drive around looking, it's a big state."

"I'll use the rest room while you're calling." Without waiting for an answer, Mike pulled open the door and got out. The fresh air felt good.

As Mike walked in the rest room, he found Dusty in front of the sink. His friend was washing his hands, over and over. Mike used the facilities and came up to the sink.

"Dusty?"

He just kept rubbing his hands under the water.

Mike tried again. "Dusty, I think you got it with handwashing."

There was no indication Dusty heard him.

"Enough." He turned off the water and pulled Dusty over to the hand dryers. "Time to move on, buddy."

Dusty complied, but Mike was pretty sure if he hadn't come in when he did, Dusty would still be washing his hands.

They walked out to the car. Roberto was on the phone. As they got up to the car, he hung up.

Mike studied the detective's face for a clue. "Well?"

"Nothing." Roberto shook his head. "Nobody's sighted the truck on the highway cams. Doesn't mean it's not here, just means we don't have any idea where."

"What now?" said Dusty in a dead voice.

"We head back and wait for more information." Roberto's face softened. "It probably won't take that long. There's literally cams over all the major highways."

Dusty sat silently in the back seat.

The detective pulled onto the freeway. The air in the car had grown heavy with disappointment. He fiddled with the radio dial, but it only emitted static. The sun was dropping in the sky and backlit the cactus and rocks in bright orange and fiery red as they sped along the highway.

Ahead of them Roberto noticed an RV pulled over. A white-haired man appeared to be struggling with a tire. Eager to escape the pall of the Explorer, Roberto said, "How about we do our good deed for the day?"

"Probably ought to." Mike nodded. "We're pretty far from a gas station out here." He looked around. "In fact, we're pretty far from anywhere."

Pulling in behind the RV, Mike and Roberto got out. Dusty followed silently.

The man in a light-blue polo shirt, tan cargo shorts and Birkenstocks stood up. "Well, hello, fellows. Am I glad to see you." He took a quick look at Dusty's blank stare. "I think."

Mike jumped in. "Oh, he's just had a rough time lately, he's really a good guy." Then looking over at the tire. "You got a flat?"

"Yeah, you know, they keep making these darn things heavier and heavier." He laughed. "Triple A is a little out of range around here. I tried, but I don't have any cell service."

"That's a fact," agreed Roberto. "I live over in Apache Junction and things are hit and miss the further out you get."

"Let's see your tire." Mike bent over.

Mike and Roberto made short work of the tire change, Dusty mechanically helping.

Birkenstocks rambled on. "Yeah, I've been doing a lot of sightseeing with the missus on this trip. We've been to all kinds of great places." He proceeded to name them off. "I really loved Tombstone, but I gotta say the total best one was Cochise's Stronghold."

"Is that right?" said Mike absently.

"Oh, yeah." The older man was warming to his topic now. "When you think about Cochise hiding his entire village in that place, well, it's just so amazing. And when you get there and you see it. Oh, yeah, water, grass, trees, tons of area to hide out in."

Roberto raised his head. "A good hideout, huh?"

"Oh, definitely. I don't think they've changed it much since he was there."

"Well, maybe we should check it out."

Birkenstocks nodded his head emphatically. "You definitely should." Laughing he said, "I must be a good salesman, you'll be my second guy today that's heading over there."

Mike looked up. "Who's the first one?"

"Well, I don't know his name, but he was driving a furniture truck or some damn thing. Said he was camping, so I told him all about it. Said he was going to try it out."

Dusty came to life like someone had turned on a light. "How long ago was that?"

Birkenstocks jumped at the sound of a new voice. "Oh…maybe two, three hours ago. I get a little messed up on time with being retired. And then this tire, not quite sure how long we've been here." He winked at them. "But I can find out."

The white-haired man walked up to the cab of the RV. He came back in a minute. "My wife said we were at the rest area at 2:30, that's about right. She said we got this flat tire at 2:45, so not much after."

"He's not that far ahead!" Dusty shouted excitedly.

Birkenstocks looked uncomfortable. "I hope I didn't do anything wrong."

"On the contrary," said Mike. "We've got a kidnapped woman. She's in that furniture truck. You've just helped us more than you will know."

Birkenstocks gasped. "Oh, my gosh. I had no idea!"

Roberto handed him a card and then moved quickly towards the car, "Give me your contact information in case something comes up, or if you think of anything else."

"No problem." The man's face was pale.

They got back in the Explorer and Roberto drove as fast as he could toward Cochise's Stronghold.

Dusty had switched out seats with Mike again, jumping in the front. Hope filled the hollow spot in his chest. *We will get her back this time*. The flat tire and the man in Birkenstocks—it was meant to be.

# Chapter Thirty-Three

Javier pulled into Cochise Stronghold at dusk. *Thank goodness that Gringo told me where to park, or I would have never found it.* Pulling into an unmarked road right before the equestrian day parking, he found what was clearly a camping area. It had no improvements, but a few scattered fire rings told the story of past occupants.

He parked and got out. He had a couple of options; they could spend the night in the furniture truck, or leave tonight. Memories of the crazy, psycho white giant roaring and punching him decided the question. There was no way he would sleep at all if there was even a chance that that monster may find him. Javier walked to the back of the truck and threw open the door.

Cassie lay in the same position he'd left her. She didn't look like she'd be in any shape to walk anywhere. He was going to have to carry her. He went back to the cab and flipped the seat forward. He picked up his knapsack and some essentials he'd been collecting. A ground cover and sleeping bag, flashlight. He picked up his gun and stuck it in the back of his pants. This was going to take more than one trip. Slamming the truck door, he walked back to the roll-up door. Making sure the latch was secured from the outside he murmured, "I'll be back soon, *amorcita.*" Javier turned and walked into the woods.

He saw where the main trail was located, so he avoided it.

Hiking higher, he began paralleling the trail. Javier was surprised at all the vegetation and so many trees. Green grass spurted up intermittently with clumps of wildflowers. He paused. A small stream gurgled in front of him, mossy rocks lined the sides, green and dripping. Looking into the water, Javier marveled at the crystal clearness of it. Beautiful. Mesmerized, he almost forgot why he was there. Suddenly remembering, he continued onward, keeping an eye on the red rock above him.

Javier saw some dark shadows in the rocks. It could be a cave. Keeping his eyes on the spot, he clumsily climbed up the rocky hill. As he got to the top, he felt a cold breeze. The opening was narrow. Slipping his pack off, he got down on his knees and crawled through. As he made it between the rocks, he sat up in a large room. A few sparkling stars shown through a gap in the rock slabs above him.

He looked around in amazement. A small stream trickled down one wall into a clear pool at the bottom. The cave was sandstone. Smooth. Seeing something on the walls, Javier squinted and walked closer to inspect it. Small creatures were etched into the wall. Drawings. He'd heard of that kind of thing before, the Anasazi, but never had he seen it with his own eyes. It gave a kind of reverence, living proof of others before him in this place. He carefully ran his finger over the figures.

Deep in thought he looked around once more. He needed to get the lay of the land. Were there any escape routes? Other rooms? Snakes? He shuddered. Well, if there were any, he needed to know. He paused and listened.

The only thing he heard was the trickling of water into the pond. This would work. He found a place by the wall that would make an excellent bed for Cassie. He frowned. Her sickness was an inconvenience. Then he smiled. That would be quickly remedied. Before he let his mind wander farther down that path, he left his backpack and squeezed through the opening. Sliding down the rocks and sand, he hit the trail and quickly walked back to the truck. The sooner he got her up here, the better.

Javier wiped the sweat from his eyes, huffing, as he finally got to the truck in the camping area. He hurried to the back and threw up the roll-up door. Without hesitating, he pulled himself in and crawled to Cassie. She lay in the same position she'd been in earlier. He carefully wrapped her in a blanket and carried her out of the truck. Setting her on the end, he got out, put her over his shoulder, and then shut the door.

Heading back to the hideout was difficult. The sandy trail was easy to walk on alone, but the added weight made him sink. The sky darkened and the trail filled with shadows. As Javier looked up for the cave, the red rocks were now dark, backlit by purple sky and golden twinkling stars. He groaned. It wasn't helping him to see.

Cassie lay quiet in his arms, but she was dead weight. After stumbling along, he stopped to rest. Setting her down, he pulled his flashlight out of his pocket. Checking the ground, he located his track. Luckily, he was at the part where he began the trek upwards. "Thank God," he said aloud. Awkwardly plunging up the hill, after several rests, Javier made it to the top, half dropping Cassie to the ground. His lungs were on fire and his breathing became labored. He leaned against a rock, gathering his breath for the final push. Cassie lay breathing, and occasionally groaning. She was going to be no help getting into the cave.

Javier pulled Cassie's feet close to the opening. Then sliding on his stomach into the cave, he turned around and grabbed onto Cassie's ankles. Pulling as hard as he could, he slid her into the room. Victory filled his chest, he put his arms around her sweating body and breathed. "We've made it, *amorcita*, to our little love nest." He strutted around the cave. At the level spot by the wall, he shook out his ground cover. Carefully, he picked up Cassie and deposited her and the moving blanket in the middle of the cover. Reaching into his backpack he found a rag. Crab-walking over to the pool, Javier dipped it into the ice-cold water and laid it on Cassie's forehead.

He leaned his head next to hers and whispered in her ear, "I will be back shortly, *amorcita*, I must take care of the truck." Caressing her cheek one last time, he hurried out the opening.

All the driving and walking up and down the hill to the cave were beginning to take a toll on him. He was tired. By the time he got back to the truck, the evening sky was black and the moon large. He opened the creaky door and jumped in. As if to ridicule him, the truck instantly turned over. Javier slowly toured the camping area. A couple of RVs and a black truck and trailer off to one side. As he continued, the area seemed deserted. What luck! It didn't take long for him to find what he was looking for, a remote corner campsite with lots of foliage around it. Javier pulled the truck in. Getting out, he grabbed the rest of the food and bags. Scouting along the perimeters of the camp, he saw a flat area down a short slope beneath some Juniper trees.

He hopped back in the truck and pulled it underneath the trees, their branches blocking it from view. Scooping up his bags, he ran back into the camp site. Pulling out his flashlight, he dropped the beam on the location of the truck. Nothing but dark trees. Javier's heart quickened in pleasure. "Perfect." He smiled. "Let that big lout of a man try and find me now."

He whistled as he walked through the darkness, carrying his grocery bags. It was just like a fairytale, Javier and his princess, alone together forever.

# Chapter Thirty-Four

"Mike, how much farther is Cochise's Stronghold?" Dusty sat on the edge of the seat.

Mike consulted his phone GPS. "According to this, just a few more minutes. We've already passed through the town of Cochise."

Dusty grunted. "I've always wanted to see this place. I've heard a lot about it." Quickly correcting himself, "But not under these circumstances."

"It's not that big of a campground, so looking for the furniture truck shouldn't be that hard," said Roberto.

"There's nothing about this whole thing that's been easy." Dusty grimaced. "I have no expectations about the Stronghold either."

"True," agreed Mike philosophically. "We can only hope."

The moon shone as they pulled into the U.S. Forest service area. The light made driving easy, but looking into the shadows was a different matter. Roberto slowly drove down the road. He pointed at the Equestrian Day Parking sign on the left and kept going. Scanning the countryside as best they could, the asphalt road ended in an RV park. Roberto slowly drove through, Dusty and Mike each taking a side and scanning for the furniture truck.

Dusty's heart sank. "I see no truck."

"Plenty of RVs though," said Mike. "With all kinds of out-of-state license plates.

"It's a tourist attraction." Roberto shifted gears.

Mike turned to look out the back. "Let's go and see if we can find the dispersed camping."

Roberto guided the Explorer slowly over the speed bumps, and they soon found themselves just about out of the park. As they passed the office, a figure suddenly jumped out in front of them. "Damn it." Roberto slammed on the brakes.

A man who appeared to be in his sixties, with gray hair, and wearing sweatpants stopped them.

"This is an RV park. What can I do for you gentlemen at this hour?" The man flashed his light on their faces as he spoke. Without waiting for an answer, he continued in an annoyed voice. "We like to close things down here at 10 o'clock."

Roberto flashed his ID. "Sorry to disturb you. We have a suspect that may be here. Time is of the essence that we find him."

The attendant stepped back, clearly surprised at Roberto's response. "Why? What has he done?"

"Abduction," said Roberto simply. "We have reason to believe he's holding a woman hostage."

"No," breathed the park attendant.

Dusty cut in. "Have you seen a furniture truck around here anywhere?"

"Furniture truck?" the man repeated.

Mike said, "Yeah, an old weather-beaten truck with green lettering on the side. It's kind of hard to read. The truck looks brown and has a big roll-up door on the back."

The man scratched his head. "I haven't seen anything like that in the park."

"Is there anywhere else where people could camp?" asked Roberto.

"Like dispersed camping?" inquired Dusty.

"Yes, it's not well marked, but as you're coming in there's a dirt road just before the equestrian day parking on the opposite side." The man rubbed his eyes. "It's all gravel roads; people can camp there with no amenities."

Roberto was already putting the Explorer into gear. "Thank you so much. And if you see anything, please call me." He shoved a card out the window and they drove down the road, headlights illuminating the way.

As they came back and turned down the unmarked road, they saw an older black gooseneck trailer and truck parked under a tree. It appeared to have red lettering on it. Dusty strained, but couldn't read it in the dark. A pull trailer in another area. And a third small RV sat alone. All the campers were far apart with a few random fire rings connected by gravel roads. Trees, brush and grass dotted the area.

After driving around three times, Roberto said, "No sign of him so far. I think we're going to need to wait until daylight to look further."

"We can see a lot better then," agreed Mike.

Dusty was ready to get out and begin the search, but he understood what they were saying made sense. "Okay," he said reluctantly.

"Somebody can have the front seat." Roberto looked directly at Mike. "And the back two seats fold down, so we can probably all fit."

"Oh yay," said Mike sarcastically.

"Déjà vu," said Dusty. "I already slept in here once."

Roberto ignored them and opened the back, pulling a couple of levers and soon both backseats were flat. Despite the conditions, all three men were asleep within minutes.

Dusty opened his eyes. It took him a few minutes to remember where he was; the sun shone brightly in the windows, momentarily blinding him. He rubbed his eyes and then sat up. Mike snored in the front seat, and Roberto lay in the back next to him, a blanket and their bags shoved between them.

"Mike," Dusty said loudly.

The snore turned into a snort. "Huh?"

"Let's go look for tire tracks."

Mike sat up, squinting in the bright light. “Coffee?” he asked hopefully.

“Sorry,” said Dusty.

Roberto sat up. “What are we waiting for?”

Dusty pushed open a passenger door and slipped both feet onto the ground. He began walking before he was sure he was awake.

They circled the camping area, checking not only the vehicles, but anything else suspicious.

Mike was the first to see it. “Hey, you guys come over here,” he said waving them over. “Take a look.”

Dusty and Roberto arrived simultaneously. “Nice work, Mike.” Roberto patted him on the back. Both men looked at the ground and saw unmistakable truck tire tracks.

They followed the tracks until they stopped abruptly. Dusty and Roberto stared at the ground, while Mike kept walking. The end campsite had thick trees behind it. Mike trotted down a small hill. Walking behind a copse of trees, he shouted, “Bingo!”

Dusty and Roberto ran down the hill. The outline of a brown furniture truck sat silently behind the cover of vegetation.

Dusty rushed forward, flipped the hook and threw up the roll-up door.

Their eyes were riveted to the inside of the truck. The interior was dark, moving blankets strewn about. The smell of vomit and urine permeated the air. Not flinching, Roberto pulled his pen light out and flashed it around the interior. Packages from tamales littered the floor. A couple of wrappers from frozen peas lay by the blankets. “That’s curious.”

“That’s the oldest cure in the book for fever,” said Mike. “You take a bag of frozen peas and put them under each armpit. It helps to take a temperature down.”

Dusty flashed his own light on the trailer contents. “Good point. There’s empty Motrin packages on the floor. Where to now?”

“Let me call my office and ask them to send re-enforcements up here. We’ll need a forensic examiner to check for prints.”

Dusty sighed. “I wish I had my horse.”

Roberto nodded at him as he talked on the phone. "We need everybody we can get up here at Cochise Stronghold." The conversation continued for a few minutes. Then he said, "Could we please have an officer swing by the Red Rock Stables and pick up a couple horses and their gear, too?" He winked at Dusty as he spoke. "Just a minute." He handed the phone to Dusty. "Give him the details."

Mike and Dusty exchanged smiles. "Great. It's a large area to cover on foot." Dusty took the phone.

Mike nodded. "If anybody can find Cassie, Prince can."

"That's for sure," agreed Dusty. "And thank God for hide-a-keys and officers that know horses and dogs."

# Chapter Thirty-Five

Dusty clicked the phone off.

"What now, boss?" asked Mike.

"It's going to take them some time to get here. I'm going to take a look around." Dusty walked towards the trailhead.

"I'll go with you." Mike fell in stride next to his friend.

Roberto dusted off his hands. "Okay, I'm going to stay here." He looked at his watch. "It's almost eight, why don't you come back by noon? Everyone should be here by then and you can fill us in on what you find."

"Will do," said Mike.

"If we don't find her by then." Dusty said, his jaw set.

"That is our first hope." Roberto spoke softly. "Hang in there, Dusty; we're closing in."

Dusty flashed a smile and trudged down the road toward the trailhead.

The terrain was dry. Clouds of dust poofed up as they walked—it always reminded Dusty of powdered sugar. Despite the aridity, the area was alive with vegetation. Lots of Junipers.

The morning air felt moist against his skin and the exercise felt good. He was doing something, moving forward.

The sound of Mike's footfalls was all that he heard behind him. Dusty missed the clomping of Muley's hooves in the ground. A sharp pain hit him in the chest. *I miss Muley and Scout.* They had been his only family for some time now. His mind turned painfully to Cassie.

The sense of loss sliced through him like a knife. *Part of my family is missing.* He winced. Dusty hadn't allowed himself to think about that part of it, he didn't want to lose his focus on finding her. But there it was: his future. Pain tightened the pit of his stomach into a fist throbbing from the inside. He shook his head emphatically. *I will get Cassie back. I know it.*

"Hey, Dusty." Mike interrupted his thoughts.

"What?" Dusty answered almost urgently.

Catching his friend's mood, Mike waved it off. "Oh, nothing, I was just thinking about where a person would hide out in these hills."

Dusty stopped and considered it. The valley was vast and horseshoe shaped. Green trees, rocks and streams filled the basin. The trail wove up the valley on one side and snaked around the huge boulders to the top. Dusty wasn't sure, but by his reckoning, the backside wouldn't be too far from Tombstone.

"How about in the rocks?" Mike suggested.

Dusty looked where he pointed, large boulders lay next to each other; they almost looked like the stunt rocks you'd see in Hollywood.

"Maybe…" Dusty said slowly.

Footsteps sounded on the trail around a bend. Dusty reached for his gun and Mike followed suit. For a couple of tense seconds only muted footfalls sounded, padding through the dust.

Quickly glancing around, Dusty saw a large rock that could be used for cover. Silently he jerked his head toward it, they stepped behind it and waited.

Seconds later a hiker came around the corner. He was wearing New Balance running shorts, no shirt and a headband. Sweat glistened on his chest as he strode by. He dipped his head in a brief acknowledgment of Dusty and Mike and disappeared around a bend.

Dusty let his breath out in a long whoosh. He hadn't realized he'd been holding it.

Mike laughed. "You okay, Dusty? That was a lot of air."

"Yeah, I guess I'm not really used to this kind of stuff. It doesn't come up that much in my line of work."

"Huh. I wish I could say the same."

"You're in better shape than being a chair jockey." Dusty motioned at the trail. "Shall we?"

"By all means." Mike set off, and they continued their climb.

The foliage remained thick and the trail twisted and turned. Then it abruptly dipped down, and Dusty and Mike found themselves staring into a large pond of water, enshrouded by trees.

"Looks like a catch pool," said Dusty. "Man made."

"This place is full of surprises." Mike shook his head.

They sat on rocks in the shade catching their breath. Dusty looked at his watch. "We may as well turn around now, it's after eleven." He added hopefully, "The horses ought to be here."

"That will be nice," said Mike, wistfully. He pushed his hat back and wiped the sweat off his forehead. "What about your living quarters, is that coming?"

"I hope so, it's got all my feed and gear in it."

"Great. The good thing about this place is it has cell reception, I noticed that Roberto got out no problem." Lowering his gaze, he said, "I'll give Terri a call tonight." He quickly added, "And see how the horses are doing."

"Good idea." Dusty felt a deep pang of longing to call Cassie—but soon enough.

"Well, shall we?" He rose and stopped abruptly as a soft jingling sound came down the trail. "Do you hear that?"

"Yeah," Mike answered. "It almost sounds like—"

"Jingle Bobs," finished Dusty.

Before they could say anymore, a mule and rider appeared between the rocks and trees of the trail on the other side of the pond.

The mule was unusual, a tan, almost buckskin color; Dusty had heard it referred to as gruella in the past. The mule's legs bore a pattern resembling zebra stripes. The rider wore a short-brimmed silver belly Stetson, white Oxford shirt and leather vest. His blue jeans were trail worn, but other than that Dusty was pretty sure he'd ridden off the cover of Western Horseman.

The mule smartly stepped the distance up to Dusty and Mike, her ears alert and pointed at them.

"Howdy." The rider dipped his hat and reined to a stop.

"How's it going?" said Dusty cautiously.

"Beautiful day and a fine mule, that's about as good as it gets." He smiled. "Name's Oatmeal."

"Oatmeal." Dusty tested it out.

"Yeah, my grandma called me that and the name stuck." He sat back and lit a cigarette. "She said it was because I always wanted oatmeal for breakfast." He laughed and blew out a puff of smoke.

"I'm Dusty and my friend's name is Mike."

"Well, good morning to you."

"Nice Jingle Bobs," said Mike.

"Thanks." Oatmeal dipped his head again.

"We could hear you coming," said Mike.

Dusty looked up. "You must have got up pretty early to be coming down already."

"It's Lucille, she's an early riser."

Dusty and Mike looked at him uncertainly.

"She's my mule." He patted her neck affectionately.

Lucille responded by flicking an ear backwards, then forward again, always keeping one focused on Dusty and Mike.

"Have you seen anyone up here today?" asked Dusty.

"There was one hiker—I guess you'd call him a hiker. Then you guys and that's it."

"Oh, okay. Thanks."

"Why? You lookin' for somebody?"

Dusty hesitated and Mike jumped in. "As a matter of fact we are." Glancing at Dusty, "We're looking for a Hispanic male and a white female."

"Long light brown hair, and beautiful blue eyes." Dusty couldn't help himself. "She's about 5'9".

Oatmeal whistled. "I'm sure I would have noticed her."

"You would have," said Dusty with finality.

"Well, we better be heading back down." Mike turned. "The horses are going to be arriving shortly."

"You got horses?"

"Yeah," said Dusty. "Figured we could cover more ground that way."

"I'd be happy to follow along with you and give whatever help I could," the mule rider offered.

"The more eyes the better." Mike grinned. "We're camping in the dispersed area."

"Perfect. Me too." He gave the mule her head, and she stepped out in a swift walk, head bobbing, ears flopping forward and back. "See you down there." Oatmeal waved as he disappeared behind the rocks.

"Let's go." Dusty headed down the trail.

"I miss my horse." Mike followed behind.

Dusty and Mike crossed the street into the camping area. The scene was much busier than when they'd left. Search and Rescue personnel stood around and a handful of sheriff's cars were parked nearby. A group of uniforms talked gathered, and just beyond that sat Dusty's living quarters with Muley and Prince tied outside.

Before he could get to the trailer, Scout and Sammy ran towards him, barking in excitement.

Dusty patted both their heads. "Hey, you guys."

Seeing his outfit made Dusty feel lighter inside. He walked up to Muley. The big roan eyed him indignantly and then lay his soft muzzle on Dusty's shoulder. Wrapping his arms around his horse, a lump formed in Dusty's throat and tears burned his eyes. Muley, normally standoffish, seemed to understand and remained with his head on Dusty's shoulder.

Dusty hung on as the wave of grief passed and he collected himself. The ground that had fallen away some time ago came back. He felt more solid than he had for days. And how long had it been? It seemed like weeks. Time had become indeterminate. But with Muley here, he knew it was going to be okay. Dusty released his horse and walked to the truck, his keys lay on the seat. The LQ keys were on the chain. He walked to the trailer and unlocked the door, planning to put out the slideout and get his gear. The first waft of the living quarters smelled familiar, but an additional scent—perfume? It was Cassie's. His stomach contracted painfully as he stepped in the door.

Roberto walked up as Dusty and Mike were brushing the horses and getting ready to saddle. "You got your horses."

Dusty grunted. "Uh-huh."

"We've been putting together a team. Some of the locals came up, so we can isolate the area in a grid and methodically search." Roberto smiled encouragingly. "We've got them now. It won't be much longer."

"Yup," replied Dusty flatly. He threaded the latigo through the cinch ring and pulled it snug. Muley whipped his head around, teeth bared.

Roberto stepped back. "Geez, what kind of a horse is that?"

Dusty smiled. "A good one." Ignoring Muley's threat, he pulled down the stirrup leather with a snap.

"They say there's some caves around here, used to be hideouts in the day. Those are most likely where they're going to look," Roberto said. "Come on over before you leave and take a look at the map."

Mike walked around the trailer. "Prince is saddled, that much I can say. How the ride will go remains another story."

Dusty grinned. "You looked like you got the wire edge off him back at the Red Rock Stables, so this ought to be a better ride."

Mike shrugged, "We can only hope."

They followed Roberto over to the old fire ring, which had become the new command post. A man stood over a foldable table with a map stretched out. He was Caucasian, in his mid-fifties, balding with faint wisps of reddish hair in a Friar Tuck look. Perspiration dripped down his forehead and his cheeks were flushed. His dark uniform had Cochise County emblazoned on the shoulder patch.

"Sheriff, this is Dusty Rose and his friend Mike."

"Nice to meet you," he stuck out his hand. "Call me Mike."

The sheriff shook it. "Chief Doug Red Eagle, nice meeting you."

Dusty put out his hand and faltered midstream.

Grabbing the proffered hand, and giving it a firm shake, Sheriff Red Eagle said, "It's a long story. You know, family stuff."

Dusty liked him already.

Sheriff Red Eagle laid out the plan and showed Dusty and Mike the area he wanted them to check. "Since you guys are mounted, it makes sense that you take the furthest area. I want you to look around for caves or other possible hiding spots up by the pass." He picked up his hat and blotted his head with a handkerchief. "Any questions?"

"No." Dusty and Mike turned to leave.

"One more thing," said Sheriff Red Eagle.

The men stopped and waited.

"Take him alive, if at all possible."

"Will do." Dusty clenched his jaw. *That was going to be impossible.*

"We'll, do our best, sir," said Mike, looking away from Dusty.

"Let's get this show on the road." Dusty said, walking towards the horses.

# Chapter Thirty-Six

Cassie shivered. Groaning, she rolled over. Heat poured off her skin. Her throat dry, she licked her lips, they were so cracked it did nothing. Squinting, she slowly looked around. The reddish-brown dirt was everywhere: the floor, the walls, the ceiling. *What is this?* Groggily, she remembered. Nightmarish scenes passed through her mind: Javier. Her stomach convulsed. *Where is he?* A deep groan and the sound of flatulence erupted from the far side of the cave. She turned her head slightly. Right there.

Javier lay on his side, wrapped in his own moving blankets. His face, relaxed in sleep, made him appear young, childlike. Nothing like the ruthless, unpredictable captor he was. Cassie looked around the cave. A few rays of light streamed through the rocks on top. A knife of pain shot through her head and her throat convulsed, so dry she couldn't swallow. An involuntary moan escaped from her lips, and in spite of her pain she froze.

Javier's eyes flickered open. He sat up. Cassie quickly dropped her lids and lay still. She heard him get up. Heavy footsteps sounded close. A meaty hand dropped on her forehead. It pulled away.

"*Amorcita*, I will get you water. You are so hot." The steps moved away and came back. She felt a cool cloth on her head.

Water. She must have some. "Water," she croaked weakly.

She felt Javier jump back. "You're awake." Recovering he said,

"Of course, I will get you some immediately." A cold metal cup pressed against her lips, she drank greedily, water running down her chin.

A deep laugh. "Oh, *amorcita*, not so fast, you will make yourself sick."

She felt herself lifted, her head placed in his lap. He carefully held her and poured the water slowly in her mouth.

Her need for water outweighed her revulsion for him. She ignored his touch and drank. The cup was empty. Javier did not put her down. He continued to cradle her. "I was so worried about you." He rocked her gently. "I thought I was going to lose you."

Cassie was no longer thirsty, but her head throbbed. After what seemed like hours, he set her carefully back on the ground. She pretended to be asleep. A wave of fear passed over her, *He's surely not going to try to rape me again?*

Her question was soon answered. "You are too hot, Senorita. I'll help you cool off." He began unbuttoning her blouse and her jeans. She weakly tried to push him away. He purred, "You will see, you will be begging for Javier." He laughed deeply as he set about his work. "Javier, more, more." Pulling her socks and shoes, her pants, underwear, shirt and finally her bra. He stood in front of her, she felt him staring at her.

She burned with shame and fever. And something else, rage grew inside her, a primal anger. How dare he? With the coolness that she shot the man at Sheep Lake a couple years ago, she waited for his next move. She had no plan, but she would make sure he was going down.

Cassie heard his pants zipper and the soft thud of his clothes dropping to the ground. In the next minute Javier's sweaty body covered hers. The smell of armpit, tobacco and stinky body odor assaulted her nostrils. He whispered endearments and he plunged his dirty head into her breasts. His blubbery body brought a fleeting image of the hog she saw one time in the farm by the freeway. It was engaged in sex and the fat rippled from one end of its body to the other. She shuddered and bile filled her throat.

As he moaned and his filthy hands groped her, she didn't respond. With one arm outstretched over her head, she slowly closed her fingers around a big jagged rock. As she reached, he groaned in pleasure, apparently mistaking her movement for enjoyment. With both hands she brought it down on his head as hard as she could. His body ceased writhing and lay still. Cassie pushed him off her. Half walking, half crawling, she made it over to the small pool. She plunged her hands in and washed his stench off herself frantically, taking glances over at him to make sure he hadn't moved. She stood, walked over to the naked mound of flesh, and pulled her jeans and shirt out from under his legs. Her rage at the boiling point, she kicked him as hard as she could in the crotch. He groaned and moved into the fetal position.

Her stomach convulsed. She stopped and vomited. Two times he'd assaulted her, so close to raping her. That he'd touched her was bad enough. She would never, never go anywhere without a sidearm again, she promised herself. Head throbbing, she slipped her jeans on and buttoned her shirt. Her vision turned gray and she sat for a minute. Looking up, she saw light shining above her. She wondered absently what time it was, not that it made a difference. She shook her head. What mattered was leaving.

The rocks seemed to completely enclose the cave, but they had come in somewhere. Cassie studied the sand. Tracks came from one side of the wall. She stumbled over. Light poured in through an opening between medium-sized rocks. She lay flat on her stomach and crawled through. Fresh air hit her in the face as she neared the end. Her hands felt the warm sand of outside and elation filled her. Suddenly, something caught her foot. She struggled to pull it out, but she was being pulled back into the cave! Frantically she raked her nails over the smooth rocks on the sides, grabbed hunks of the red, sandy soil. It all gave way as she went backward into the cave.

Dusty, Oatmeal, and Mike rode up the trail to the pass. It was the same way they had walked earlier, but now on horseback they covered ground swiftly.

"Hey, Dusty, what about if we cut off the main trail and check those rocks below that catch basin. It seems like there may be some caves in that area." Mike gestured in the direction.

Dusty nodded. "Yeah, that's what I was thinking, too."

"Oatmeal, you up for it?" Mike asked.

"I'm just along for the ride. Proceed, sir."

Mike turned in his saddle and pointed a gloved finger at him. "Doc Holliday, Tombstone."

Oatmeal beamed. "My favorite."

Mike grinned. "Mine too. That was some shooting, wasn't it?"

"The best part." Said Oatmeal.

Dusty's mind drifted as he heard the voices of Mike and Oatmeal in conversation. He glanced over at the big rocks. *Is she there? So close?* Suddenly Oatmeal said something that drew him back to the present, "Did I just hear you say that you used to be a mounted cowboy action shooter?"

Oatmeal shrugged. "Yeah, I done some shooting."

"Like at the World competition." Mike grinned.

The old cowboy smiled. "I have to admit, I enjoy shooting guns."

Dusty laughed tightly. "Well, hopefully we can stir you up a good target here shortly."

They dropped off the trail and began riding cross country toward the rocks.

"Mike, what did Terri say about the horses?" Dusty asked.

"She wasn't home."

Dusty frowned. "When did you try?"

"Last night, then early this morning and then right before we left riding."

Dusty considered it. "That seems like a lot of times, is that usual?"

Mike cleared his throat. "No. Not at all."

"Maybe we'll need to get a search party for her next," joked Oatmeal.

"One missing person is enough," Mike said flatly.

Still naked, Javier roughly pulled Cassie into the cave. He shook in rage. "Get up," he bellowed.

The back of his head was covered in blood. Cassie kept herself devoid of emotion as she slowly raised up. Before she had time to completely stand, Javier backhanded her hard across the face. The force wrenched her head back and she went over backwards, her head thudding into the sand, just missing a rock.

"Bitch," Javier spat. He stormed over and got his pants. "You were special to me," he snarled. "Not anymore." He snapped his pants and pulled on his shirt. "We're going back to Mexico. This time I'm selling you."

He walked over and kicked her in the side. "Get up."

Her jaw and neck ached from the blows. The kick was more pain. She rose mechanically, clutching sand in each hand. Fear gone, cool rage boiled within her. Javier came at her again to slap her. She ducked and threw sand into his eyes.

His yowl let her know she'd hit a bullseye. Without hesitation, she whirled and headed for the cave opening and freedom.

# Chapter Thirty-Seven

Dusty stopped in his tracks. "Did you hear that?"

"I heard something." Mike scanned the rocks in front of them.

"It sounded like a yell," agreed Oatmeal.

Dusty rode over to the side of the trail. "We can make it down over here." He turned his horse and dropped over the edge.

Mike looked at Oatmeal questioningly.

"Hey, I got a mule," he replied.

Lucille and Prince followed Muley down the side.

The terrain wasn't as steep as it was rocky. The riders wove and plunged around the boulders. Dusty abruptly stopped. "Let's tie up here and walk the rest of the way. We can probably go faster."

"I think so," said Mike.

Tying to some scrub Junipers, they picked their way down the hillside, guns drawn.

Cassie made it through the tunnel to the outside. Her neck and face burned with pain, but she pushed herself onward. One thing was for certain, he would be coming after her. *I need to keep moving.*

The combination of hunger, pain, fever and bright sunlight made her feel faint. She fought the weakness in her knees and head. Glancing back periodically at the cave opening behind her, she stayed close to the ground, carefully picking her way around the rocks.

Cassie took a deep breath of air. She dared think about Dusty and her heart swelled with elation. She never saw the rock give way. Her body tumbled head over heels down the steep hillside. The blinding pain stopped as she slipped into darkness.

The men had just reached the bottom of the draw when they heard the commotion. Three guns pointed at the form rolling down the hill, finally coming to rest in the sandy bottom of the draw. Dusty ran over and turned it. He found himself staring into Cassie's beaten up, dirty face. Dumbfounded, he stared at her for a moment.

"Who is it?" Mike came up behind him. "Is it Cassie?"

Finally reacting, Dusty grabbed her up in his arms and buried his head in her hair. "It's Cassie." Hot tears poured down his cheeks. All his fear and doubt burst inside of him. It was finally over. "Thank God you're alive," he repeated almost in a chant, holding her and gently rocking.

"Dusty," Cassie croaked, more of a statement than a question. "I knew you'd come."

Not willing or able to put her down, Dusty said, "Mike, can you call down? Tell them we need a medic ASAP."

"Already on it." Mike had his phone to his ear. "Roberto, we have Cassie. Can you send up medical?" He stopped and squinted up at the hillside. "He's close, too, but we haven't actually seen him yet."

Hanging up, Mike turned to Cassie. Softly he said, "Can you tell us where Javier is?

"There's a…a cave just at the top of the rocks. You have to… kneel down to get into it, but you'll see…thc tracks." Exhausted, she laid her head back down on Dusty's chest.

Mike looked at Oatmeal. "You ready?"

"Let's go." He pulled out his 1911 semi-auto.

The two men crawled toward the cave, careful to take shelter as they went. A bullet bounced off a rock next to Mike. "We got him."

More shots rained off the rock above Oatmeal.

"How many more does he have?" Mike frowned.

Oatmeal peeked around the boulder. "Depends on how much extra he's got with him."

"Good point." Mike took aim and fired. When he stopped, Oatmeal shot, spraying a rain of bullets over Javier.

Dusty was torn. He wanted to go after that SOB. Every fiber of his being wanted to destroy the psycho that had done this to Cassie. But holding her, battered and broken, he didn't dare put her down. The sounds of gunfire continued.

"Right up there." Oatmeal pointed toward a large reddish boulder.

Squinting, Mike could see the barrel of a gun flash as a bullet whizzed by. "He's got a better view."

"Let's just give him a few minutes. We get quiet, and he's going to wonder what's going on."

Mike sent him a side glance. "You do this often, do you?"

Oatmeal smiled. "No, but I seen a lot of Westerns."

Mike gave a short laugh. "Okay, cowboy, we'll try it your way."

A few more shots rang out until Javier apparently noticed he was the only one shooting.

Taking advantage of the pause, Mike called out, "Give it up, Javier, we've got you surrounded."

"Give me the girl, and I'll go."

"Are you cra—" Mike started to ask, but he caught himself, realizing it was obvious.

He tried a different tact. "Why don't you come down and we'll talk about it?"

Silence followed.

"Just throw your guns down first."

"Gringo, you think I'm stupid. I throw my guns down and you kill me."

Mike leaned forward. "No one wants to kill anyone, Javier. We just want to get you some help."

"Ha, help. That is a good one," the shooter scoffed.

Mike looked at Oatmeal. "We've got two choices. Hold him here and wait for help, or one of us go around behind him and see if we can get him that way."

The old cowboy considered. "This is more exciting than cowboy action shooting." He paused, "I think I'll go around behind and see what I can do."

"It's a lot more dangerous, too," warned Mike.

His statement was met by the cowboy's back as he slipped behind the rocks.

No more shots were fired. Mike waited for what seemed like hours. He called out. "Javier, you okay? Need any water? Food?" No reply.

On the ridge above the rocks and below the cave, he caught sight of Oatmeal, slowly making his way to Javier.

Mike waited, tension knotting his shoulders. *I should have gone. It really is dangerous up there. Javier is insane.*

Oatmeal was right above the rock now. Mike saw the glint of his gun in the sunlight. The seconds dragged by.

Then the cowboy stood up. "He's gone."

Gun in hand, Mike ran up the hill.

# Chapter Thirty-Eight

Reaching the top, Mike saw the opening to the cave. Several footprints marked the sand. He paused, uncertain what to do next. Something caught the corner of his eye. More tracks going the opposite direction from the cave and blood drops. Javier had been hit!

Oatmeal stood with him at the top of the hill. "See anything?" Gun drawn, the cowboy scanned the rocks and scrub around them.

"Not yet, but take a look at that." Mike pointed at the tracks.

"We at least winged him." Oatmeal squatted to take a closer look.

"It doesn't look like he went back into the cave," Mike said.

"Let's check the ridgetop." Oatmeal was already headed that way.

Mike hurried and dropped in next to him. "I think this intersects the main trail,"

"I think you're right," whispered Oatmeal.

Watching the tracks in front of them, they followed the ridge, which dropped down and hit the trail.

Mike scanned the area. "Where do you think he's headed?"

"I've been riding up here for a few days," said Oatmeal. "If you follow the trail all the way to the top, you come to a pass. It gets quite a bit steeper and narrower from there, but if you can stay on it, it will eventually take you down to the bottom." He leaned against a rock and lit a cigarette. Taking a deep inhale, he blew out the smoke. "Which doesn't put you that far from Tombstone."

"I hadn't realized we were so close." Mike began walking again. "We've got to get him before he gets down."

Oatmeal followed. "He can't be going that fast if he's shot."

The trail dropped through rocks and scrub, and they came back to the catch pond where they'd met Oatmeal earlier. Mike shook his head. Seems like days ago now.

"The trail hits some switchbacks and then opens up. He'll have a clear shot at us there," cautioned the cowboy.

"Or us at him," said Mike.

They carefully picked their way up the trail.

Just as Oatmeal had said, rocks took the place of the thick foliage. To the right plunged a ravine backed by jagged rock formations. The raw beauty of it transfixed Mike for a second. "Wow."

Coming up behind him, Oatmeal followed his gaze. "It is beautiful…" A bullet zinged off the rock above his head. "Oh crap, found him."

Both men dropped to the ground.

Mike scanned the area from where the shot had come. The trail planed out on the right side and the remains of a campfire ring with a few "rock seats" surrounding it. Probably a popular spot for hikers to admire the beauty. *I hope no one's here today.*

He and Oatmeal belly crawled to a spot over the sandy platform. Javier leaned against a rock. The side of his face was bloody, and either it had dripped down his arm, or he had more wounds.

Wordlessly, Mike pointed at Javier.

Oatmeal nodded and pointed his gun, steadying it on a rock.

"Give it up, Javier. We've got you covered," Mike said. "Drop your gun. It's over now."

Javier giggled, a shrill high-pitched tone. "Over? No, senor, it's not over at all." He aimed and fired at Mike.

Instantly Oatmeal fired a round at Javier. The kidnapper gave a slight scream and rolled away, over the hill.

Javier's bullet came within a fraction of an inch from Mike's head, splitting the rock off next to him and cutting his face. He reached up and pulled back fingers covered in fresh blood from his cheek.

"What the heck? Oatmeal, I thought you were a cowboy action shooter! He got away again."

The old cowboy shrugged. "We shoot at balloons off a galloping horse. This is different." He stood. "This is my first go at hunting humans."

"Let's get him," said Mike. "Now I'm pissed off."

They crawled through the rocks for a better look at where Javier had gone.

As they inched closer, the clatter of rolling rocks echoed off the gully walls.

Mike and Oatmeal crawled to the edge and saw a wide ledge below them. Javier had apparently lost his footing and rolled. He lay at the bottom of the gully. Mike couldn't tell if he was dead, unconscious, or just stunned. It didn't take long; a deep moan came from the inert man.

"Javier, are you okay?"

Upon hearing Mike's voice, the man seemed to awaken. He frantically patted the dirt around him. Finding nothing, he called up, "No, I am not okay." A sob then filled his voice. "I have lost it all."

Mike thought about what he could say. It was so true. Meanwhile, he heard a strange buzzing in the background. Despite shaking his head to clear it, the noise was still there. He looked at Oatmeal. "Do you hear that?"

"Yeah, almost sounds like honey bees."

Before Mike could answer, a small black dot came over the pass, heading straight toward them. It got larger as it approached. Prickles of fear hit Mike in the back of the neck. The buzzing formation resembled a large lawn chair flying over the terrain. It seemed to operate as one body. Gruesomely transfixed, Mike watched as it flew above Javier and hesitated, then suddenly dive-bombed. Within seconds his body was indiscernible from the mass of swarming insects.

"Aiehhheeeee! Help me! Help me!" His anguished voice screamed. Mike wanted to turn his head, but he couldn't take his eyes off the horror. Javier thrashed, high pitched screams followed by low gurgling moans. Then silence. The only sound was a determined buzzing bouncing off the rock walls.

Mike's stomach clenched. He felt like he was going to throw up. Turning his eyes from Javier, he looked at Oatmeal.

The old cowboy shook his head slowly. "I'll be damned. I've never seen anything like that before."

"Killer bees," said Mike. "I've heard of them, but never seen them."

Oatmeal stood up. "I gotta get back to Lucille."

The men hurried down the trail to their stock.

Dusty and Cassie were still by the horses and Lucille, where they'd left them earlier. Mike puffed. "Did you hear that?"

Cassie lay with her head in Dusty's lap. He said, "We heard shooting and then screaming. What in the heck happened?"

Oatmeal came up behind Mike. "Killer bees."

"Killer bees? Dusty repeated incredulously.

Mike grimaced. "It was absolutely horrific."

A grim smile crossed Dusty's face. "That so?"

Mike felt a shift inside; the horror of Javier's death played in his mind. Seeing anybody go that way was something he knew he would never forget. At the same time, watching Dusty suffering the anguish Javier had put him through the last few weeks, thinking Cassie was dead, or worse, sold to the sex trade, was something he also knew he would never forget.

A voice yelled. "Here they are!" Mike looked up. A search and rescue crew came down the trail, carrying a litter, Roberto leading the way.

He trotted up to Mike as the paramedics surrounded Cassie. "Did you get Javier?"

"Oh, yeah," said Mike. "We got him all right."

# Chapter Thirty-Nine

Mike and Oatmeal sat by the fire. The stars sparkled in the sky. All was silent but an occasional pop from the fire and a burst of sparks. Mike looked around. He and the cowboy were the only ones left in the campsite. Dusty had given Mike the keys to the horse trailer and had gone with Cassie to the hospital. Metal striking stone caught his attention. Mike looked over at the horses. Prince and Muley stood under the highline, their large frames dark silhouettes in the moonlight. The sound had come from Muley repositioning himself and nuzzling hopefully at the dirt, his lips pulling at any leftover pieces of hay.

Stretching his legs in front of him, Mike relaxed. Oatmeal lit a cigarette and the ember glowed red in the firelight. "Seems like nobody was ever here."

"Yeah." Mike took a deep breath "After all the commotion today the silence feels pretty good."

"Sure does." Oatmeal took another contemplative drag on his cigarette.

Scout and Sammy lay by Mike's feet. He petted each one. It had been a traumatic time for the dogs too. Especially Sammy. When she saw Cassie, the paramedics couldn't keep her off. Cassie had laughed—*at least I think that's what it was*. She had thrown her arms around her dog and buried her face in Sammy's thick fur.

Even now, Mike felt tears burn in his eyes. It has sure been a difficult couple of weeks.

He leaned down and poked a stick in the fire. Dusty was an amazing guy. Mike had always admired him. He was an excellent rider and a great person to have along on a crazy adventure. The voice of reason. Going through what they had in the last couple of weeks physically and emotionally drained him. He saw his big, vibrant best friend turn into a hollow-eyed shell. Mike's stomach tightened. He felt the burn behind his eyelids again.

"You're one heck of a guy, Mike."

Mike started. He'd been so lost in his thoughts he'd even forgotten Oatmeal was there.

His cheeks felt warm. "That obvious, huh?"

Oatmeal sat back in his chair, relaxed in front of the fire. "Well, I haven't known you guys long, but—"

"Yeah." Mike gave a feeble laugh. "I think we're coming up on our two-day anniversary here."

"Really?" Oatmeal cocked his head. "Seems longer." He blew out some smoke. "Big adventures can do that to you."

"Seriously, Oatmeal, I can't thank you enough for being here for us." Mike didn't know how much longer he was going to be able to hold the tears back. "I don't know what we would have done without you."

The cowboy waved his hand in the air. "You don't have to thank me for anything. The good Lord puts me where he sees fit." He looked at Mike. "If you want to thank someone, I'd go right to the source."

"You're a believer."

"Yup," said the old cowboy. "He's shown me more than once He's there for me."

Mike stared into the fire. "I don't know what I am."

Oatmeal stood up. "Well, I know who you are, both you and Dusty. You're my brothers. The Lord's never wrong." He tossed his cigarette in the fire. "I'm going to turn in. Me and Lucille got some ground to cover in the morning."

"Night," Mike, stirred the coals with a stick, the embers glowed bright red in the surrounding darkness.

The cowboy disappeared into the dark.

Mike heard the mule nicker and Oatmeal's low voice. Mike felt tired down to his bones but couldn't stop thinking about what he'd said. He had always felt close to God; it was one of the reasons he loved the mountains. The gifts from heaven, uninterrupted by the noise of society. Sitting now at the fire alone, it struck him—how else could they have gotten Javier? Oatmeal. The Lord again at work. A surge of gratitude passed through him. For the first time in days he felt warm inside.

Mike stood and banked the fire. He had a light jacket on, hard to believe how temperate the weather was down here—knowing how cold it was at home. He stopped in his tracks. Home. *I need to call Terri again.* She still hadn't answered any calls. What was she doing? It was not like her at all. He quickly checked the horses and offered them a final bucket of water. They just sniffed at it. He set the bucket down and went into the trailer.

His phone lay on the table where he had left it. Picking it up, he punched in Terri's number and waited. It rang several times and eventually the voicemail picked up. Her voice chirped out that she wasn't available just now, but please leave a message and she would call back. "Hey, where are you, Terri? This is Mike. It's kind of late to be feeding the horses. Please call me back when you get in." He hesitated. "Any time you get in."

As he hung up the phone, his stomach knotted. The feeling of missing her washed over him in a deep pang. How long had it been anyway? *I've been so caught up in this thing with Cassie, it's been days since I've spoken to he*r. He wracked his brain. At least two or three days. Making up his mind, he punched in the numbers.

A sleepy female voice answered, "He-hello."

"Shelley," he said urgently, "This is Mike."

"Mike?" She sounded confused for a minute.

He tried again. "Dusty's friend, Mike."

"Oh, hey," she said, "Sorry, I think I was asleep."

"Sorry to wake you," his voice faltered.

"What time is it anyway?" A fumbling came over the phone, "Eleven o'clock," she squeaked, "Is something wrong?"

"No." Mike tried to keep his voice even. "Or at least I hope not. It's just I can't get ahold of Terri. Have you seen her?"

"Not lately," said Shelley. "She wasn't at the Backcountry Horsemen meeting last night, which was kind of strange."

Mike felt his stomach drop. "I'm still down here in Arizona with Dusty and Cassie's horses."

"What is going on with that? They were talking about something about a kidnapping at the meeting. Is Cassie okay?"

"She is now. She was taken, we got her back today." Mike outlined what had taken place.

"Oh my God!" exclaimed Shelley. "What can I do? Do you guys need anything?"

"I haven't been able to get ahold of Terri for about three days," he said flatly. "I was wondering if you could go out there and see what's going on. Maybe check on the horses."

"The horses?"

"She's feeding one of Dusty's, one of Cassie's, both of mine and hers."

"Wow, all in one place?"

"I'm not sure what she's got worked out, she said she was going to take them all to her place. I would really appreciate it if you could check on it. Find out what's happened to her."

"I'd be happy to do that, Mike." She paused. "Would you mind if I waited until daylight? I'm not a real big one to go out in the middle of the night checking on things."

A tight laugh came from his throat. "That would be great, Shelley. And no, I didn't mean the minute you hung up the phone." He cleared his throat. "I'm down here at Cochise Stronghold, I'm going to be starting back tomorrow with Dusty's rig and the horses. Could you ask Terri to call me when you get out there? And if you don't find her, call me and let me know what's going on?"

"No problem, Mike. I'll head out at first light."

"I really appreciate it." He disconnected, threw his sleeping bag on the bed, and lay down. Sleep eluded him. Instead, a drum beat in his head. *Something's not right.*

# Chapter Forty

Mike rose before daylight and fed the horses. He went back in the trailer and made a cup of coffee. He couldn't stop thinking about Terri. Picking up his phone he hit redial, the rings clicked to the chipper voice which turned to voicemail. He started to hang up when he heard, "This voicemail is full, please call back later."

Mike froze. How long since she picked up her messages? Willing himself to be calm, he went back outside the trailer, checked on the horses, and offered them a drink. Water dripped from Prince's mouth as he turned and plunged his head into the hay bag.

Walking around to the back of the trailer, Mike let Scout and Sammy out. The dogs bounded into the darkness. Light had just begun to touch the mountains in the distance. Watching the dogs and horses, Mike felt peace. The routine and predictability of animals relaxed him. *You can depend on what they will do.* People are so different.

His mind turned back to the phone in his pocket. Never had he yearned more for a call, but at the same time dreading it. The last couple weeks had not been good. Mike wasn't sure he could take any more bad news. He busied himself shoveling manure and cleaning up his camp. He put out some food for the dogs and stowed everything in the trailer to ready it for travel. Prince and Muley raised their heads from their hay bags and kept them there, signaling they were finished. Mike tied the horses to the trailer, took off the hay bags, and coiled his highline.

He loaded the horses and started his truck. Leaving it to warm up, he walked over to the cowboy's camp.

"Thanks for all your help, Oatmeal." Mike held out his hand.

"You don't need to thank me. This was the best adventure I've had in years." Oatmeal took Mike's hand and firmly clasped it.

Mike's face creased in a wry grin. "Yes, it was that."

"I'd be happy to team up with you and Dusty any day of the week. Next time give me a little warning, so I can practice my aim and be ready."

Mike laughed. "Will do."

"Funniest thing," said Oatmeal.

"What's that?"

Oatmeal cocked his head. "I feel like I've met you before."

"Really?" Mike cocked his head. "Me?"

"Both of you," said Oatmeal firmly. "Maybe I read about you somewhere or something?"

"Doubt that." Mike caught off guard, stepped back.

The old cowboy winked at him. "Have a good trip, Mike. Say 'bye to that friend of yours."

"Take care, Oatmeal." Mike turned and walked back to his trailer, feeling hollow inside.

The call finally came just as Mike turned into a truck stop to fuel up. He pulled over and parked. Snatching up the phone he barked, "Hello."

Shelley's voice sounded flat. "Mike, I just got back."

"Is Terri okay?" He couldn't wait, he had to know.

"I… I don't know, I couldn't find her." Her voice quavered.

"Wait, just tell me the whole thing. What did you do?"

"I went out to Terri's place first. She had her horses and Cassie's other horse in her pasture. The minute they saw the car they started nickering and charging up and down the fence line. They were hungry."

"Was Terri's car there?" Mike cut in.

"Yes. That was the strange thing, both her car and truck were parked by the house." Shelley cleared her throat and went on. "I fed the horses and went to the door. It was unlocked. I beat on it and called her name. No one came, so I pushed it open."

Mike went still inside. He'd been there so many times himself, he could picture the whole thing. *But this time Terri's not there.*

"The house looked normal. Her purse, keys and cell phone were on the table. I walked back through the bedrooms calling and..." Shelley's voice cracked, sobs filled the line. "Her bed hadn't been slept in, Mike." She finally managed. "It...it scared me. I ran out of there and back to my car."

"Then what?" Ice flowed through his veins.

"I didn't know what to do. This has never happened to me before," replied Shelley in a ragged voice. "I told you I'd check on the horses. I thought I'd better at least finish that, so I drove to Dusty's place."

"How was that?"

"I didn't get out of the car. Driving back in there it's so isolated, and I didn't see Cheyenne anywhere. I was afraid." She blew her nose. "That place is creepy enough with the dark woods and the mist from the rain."

Rain, Mike thought abstractly, hard to imagine in the arid climate where he was. "Then what did you do?" If he got any tighter inside, he thought he would snap.

"I... I went to your house."

"And?"

"Dusty's other horse, Cheyenne, was there with your horses."

"How were they?"

"Crazy hungry too, Mike. I got out and fed them. They tore into it like they hadn't eaten for days." She hesitated. "Your truck was parked in the driveway, so I just thought I'd check the house. When I got up to the door, it looked like it had been kicked in. The doorjamb was broken out and black scuff marks on the paint. I barely pushed and it fell open."

Dread filled Mike. "Did you go in?"

"No, from what I could see, the place was trashed."

"Trashed," breathed Mike.

"Yes, everything was everywhere. I didn't stay. I was really scared. I ran back into my car and drove home." She sobbed. "Mike, who would do this? She took a ragged breath. "What do you want me to do?"

The miles between him and Washington loomed large in front of him. He wanted to be the first on the scene. *Terri's missing. That's the most important thing*. "You better call the sheriff. We need to find Terri."

"Okay." She paused, "I just wanted to hear it from you."

"I'll be there as soon as I possibly can. It's going to take a couple days. I'll have to stop at least once to sleep."

"Don't worry about the horses, I'll feed them until you get back."

"Thanks, Shelley." He clicked off his cell phone. Overwhelmed, he rested his forehead on the steering wheel. Breathing in and out calmed him. He sat up, picked up his phone and punched in a number.

Dusty answered in a couple rings. "What's up, Mike?"

"I called Shelley to go check on Terri."

He could sense Dusty listening intently on the other end of the line.

"She said the horses looked like they hadn't been fed in a while."

Mike heard Dusty's intake of breath.

"My—my house had been trashed."

"What in the heck?"

"And Terri's gone." Mike choked out the words. "She's missing, Dusty."

"Oh, no," Dusty said quietly.

"Shelley's calling the sheriff now."

"We're at the University Medical Center in Phoenix. Cassie's okay. The airport's right here. I'll be on the next plane, buddy."

Mike hadn't realized he was holding his breath until it came out in a rush. "I'll get there as soon as I can."

"Yeah, with my rig," Dusty said ruefully. "I'm sorry."

"Just fill me in on what you find out."

"Don't worry, I will." Dusty paused. "We'll get her back, Mike."

Mike felt shades of déjà vu pass over him. "Yeah, we will," he said weakly. Punching the phone off, he rested his head on the steering wheel again and waited for the tears to pass. Scout and Sammy jumped from the back seat. They pressed their furry bodies against him. Aussie muzzles licked his face, and both dogs fought for lap space. Mike raised his head and put his arms around them. Their fur was soft and smelled of hay and outdoors. Scout and Sammy quit pushing and rested their heads on either side of his neck, their breathing slow and steady.

Feeling new strength, Mike finally moved them over. "We gotta go now." The dogs seemed to understand. Scout stayed next to him and laid his head on Mike's lap. Sammy sat by the door with her head on Scout. Mike put the truck in gear and drove over to the fuel pumps.

# Chapter Forty-One

A light rain drizzled as they pulled away from the airport. "Thanks a lot for picking me up, Shelley."

"Oh, sure." She pushed her hair back from her face, bracelets rattling.

Dusty started absently out the window at the starting and stopping traffic, the sea of red tail lights blinking on and off in front of them. Weariness engulfed him, all the way down to his bones. Cassie was safe now. Roberto had promised he would keep an eye on her. After what she'd been through, it was amazing she was as healthy as she was. They wanted to keep her under observation for another day at least, but once her fever was gone, she'd be discharged. He breathed deeply.

His thoughts turned to Terri. What could have possibly happened? Was it related? Dusty wracked his brain. How could it be? Javier had popped up out of nowhere in Alamo. What is the common denominator to Terri?

"Dusty?"

Hearing his name brought him back to the moment. "Yeah, sorry, Shelley, I missed what you said?"

"What are you going to do?" Her blue polished fingernails clutched the steering wheel, her hands white. The bangle bracelets hung limply on her wrists. She wore a winter coat with fur trimmed hood and sleeves and her signature low-cut top with her breasts threatening to topple out of it. Dusty knew that's just who Shelley was; at one point not so long ago it had been a different story.

The word was out now at Backcountry Horsemen that he was seeing Cassie. Before that, whenever he and Mike would come to a meeting, they would be swarmed by the single hopeful women who wanted to meet a cowboy. The ratio in BCHW were very high on women to men. Every girl wanted a guy to ride with, the problem was not many guys wanted to ride horses. That made meetings difficult, if not treacherous at times, to navigate. Dusty had enjoyed the group mainly for the trail work. He believed in giving back.

Shelley was more aggressive than most, and pretty soon she began to turn up at his favorite café. Dusty winced inwardly at the memories. Mike had thoroughly enjoyed Dusty's discomfort at the time, but he was also able to smooth things out. Dusty felt a wave of warmth, Mike was a good friend, and he was going to be one back. The result of all that was Shelley had become a very good friend to him, Mike, Cassie and Terri. Despite her appearance, she deeply cared about people and would do anything for her friends. Dusty was thankful for that—especially today.

"I'm going to go home and get my car. To start off with anyway."

"If you need me to do anything, just let me know." Shelley looked at him wide-eyed.

Dusty reached over and squeezed her shoulder. "You're a great friend, Shelley. I really appreciate all your help."

Pink suffused her cheeks. "You guys are my friends."

Riding in silence, Shelley finally turned into his driveway, a wall of trees with a gravel road splitting them. They pulled into a large parking area strewn with pine needles and a red garage with white trim. A stately log cabin stood in the clearing. Chinks were packed with cement, repacked in some areas with more up-to-date caulking. On the large front porch sat two wooden Adirondack chairs. Water dripped off the porch from the rain. Hydrangea plants hugged up to the side of the house. An old mossy wood picket fence lined the yard around the cabin, and lawn surrounded the house.

Mist swirled from the rain and fog in the late morning. Shelley pulled the car to a stop.

"Your place always kind of creeps me out." She shuddered. "Especially with the fog, looks like a horror movie."

Dusty grinned. "Yeah, you get used to it though." He got out and pulled his bag out of the back seat. He didn't have much, most of his gear was still in the horse trailer with Mike. He slammed the back door and leaned in one more time in the front. "Thanks for everything, Shelley, I'll keep you posted."

"No problem, Dusty. If you need help with feeding or anything, just let me know."

"I appreciate it." He shut the door and went to his cabin.

On the back porch the chopping block and ax were just where he left them, a pile of wood ready. Putting his key in the lock, he walked through the laundry/mud room and then the second door into the house. The minute he walked in, the comforting smell of wood and campfire smoke filled his nostrils.

He set his bag by the kitchen table and made a pot of coffee. He took a quick shower and poured himself a cup. Downing it quickly, he turned off the pot, grabbed his lined jean jacket off the hook by the door, and setting his Stetson on his head, he locked up and went to his car.

He drove straight to Terri's house. A black SUV with "Sheriff" on the side sat in the driveway. Dusty got out and went to the door. He knocked. "Hello?" It was halfway open, so he pushed it the rest of the way. "Anyone here?"

"Yeah." A uniformed sheriff's deputy stood in the living room. "Do you know Terri?"

"I'm a friend of hers."

The deputy walked toward him, "Can I see your identification?"

Dusty handed over his driver's license.

After scrutinizing it, the deputy made and note. "What are you doing here?"

His eyebrows raised, Dusty replied, "I'm looking for Terri." He gestured around the room, "She's missing."

The deputy looked down, "I know, but I have to ask."

"Any word?" Dusty asked, tucking his license back in his wallet.

"Not so far. They took her cell phone to check it for messages." He looked around, "I was just about ready to leave. They wanted me to stick around for a while in case anyone came by." He hesitated. "Do you know Mike Dracopoulos?"

"Yes," said Dusty. "He's my best friend."

"You might check by his house then," said the deputy. "We were told he was the vic"—he cleared his throat quickly, "Terri's boyfriend. A unit was sent to check it out."

"On my way."

Terri's two horses and Cassie's pack horse stood at the fence. Their coats were dripping and their ears perked toward him as he walked by. They nickered encouragingly. Dusty walked over to check them. They had water but were out of hay. He wasn't sure when they'd been fed. Shelley was taking care of feeding. It couldn't hurt though, he tossed them each a flake. Dusting off the particles of grass on his coat, he got back in his car.

Mike's house had a lot more activity. The small two-bedroom bungalow sat back in the trees. The once-white paint looked gray, strewn with pine needles on the roof, water dripped over the gutters and down the sides of the house. The windows looked like dark sad eyes in the misty rain. Three sheriff's cars were parked in the driveway next to Mike's truck. To the side of the house, Dusty saw Mike's two horses, Toby and Duke, and his own packhorse Cheyenne. He went over and checked the horses. They ran up and down the fenceline and shook their heads, whinnying encouragingly. There was plenty of water, and he tossed them another flake of hay from the blue tarp-covered, small stack next to the pen.

Walking to the house, he hesitated, the front door stood ajar. The doorjamb was shattered. Shelley was right, someone had kicked it in. He heard voices inside., Clearing his throat, he called out. “Hello.” He knew it was never a good idea to surprise people in a situation like this, especially if they were armed.

The door opened the rest of the way, a large officer in a khaki colored shirt, badge and dark coat stood in the doorway. Dusty could see behind him, the place was a mess. Mike didn’t have much, but whatever he had was strewn everywhere.

“This is a crime scene, sir. Do you know Mike Dracopoulos?”

“Yeah,” said Dusty for the second time that day, “He’s my best friend.”

“Do you have any idea who would do this to him?”

A cold chill shivered up his spine. No, I don’t.”

# Chapter Forty-Two

Dusty sat in his kitchen. The clock in the living room chimed 3 a.m. He couldn't sleep. He'd called Cassie earlier and she was feeling much better. The doctor told her she would be released in a day or two. Roberto had been a great support. Dusty could hear his voice in the background, and Cassie said he'd been a constant visitor. Mike was lucky to have such a good friend. And Dusty was grateful for his help.

The silence was split by the sound of a familiar engine. He looked out into the parking area and saw truck lights, followed by the running lights of a trailer pulling in. Slipping on his headlamp, Dusty went outside, and greeted Mike before he even got the engine shut off.

Dusty opened the truck door. Even in yard light Mike looked gray and tired. He slid out of the truck. "How was the drive?" asked Dusty.

"Long." Mike sighed. "Any word on Terri?"

"Not yet." Dusty's friend winced. He touched Mike's shoulder. "You told me once we'd get Cassie, I'm telling you now the same thing."

"We'll get Cassie?" Mike said in a deadpan voice in spite of himself.

Dusty felt lighter, at least Mike could still joke. "Both of them." He turned and walked to the back of the trailer. "I'll get the horses. Why don't you head in the house? I've got some coffee on and we need to talk." He hesitated. "Unless you want to catch some sleep first?"

Mike waved him off. "Plenty of time for that later. I want to find out what's happening."

"Okay, you know where everything is. I'll be back in a minute." Dusty led the two horses to the corral. Shelley had brought her trailer out and helped him bring Mike's two horses and over; he'd put them in the back pasture to make feeding easier.

Cheyenne came back too, and waited in the front pasture, calling to Muley. Prince snorted loudly at the new surroundings.

"It's okay, boy. You'll have your own spot," Dusty assured the big gray. He put Muley in with Cheyenne, closed the gate. There was a small paneled area in the front that he used when he didn't want to have to walk all the way out to catch Muley and Cheyenne. It came in handy now for Prince. Dusty threw them all hay and filled Prince's water bucket. Both dogs followed closely at his heels. He stopped and surveyed the horses with his headlamp. All were eating. He turned and went to the house.

Mike sat at the kitchen table, both hands around his coffee cup. He turned bloodshot eyes up to Dusty. "Fill me in. Why did I need to come here first?"

Dusty poured another cup of coffee. Sleep far from his mind. "You should plan on staying here for a while. Your house is in bad shape."

"Shelley said it had been trashed."

"That's putting it mildly," said Dusty flatly. He told Mike all the events to-date.

Mike looked mystified. "Why?" He shook his head. "What could they possibly think they were going to find at my house?"

"It's got to have something to do with Arizona." Dusty took a sip of coffee. "Whoever did it knew you were gone."

"But what about Terri? She wasn't there."

"Mike, it's something with you. That's all I can think. The only connection to Terri is you." Dusty's voice was gentle, but he could see the pain in Mike's tired face.

"It's got to be." Mike nodded.

"Let's get some sleep, you look like you could use it."

"Sleep," Mike repeated and laughed hopelessly.

"At least lay down for a couple hours. We've got a big day in front of us."

Mike finally capitulated, he set down his coffee cup and rose.

"Take the first bedroom at the top of the stairs."

"Okay."

Dusty watched him walk. He looked like a much older man as he shuffled forward, shoulders slumped, feet dragging.

Dusty picked up the cups and put them in the sink. Something kept bothering him, but he couldn't put it together. What was it?

Terri lay in the hotel room bedroom. She heard the city sounds outside the window. The men had blindfolded her at the house, so she couldn't see where they'd gone. She thought back to how she'd gotten here.

After feeding the horses, she was getting ready to go to go a deposition in Puyallup. She had talked to Mike. They were back in the U.S. now; he would be able to find Cassie. Warmth washed over her when she thought of him, his gentle way with animals and people. He would do it.

A sharp knock at the door jarred her from her thoughts. She'd had her purse and keys in her hand, so close to leaving her house. Setting them on the table, nervously she started toward the door. She lived just far enough out that people didn't knock on her door very often. And when they did, it always made her feel vulnerable. She mentally chastised herself. It was probably just the Jehovah Witnesses. They were the main visitors out here. She plastered a polite but resolute smile on her face as she opened the door.

The man pushed in, gun thrust in her chest. Terri stumbled back, filled with a combination of shock, and worst of all, icy cold fear. He wasn't tall, but it was his eyes, hard, cold shards of copper. He was tan-skinned with several tattoos on his hands and neck. Marks on his face looked like tears from his eye. A murderer! Terri's mind flashed back to gang-related trials she'd taken in court. Tears from the corner of the eye signified they'd committed murder. Her heart beat so fast she felt faint. Three more men piled in the door after the first, slamming it shut behind them. The air filled with rapid Spanish. Terri didn't understand it, but she was familiar enough to know what language they were speaking. The first man held the gun on her chest and the other three searched her house. "Why?" was all she could manage. Wracking her paralyzed mind, she couldn't think of any recent robberies in the area.

The men came back in seconds. "*No hay gente*."

The man with the gun nodded. "*Buena*."

Terri was rooted to her spot. What next? Rape? Murder? She couldn't think. Then she felt the metal through her rain coat. "*Vamos*." The man pushed her shoulder toward the front door. Her heart sank. Kidnap.

"*Parada*!" barked one of the men behind her. A dirty handkerchief was pulled over her eyes, she could feel it tied tightly behind her head. "*Ahoya vaya*." She was pushed forward, stumbling out the door.

Sitting in the car, Terri heard traffic outside and felt the car move and stop, move and stop. A motion she was very familiar with on the freeways of Seattle. The apparent leader barked, "*Callado*," to the other men and they stopped talking. He sounded like he was on the phone. He spoke rapidly in a deep voice, then chuckled. The hair on the back of her neck stood up. She didn't like the laugh. It was a cold imitation.

The blindfold made time difficult to tell, but eventually after much starting and stopping, it felt like downhill. They came to a halt.

The driver got out and slammed the door, while the other men talked and laughed. Within minutes he was back and she was jerked from her seat. Powerful arms picked her up and she lay on the man's shoulder. He roughly pulled her hood over her head. He smelled strongly of cigarettes, alcohol and aftershave. Carrying her into the building, she could hear the other men next to them.

They hesitated at what must have been a check-in. The driver said, "*Infermo*."

A knowing laugh from a young male voice. "Oh, yeah, sick all right.

The four men laughed in return. She felt herself carried up a flight of stairs. The building smelled old. The steps creaked in protest as they climbed. Despair welled up inside of her and she willed it back down. *As long as I'm alive, I can help myself.*

# Chapter Forty-Three

When Dusty woke it was still dark out. He felt like he'd barely rested rather than sleeping all night. Checking the clock, 6 a.m. He rubbed his eyes. It had been a short nap. As his brain began to focus, he thought about Cassie. He missed her. This was new for him. He'd never felt that way about anyone before, not even his ex-wife in the day. This had turned out to be some bumpy ride. He winced. Hopefully once she was home they could try to get on track with their relationship. A wet nose interrupted his reverie, followed by a second one. "So, Scout, you have reinforcements." Two shaggy dog muzzles thrust at his hand to be patted.

"Hold on." Dusty pushed them back as he swung his feet onto the floor. He grabbed a shirt and jeans. No reason even pretending he would be sitting around this morning. They had to find Terri and figure out what the heck was going on. "I know it's all related. But how?"

He started up the coffee maker and got a quick shower. Walking out to the kitchen, he saw Mike seated at the table drinking coffee. "You're up early."

"Sleeping is not high on my list at the moment." Mike hunched over his cup.

"I can completely understand that." Dusty poured himself a cup of coffee.

Mike was silent.

Sitting down, Dusty took a drink. "Something has been bothering me, but I've been having a hard time putting a finger on it."

Mike looked up at him, his eyes intent.

"Just the way all of this has come down." He set his cup on the table. "So we meet Javier at Alamo, right?"

Mike nodded.

"We know now that he made the decision to abduct Cassie after that meeting. And it was probably a chance thing, since as far as I know we'd never run into him anywhere before."

Mike added, "So he abducts Cassie and we go to the Sheriff's Department and find Roberto to help us."

"Yes." Dusty nodded. "And we start the pursuit."

"Yeah. So?" Mike was confused.

"Well, hang on, let's just walk through this." Dusty took another drink of coffee. "We get into Mexico and everywhere we go we almost catch Javier, but just miss him."

"Even when we can see him."

Dusty nodded emphatically. "And what was Roberto saying to the police officers? Because whatever it was, they let Javier go."

"Not knowing Spanish didn't help."

"Right. But why?" Dusty said slowly. "Unless they were told something different."

Mike's hand with his coffee cup froze in midair. He set the cup back down and looked at Dusty. "Meaning what?"

Dusty felt ice running through his veins, but suddenly knew he was right. Standing up abruptly he said, "I've got to call Cassie."

Running, taking the stairs two at a time, he picked up his cell phone by his bedstand. He punched in Cassie's cell, the phone rang and went to voicemail. Quickly he scanned his past calls and hit redial on the Phoenix area code for the hospital. It took forever. Finally, a nurse answered. "Fifth floor."

"Can I speak to Cassie Martin, please?" Dusty tried to control his rapid breathing.

There was a hesitation. "Do you know which room she's in?"

Dusty snapped, "No! For heaven's sake, you work there, don't you?"

The nurse stammered, "I'm filling in. Hang on, I'll ask someone."

Dusty's heart hammered so loudly he could feel it thumping in his ears. *What if I'm too late?*

After what seemed an eternity, another female voice came on the line, this one sounded a lot more assured. "Nurse Wyatt here. I understand you're looking for Cassie Martin."

"Yes," Dusty answered quickly.

"She's sleeping."

Relief flooded through his body. He couldn't remember being so thankful.

"Can I take a message and have her call you when she wakes up?" The nurse lowered her voice confidentially. "She's been having a really hard time sleeping lately."

"Sure. Could you have her call me the minute she's awake? I need to talk to her."

"Of course."

Dusty clicked off and stared at his phone for a minute, as if the answers were there. He put it in his pocket and hurried downstairs.

"Did you talk to her?" asked Mike grimly.

"No, but they said she was still asleep."

"Thank God." Mike hesitated. "You know, I just flashed on something. When we were originally at Roberto's office, he was telling me about female trafficking. You had already gone out to the truck. I told him I was worried about that happening with Cassie. He just pooh-poohed me, said not at her age. So I pulled up one on my phone."

Dusty's face was blank, devoid of emotion. Mike continued. "He said they usually went for younger girls, twenties and below, but when I showed him the photo he said, 'Unless they look like her.'" Mike paused. "It was just the look on his face, shock and then something else bothered me—in hindsight it almost looked like calculation."

Dusty slammed his fist on the table. "That's it," he roared. "You were already on your way back to Washington with my rig. How to get rid of me? Take Terri so you'd need help. And Roberto knew I'd go." The last part came out sounding like a wounded cry more than a statement.

"What now?" Mike facial expression.

Dusty stood and pushed his chair back. "I'm going back to Phoenix on the first flight I can get."

"I'll get ahold of Seattle Police Department." Mike rose from the table. "Those detectives have a lot of resources."

"Good idea, because when Roberto doesn't get Cassie, there's probably going to be a change of whatever plans they had." Dusty shrugged into his coat and put on his Stetson. "I'll unhook the truck and give you a ride over to your place." Punching Cassie's cell number, he walked out the door with the phone at his ear.

The phone rang five times. Then a sleepy voice said, "Hello."

"Cassie." Relief flooded through him.

"Oh, hi," she said weakly. "Did you find Terri?"

"Not yet."

"Oh?" Cassie sounded puzzled.

"Listen," Dusty said seriously, "Something has come up. I don't want to scare you."

"Scare me?" Cassie suddenly sounded wide awake. "Doubt that."

"Where's your gun?" Dusty said abruptly.

"It's right here." She touched in in the pocket of her robe. "Do you think I'd ever be without it again?"

"No, I don't, that's why I brought it for you." Then he added in a low voice, "Do not go anywhere with Roberto."

"Really?" asked Cassie.

"Yes." Dusty spoke in an emphatic tone.

"Why am I not surprised?."

Dusty stumbled, "W-Why?"

"Yes. Ever since you left, he's been acting strange. As if he owns me." She hesitated. "It just feels wrong."

"I'm coming back on the next flight, so just relax."

"What about Terri?" she asked.

"Mike's got this, I'm afraid once they don't have you, things are going to move quickly."

"Okay. See you soon."

"You will," Dusty affirmed. "Love you, babe."

"Love you too." She clicked off her cell phone and set it on the bed stand.

"When is he coming back?" A deep voice startled her.

She felt the blood drain from her face. Looking up, she saw Roberto leaning against the door frame, his face a dark mask.

# Chapter Forty-Four

Mike stood in what was left of his living room—furniture overturned and books from his bookcase dumped everywhere. He didn't have a lot of stuff, but what he did have lay broken and strewn about. Glancing into the kitchen, he shook his head and sighed deeply. Even the drawers had been pulled and emptied.

He turned and walked into his bedroom. "Really?" His bed had been sliced with a knife, feathers and mattress stuffing littered the room. Years of investigative work confirmed to him that the perpetrators were not looking for anything. This was a setup. Dusty was absolutely right, taking Terri was a means to get him out of Phoenix. Trashing his house was just a cover-up, something to slow them down on the real reason: Cassie's abduction.

Mike's mind raced and his blood pounded. Time was running out, he had to get Terri. Images of what they would do to her flashed in his mind. His stomach roiled, and he forced himself to stop. *I can't go there, because if I do, I can't think clearly.* He hurried out the door and jumped in his old blue Ford pickup. The ignition turned over on the first try. He slammed it into reverse and backed out of the driveway, pausing only to dial Seattle PD.

By the time he'd worked his way through the system and gotten into the detective's division, Mike pulled onto Highway 167. "Detective O'Rourke," came the clipped response. Mike introduced himself and launched into his story.

The detective remained silent until he finished. "Let me do some checking, we have sources downtown." Mike could hear papers rustling. "Give me your contact information."

Mike did. "I'm on my way down there right now. I've got pictures of Terri I can give you." He rushed on, "And I want to help."

"I'll be here. I've got paperwork all day to catch up on." The detective paused. "Unless I get a call of course."

"Oh, you're going to get one all right. The second we find out where she is, we need to get her." The line was silent. "Or I will," said Mike emphatically.

"Got you. See you shortly." The line went dead.

Mike focused on the traffic in front of him, lines of lights as far as he could see. Seattle morning traffic, probably the worst in the U.S. His heart sank as he joined the dance of starting, creeping a few feet ahead, and stopping. Taillights blinked ahead of him as the big traffic snake wove its way toward the city center.

Terri lay on the bed. They had removed her blindfold—or it had fallen off during the night. Her arms and back ached from being tied behind her back. She moaned and turned on her side, trying to relieve the tension in her muscles. Her stomach growled. She'd had nothing to eat since yesterday. Last night she smelled beer and pizza wafting into the bedroom, mixed with tobacco and marijuana smoke, the acrid odor distinguishable. Hunger wasn't as important to her as survival. She'd taken enough criminal trials, pro tem, to understand how these kinds of men operated. Human life was cheap, money and drugs ruled. A sleazy downtown Seattle hotel room was just one jump away from Elliott Bay, an easy disposal. Terri's mind raced.

The doorknob turned and a man walked in. He held a coil of rope in his hand, a sickening smile on his face. What was the rope for? The man was short, but broad. His arms were muscled with sleeve tattoos on them. Terri squirmed away. Whatever it was, she didn't want anything to do with it. He pulled out a giant knife from a sheath on his belt, the glint pulled her eyes to his face. Three ink tears fell from one eyelid. The same guy with the gangland translation of a murderer.

Mike screeched to a halt in front of the Seattle Municipal Building. He jumped out and ran inside, giving no thought to parking places or tow-away zones. Rushing into the lobby, he punched the elevator button. People crowded around him, their faces a blur. When the elevator finally arrived, he rushed in, jostling the person next to him and spilling some of his Starbucks. "Hey, take it easy." The man held his cup away from his suit. "You made me spill my coffee."

"Oh, sorry," Mike replied without conviction. He punched the elevator button and stood back. As he watched the floors tick by, his heart pounded in his eardrums. It seemed to stop at every floor. Finally, the doors opened and he hurried out, only to be stopped by a receptionist.

"I'm here to see Detective O'Rourke," he barked.

The receptionist, a girl in her twenties with dyed black hair, lots of makeup, and black painted fingernails gave him a sideways look. "One minute please, I'll see if he's in." She hit a button on the phone, spoke into the receiver, and then looked up. "He'll be out in shortly. You can have a seat." She gestured at the metal and lime green military issue furniture in the spartan waiting room.

Mike left the front desk, but he couldn't sit down. He paced back and forth as he waited. After what seemed like an eternity, a fair-skinned man in his late thirties opened the door. He had reddish brown hair and a moustache and wore a maroon tie, white dress shirt and suit pants with no jacket. "Mike?"

"Yes." Mike hurried over.

"Follow me." O'Rourke led the way back to his office.

The office was furnished in the same way as the waiting room. Metal desk and chairs with lime green cushions. A dingy window behind him looked across at another tall building. A few family pictures sat on the desk.

"I've been doing some checking around," he said. "I've got one lead, but I'm going to need a picture of Terri."

Mike reached in his wallet and pulled out two photos. One was a close-up of Terri. The second was farther away, she and Mike standing together by a campfire.

"Is she your girlfriend?"

Mike had left that part out, but he confirmed it now. "Yes."

The detective studied the photos briefly. "Okay, we have various people downtown that work with us. I put out the word this morning and got a call back on it already. Pretty lucky, usually it takes longer." He paused and looked directly at Mike as if gauging him. "He's a hotel clerk," the detective cleared his throat, "in a downtown hotel."

"Go on." Mike said impatiently.

"I'm not going to lie to you. It's not a good part of town."

"I pretty much figured that," said Mike through tightly clenched teeth.

Detective O'Rourke looked sympathetic. "The rooms usually rent by the hour." He cleared his throat. "The clerk owes us, he's working off some time, and so far, he's been pretty reliable. He said four men came in last night with a woman over one man's shoulder. They made it sound like they were there to party with her, but she was sick. He felt like something was wrong. He said from what he could see, she didn't look like a party girl."

"Where is she?" Mike blurted out.

"Just hold on. I need to scan this over to our 'friend' and see if I can get a positive identification. Meanwhile I'll assemble a team."

Mike felt the sweat trickle down his armpits.

Detective O'Rourke spoke in a soothing tone. "We're going to move on this as soon as humanly possible, okay?"

His brown eyes looked kind, and Mike instantly responded. The rising panic in his mind slowed.

O'Rourke stood. "I'll be right back."

Mike fidgeted and paced around the office. He looked out the window; throngs of people moved up and down the sidewalks. The homeless were widely represented, a few of the more industrious pushing shopping carts. Mike shook his head. So many people. He stared at the old buildings around the one he was in. *Terri, you're out there somewhere, don't worry, honey, I'm coming.*

The office door flew open and O'Rourke strode in. This time he was all business. "We got a positive I.D. The team's waiting downstairs."

"Right behind you." Mike followed the detective out the door.

As the realization hit Terri, her stomach dropped. He was going to kill her! The man smiled. It was cold and mirthless. The worst part were his eyes. Sharp black beads, they looked emotionless, soulless. He took his large knife and cut off a piece of the rope, then again, until he had four long pieces. He slipped his knife back into the sheath on his belt. Terri breathed a sigh of relief. Short lived. He grabbed one rope section and tied it to the bed frame, then the next one. Pulling out his knife again he sliced the rope off her hands, freeing them. Terri instantly rubbed them together, attempting to bring back the feeling. He grabbed one hand roughly away and tied that to one side of the bed. Realizing what he was doing, Terri fought him, attempting to pull it away. He swatted her across the face with his large beefy hand.

Terri saw a flash of bright light from the impact. Her struggling stopped as she worked to refocus her vision. She vaguely felt her last wrist bound to the bed post, then her legs. She struggled against the ropes, and he laughed.

"Let me go!" she demanded.

He stepped closer and put his hand under her chin, cruelly turning her head towards him, "Oh, I will let you go, Senorita, when we are done. *Comprehende*?" He dropped her head with a jerk, snapping it to one side. "You must dress for the occasion." He grabbed the front of her dress shirt and ripped down, tearing her bra off with it.

Tears ran down her face. Terri could feel the cool air of the hotel on her chest, at the same time she burned with shame.

Seeing her discomfort seemed to add to the tattooed man's delight. He laughed deeply. "Don't go anywhere, Senorita, we are going to play cards now." He turned toward the door and stopped. "Winner goes first."

The door shut behind him. Terri desperately tried to pull her hands out of the ropes, kicking and straining. But they held tight. She turned her head into the pillow and sobbed in despair.

# Chapter Forty-Five

Dusty arrived at the SeaTac Airport in record time. Probably the first time he was ever able to get anywhere fast on the west side of Washington. Miraculously a flight was leaving for Phoenix in fifteen minutes. He looked at his watch. He'd be there by 11:30. Not bad, especially considering when he'd woken up that morning, he didn't know he was leaving.

As the plane's engines hummed, he watched the snow-capped peaks of Washington and Oregon fall behind. All he could think about was Cassie. Again, in danger. *Why did I not notice Roberto's behavior?* He gave all kinds of tells, now that he looked back. Toys in his car? That's the oldest trick in the book to make a person look trustworthy—even Ted Bundy did that one.

Frustrated, Dusty concentrated looking out the window. He tapped his fingers on the windowsill.

"Is this seat taken?"

Surprised out of his reverie, Dusty looked up at an attractive woman with long blonde hair. "No."

The woman put out a hand. "Kayla."

Years of training kicked him. "Dusty." He politely shook the proffered hand.

Kayla had long dangling earrings and a short leather jacket that she took off and laid across her lap. "I was sitting over there," she pointed offhandedly, "But my seatmate fell asleep and, well, it got pretty loud." She smiled apologetically.

In times of old, before Cassie, Dusty would have found the woman entertaining. Not today. Not now. He nodded politely and then turned back to look out the window.

Upon the apparent cold shoulder, Kayla sighed and opened up a book. Dusty gathered from her body language that she wasn't a woman who was used to being turned down. He grinned to himself. Nobody came close to Cassie.

Roberto walked over to the bed. "I said, when is Dusty coming back?"

"Tomorrow. I think he said tomorrow."

"Don't lie to me, I heard you. You said, 'See you soon.'"

"So what?" snapped Cassie. "I will see him soon. What's it to you?"

Roberto laid a hand on her arm. "Calm down, Cassie. I was just asking," he said soothingly. "I have good news for you."

"Oh?" Cassie feigned interest.

"Yes, I talked to your nurse and she tells me that you are ready to be discharged."

"Right now?"

"Yes." Roberto allowed his hand to run down her hair. "You are so lucky. And beautiful too." He breathed in a low raspy voice.

Cassie's stomach tightened in revulsion. "Get your hands off me, Roberto," she hissed through clenched teeth.

His jaw set in a firm line, he slowly removed his hand, purposefully grazing her breast in the thin hospital gown.

Hot anger boiled through Cassie. She grabbed his hand and pushed it again from her. "You better leave, Roberto. You're not welcome here."

Roberto's previously handsome features had now transformed. He looked cruel and ruthless. "Oh, I'm leaving all right, but I'm leaving with you. Get up and get dressed," he ordered.

Cassie quickly pushed the call button on the tray next to her.

Not noticing, Roberto picked up her clothes and threw them on the bed next to her. "Would you like some help?"

Before Cassie could answer, the room door opened. A middle-aged, heavyset nurse waddled into the room. "What can I get for you, ma'am?"

Cassie's mind raced. Roberto was dangerous and armed. The nurse was hardly a match of force if it came to that, asking her for help wasn't an option. "I'm really tired." Cassie stifled a yawn. "Could you please show Roberto out?"

"Oh, of course." She stepped to one side and gestured at the door. "You heard the lady, we need to leave her alone so she can get some sleep."

"I talked to the head nurse," he said smoothly, "and she said Cassie was to be discharged."

The portly nurse frowned and stood her ground. "I've seen no paperwork." She picked up the clothes on the bed, folded them and placed them back in the drawer.

Roberto looked from one woman to the other. Finally, he apparently made his mind up. "Get your beauty sleep, I'll be back to pick you up in a little bit."

Cassie ignored him, turning on her side with her back towards him. *I'm not going anywhere with him.* It happened once, but it's not going to happen twice. She reached down in her robe pocket, wrapping her hand around the reassurance of cold steel. She smiled and closed her eyes.

Mike sat next to Detective O'Rourke in the front passenger seat. He'd been given a tactical vest and clothing with "Seattle Police Department" emblazoned on it. "Remember what I said. Just stay on the sidelines. This is a police intervention." O'Rourke glanced at Mike. "The only reason you're going is because of your training. But also, for that reason I expect you to stay out of the way."

"Will do." Mike went along, knowing full well the second he could get to Terri, he was going to do it.

Detective O'Rourke had two cars with the SWAT team following behind him. They had agreed to park a block away in an alley, so as not to alert the captors. The three cars pulled into parking spots and the police officers poured out. They huddled for a moment while the detective gave final instructions and then a mass of uniforms rushed toward the old apartment building.

Mike's heart was in his throat. *We have to get there on time!*

They covered the block in less than a minute and all funneled into the apartment lobby.

A young man at the desk gave a small wave. Wordlessly, he set an "Out to Lunch" sign on the desk and walked out the front door.

Detective O'Rourke pushed the elevator button and they waited in silence.

The poker game had gotten more raucous, and finally one man threw down his cards howling in victory. Empty beer bottles and marijuana stubs littered the tabletop. He was short, stocky, with thick greasy black hair. The tattoos on his face didn't cover up the years of acne he'd battled. He jumped up and down, beating his chest, and then went to the bedroom door. He threw it open so hard it banged against the wall, causing a picture to crash to the floor. At the sounds of breaking glass, he howled again, kicking off his pants and strutting to the bed.

Terri struggled in the constraints, turning her head from side to side trying to, if not escape, block the horror from her visage. Hoots and hollers came from the front room as they cheered on their comrade. With one final victory whoop, he threw himself upon her.

His weight knocked the wind out of her. With her sharp intake of breath, the stench of alcohol, marijuana and body odor was unbearable. She was encased in blubber with claws ripping at her skin. She felt herself slipping into darkness.

A huge bang shook the walls, wood splintered, and then a deafening roar. Through a small pinprick of light, she felt cool air as the horrible beast was pulled off her. Looking up, she saw Mike. His normally olive-colored skin was black. She had never seen him look like that before; his face transformed by rage. He punched the man in the face repeatedly. The rapist tried to feebly throw a punch, but that enraged Mike more, and he beat on him harder. Three SWAT team members tried to pull Mike off, but they could not suppress the wiry Greek. The rapist looked like he would be beaten to death, when two more SWAT team members jumped in and were finally able to handcuff Mike.

"Settle down. Just settle down," one of them said.

"Turn me loose. I need to check on my girlfriend," he roared.

"I'll let you go once you calm down and not before." The officer spoke firmly.

Mike turned his head. "Terri, Terri, honey, are you okay?"

Another officer had walked over and threw his jacket over her, while he untied her arms and legs.

"I'm okay, Mike," she whispered, "But if it had been one second later…"

"I know, baby, I know." Tears now were running down his face. "Just turn me loose, detective." He looked at a man with reddish brown hair. "Please."

"Are you going to leave that guy alone now?" asked the detective.

"Yes," Mike said quietly.

O'Rourke gestured to the officer standing next to him. "Turn him loose."

Once freed from the cuffs, Mike ran over to the bed and threw his arms around Terri, cradling her and gently rocking her. She clung to him, sobbing.

The officers went into the front room to finish securing the scene.

# Chapter Forty-Six

The plane touched down in Phoenix, the sun a golden globe in the sky. Had Dusty not been in such a hurry to get to the hospital, he might have appreciated it more after leaving the rain and fog of Washington. Having slept for most of the trip, he felt a lot better. *Cassie is going to be okay, I'm almost there.* Thinking about seeing Cassie, Dusty smiled at Kayla. She brightened. "Did you have a good nap?"

"Oh, yeah. That's the best way for me to fly." He winked. "When I don't remember it."

She laughed and threw her hair back. She sat up and started to put on her coat. Dusty helped her on with the jacket.

"Thank you," Kayla purred.

"Sure." Dusty shrugged into his own coat.

Everyone was taking down their overhead storage and gathering carry-ons to leave the plane. Kayla apparently decided to give it one more shot. "Hey, if you don't have plans, uh, maybe we could go get a drink at the airport. I flew in for a meeting, but it's actually not until tomorrow." She flashed a shy smile.

"Thanks, but I can't." He did something he'd never done before. "I've got someone special to see at the hospital."

"Oh, well, you can't blame me for trying." She smiled. "She's a lucky girl."

Dusty smiled. "I bet a woman like you doesn't have to try very hard." He nodded at her and walked out of the plane.

Cassie wasn't asleep. All she'd been doing was lying around, and she couldn't bear it anymore. She wanted to leave the hospital. Hopefully Dusty would get there pretty soon so she could. The thought of Roberto flashed through her mind. Strange how people could go from being nice to evil so quickly. She liked him when she met him, he was very helpful. Cassie could tell why Mike thought so much of him. But as soon as Dusty left, he changed. A cruel side came out. If Cassie would have been anyone else, she knew she would have been intimidated. But after what she'd just been through, along with her life before that—taking care of herself was second nature. If Javier hadn't gotten the drop on her and she'd gotten so sick, she was pretty sure he wouldn't have been able to keep her contained very long.

The nurses said the fever was gone. She was ready to leave. A tingle of excitement coursed through her as she thought about going home: to see Sammy and her horses. The door abruptly opened. In walked Roberto.

Instantly her happiness evaporated. "What do you want?" she said coldly.

"We already went over that. You're leaving with me."

"Roberto," she said firmly, "I already told you, I'm not leaving. Period." She pointed at the door. "Now leave."

His handsome face contorted in rage. Before she could react, he walked across the room and slapped her hard across the face.

Much to her annoyance, the stinging blow made involuntary tears course down her cheeks. Brushing them away with one hand, she glared at him. Her other hand closed around her Smith & Wesson 9mm Shield and slipped the safety off. "You shouldn't have done that."

Ignoring her, Roberto dug through the drawers and found her clothes, throwing them on the bed again. "Get dressed." Then he paused. "Unless you would like me to do it?"

Cassie reached over and pushed the nurse call button. Too quick for Roberto, but he pulled out his pocketknife and slit the cord immediately after she did it. "Damn you," he said, "always causing problems."

He stood by the bed, but hesitated. The nurse could be here any minute now, and he didn't want to call any more attention to himself and Cassie than necessary. He grabbed the clothes, threw them quickly into the drawer and waited.

"I'm not leaving now?" Cassie gave him a bemused grin.

His eyebrows drew together in annoyance. What was it about Cassie? She showed no fear. Any other woman would be cowering at his feet by now, waiting for another slap. With Cassie, nothing. A grudging respect for her grew inside him. No wonder Javier got himself so full of her. It would be easy to do. He straightened his shoulders. But not him. She would bring him a lot of money, and he was going to cash in. Maybe one day he'd get married, have kids. He smirked, instead of just the toys he'd thrown in the back of his Explorer and the "wife" he'd made up. He congratulated himself on the pictures in his office. It was the benefit of having lots of nieces and nephews. Mike had never changed, he was just as big a chump as back in detective training. Didn't he ever learn? There are no good guys. Just survivors and everyone else.

The door opened and a middle-aged gray-haired woman came him. "Did you need something, sweetheart?"

Roberto spoke up. "Everything's fine. It was an accident." He smiled seductively. "It just sort of went off."

The nurse gave a perceptible shake, like unwanted water off a duck's back. She cleared her throat, ignoring the detective. "Could I help you with anything?"

"I would like to get out of bed. Maybe you could help me?" Cassie asked.

The nursed walked over to one side of the bed and put the bars down. She helped Cassie put her feet on the ground. "There you go."

"Thank you so much." Cassie looking through Roberto.

His cheeks burned. Such disrespect! The anger and indignation burned inside him. He would teach Cassie her place. Apparently, Javier hadn't. He snorted. *What a bumbling fool he was!*

The nurse said, "If you need anything else, just let me know." Before Cassie could reply, the nurse's buzzer went off. Frowning, she turned it off and went out the door.

Roberto closed it behind her.

"Now you can get dressed." He went back to the drawer and pulled the clothes out, throwing them on the bed again.

"I don't think so."

That was it; he'd had it. Anger exploded inside him. He grabbed Cassie by the collar, pulled her face within inches of his and growled, "You will do as you're told."

Suddenly he felt cold steel in his stomach. "Get your hands off me." She breathed angrily. "I'm going to blow a hole in you so big you can drive a truck through it." She swallowed hard. "And after what I've just been through, I'll enjoy every second of it."

Roberto froze. His mind clouded with uncertainty.

The door opened again, but this time it wasn't the nurse. Dusty walked in. He hesitated for only a second, trying to size up what was going on. Then he grabbed the shorter man by the shirt and punched him squarely in the face. Roberto staggered back, hit the wall and slumped to the floor.

Dusty glared at him and then turned to Cassie. "Are you okay?"

"Yes, I am."

"What in the heck did you do to him?"

"Nothing much," she said casually, "just put my gun in his stomach and told him what I was going to do with it."

Dusty shook his head. "Never underestimate a woman." He pulled his cell phone out, called 9-1-1 and filled them in. He heard the operator on the phone and laid it on the bed, his attention on Cassie.

Sirens wailed faintly in the distance.

Dusty put his arms around her and silently pulled her into his chest.

"I'm just glad I didn't have to kill him." Cassie looked at him her eyes shining, "I would have you know."

Dusty smiled faintly. "Not a doubt in my mind."

A sharp knock rattled the door.

"Come in," Dusty said.

Two uniformed officers walked into the room.

# Chapter Forty-Seven

Dusty rode down the trail with an overcast sky, Mount Rainier behind a cloud. The forecast had called for snow today, but he had to ride. Muley walked briskly, passing Douglas Fir trees and salal, covered in frost. The Ranger Creek trail began a slight climb up the ridge. Dusty inhaled deeply. The fir needles and deep rich dirt of the forest filled his nostrils. He felt his shoulder drop as tension left his body.

The silence was broken only by the sound of hooves hitting dirt and striking an occasion rock. Today, Dusty found the silence therapeutic. He crested the rise. An old lean-to for hikers sat in a clearing. The logs were thick and wet, the ground dry and powdery underneath, an old fire ring near the front. He rode over to a tree and tied up Muley.

Cassie came up the hill behind him. She dismounted and tied up her big gray Tennessee Walker.

Dusty picked up dry twigs around tree bases and started a fire. Small at first, it gained size and momentum as he placed more fuel on it. Soon it was large and crackling. He sat back and enjoyed the warmth.

Cassie took a thermos and two cups out of her saddlebag. Sitting down next to Dusty, she poured coffee and handed it to him. They sat companionably next to each other for a long time, staring into the fire.

Dusty broke the silence. “It feels good to be back.”

“Yes, it does.” Cassie smiled, the corners of her mouth turned up.

Dusty set down his cup and pulled her into his arms. “God, I thought that was never going to be over.”

“That makes two of us.” Cassie rested her head on his shoulder.

Amazing himself even more, Dusty turned her head and looked into her eyes. “You’re everything to me, Cassie.” Before she could answer, he kissed her.

The fire popped and large flakes of snow fell silently, covering the trees around them.

Dusty pulled up in front of his office, got out and slammed the truck door. It felt like a lifetime since he’d been here. He walked in the door, the bell sounding his arrival.

Mrs. Phillips sat behind her desk, her gray hair pulled back in a bun and her no-nonsense white shirt and gray sweater in perfect order. She stood. “Mr. Dustin Rose, so good to see you!” She walked quickly around the desk in greeting, stopping just short of a hug, which she viewed as “nonprofessional” with her boss.

She was bubbling. “Could I get you some coffee?”

Dusty grinned at her apparent excitement. “That would be great.” He hung his jacket on the hook and set his Stetson on the hat rack. “I’m afraid to look at the mail.”

“It’s all on your desk. In order.” She stopped, “Oh, and I pulled your files and clipped your letter on top of the corresponding one.”

“Thank you.” Dusty walked past the reception desk down the short hall to his office.

Stepping through the doorway, he was confronted with a stack of files and correspondence that looked to be about a foot high. “Oh, geez,” he muttered. Gritting his teeth, he said down at his desk and began going through it.

A few minutes later a smiling Mrs. Phillips brought in a steaming cup of coffee. “I didn’t book any appointments for you until tomorrow to give you time to go through everything.”

"Great. Who am I seeing and why?" he asked half-heartedly.

"That pile is over here." The secretary pointed at a smaller stack on the corner of his desk.

The morning sped by and at noon, Mrs. Phillips appeared in his doorway. "Are you taking lunch today?"

"Oh, shoot, yes." Dusty stood up abruptly. "I'm meeting some friends. I've got to go." He flashed her a wide grin. "Thanks for the reminder."

The café was crowded, it was a little past noon. Shelley waving from the large round booth in the back caught his eye. He made his way over, almost bumping into Maude.

The waitress with her signature dyed bright red hair and matching lipstick gave out a little screech. Almost simultaneously she hugged him and gave him a quick kiss on the cheek. "We've missed you so much, Dusty. So glad you're back!"

Dusty smiled widely. "So you missed my order of the daily special? I never knew."

"Oh, you." She laughed and pushed his arm. "You've got a table full back there, better get going." She winked. "I'll go get your coffee and your daily special." In a flash of pink, she was gone.

Mike and Terri, Cassie, and Shelley all sat around the table. Dusty sat down next to Cassie and slipped his arm around her, pulling her close to him.

"You finally made it," said Shelley. "We thought you forgot."

"No, I'd never forget." He sighed. "Just work."

"Looking at the red lipstick kiss on his cheek, Cassie grinned. "Oh, just work, huh?"

"Huh?" said Dusty glancing around.

Shelly pulled a small mirror. "Here."

"Oh, gosh." He reached for a handkerchief.

"You're off the hook, boss," Mike said. "We all saw it." They burst into laughter.

"Sorry, I couldn't resist." Cassie giggled.

Mike sat next to Terri, his arm protectively around her. Dusty flashed on how hard it must have been for them too. Terri was quieter and Mike was much more attentive. They were good together, and Dusty was happy for them.

"Hey," said a soft voice next to him. "You okay?" Cassie was looking at him.

"Oh, yeah." He gazed into her light blue eyes. "Just thinking what a lucky guy I am."

"Yeah. You are."

He gave her a mock frown, and she laughed. It was a beautiful sound.

"Okay, lovebirds," said Shelley. "So how about filling everybody in on what happened? We all only have our piece of it."

Maude rushed up and poured coffee. "Your food is up next," she said and left for another table.

Mike grimaced. "Geez, Shelley, it was bad enough the first time around."

She looked so crestfallen, even her bracelets hung limply from her wrists.

Dusty leaned back in his chair. "So… Cassie and I decided to go on a trip down south with our horses…"

Thank you for reading. Please take a moment to leave a review on Amazon.com. It's greatly appreciated.

Visit me at my website www.SusieDrougas.com to sign up for my newsletter and find out about my latest publications.

# Also by Susie Drougas

The Dusty Rose Series

PACK SADDLES & GUNPOWDER
*Book 1*

MOUNTAIN COWBOYS
*Book 2*

HIGH HUNT
*Book 3*

THE BLUES
*Book 4*

Wenn die Wildnis Ruft
(Pack Saddles & Gunpowder)
*Translated and Published in Germany in 2016*

Pack Saddles & Gunpowder now available on audible.com

# About the Author

Powerful new novelist, Susie Drougas, rides with her own Greek packer, husband Mike.

Susie has written a series of exciting books set in the high county. She is a longtime court reporter in Eastern Washington and has been packing horses in the mountains for over 25 years. She has two grown daughters and lives on a small ranch in the foothills of the Cascade Mountains.

Her passion is riding and sharing the beauty of packing horses. She has effectively put us in the saddle to experience firsthand a rugged backcountry pack trip in the Pasayten Wilderness in her first novel, "Pack Saddles & Gunpowder." The ride continues in her second novel in the Cascade Mountains in "Mountain Cowboys." A return to the Pasayten Wilderness for her third book in "High Hunt." Then a trip down to the Eagle Cap in "The Blues."

Her latest novel, "Goin' South", takes us to Arizona and on what starts out as a warm couple weeks of riding in the winter and ends up in an action packed chase into Mexico.

The plots are fiction, but the trails are real. Susie and her husband Mike, have been to all of them.

www.SusieDrougas.com

Made in the USA
Middletown, DE
22 June 2019